Praise for *In The Cage*

"The architecture of this first novel is faultlessly conceived; the construction of the storytelling is meticulously crafted. Hardcastle has an abiding sympathy for the neglected rural poor. The characters we love will break our hearts; the low-lifes we fear are no less indelibly rendered. There is an aura of foreboding—of tragic inevitability—to the collision course of their lives. And, speaking strictly as a former wrestler, the details are true."—John Irving, author of *The Cider House Rules*

"With a cinematic quality comparable to Cormac McCarthy's *No Country for Old Men*, Hardcastle's *In The Cage* is a wild, unrelenting ride, filled with thugs and desperation and innocents and heartbreak. It's a damn fine book."—Donald Ray Pollock, author of *Knockemstiff*

"*In the Cage* is a potent and gripping novel that rigorously steers through rural poverty and mixed martial arts. Fighting is more than just a metaphor for what Hardcastle's endearing characters must resolve as they face increasingly difficult challenges, and their depth and richness flourish throughout his captivating narrative. The story is a precise depiction of a vital and sometimes chaotic intersection between the cultural and social forces in its rural Ontario setting, which I greatly appreciate, having grown up on a reserve in the region. And as a martial artist, I was riveted by the fighting and training passages that intimately brought me on to the mat and into the intense confines of combat."—Waubgeshig Rice, author of *Legacy*

"Hardcastle's signature style [is] a kind of rural poetry ... closer in spirit to McCarthy than Hemingway."—Steven W. Beattie, *Quill & Quire*

"Hardcastle's descriptions possess an elegant choreography that is vivid, energetic, and well-paced ... *In The Cage*—like its protagonist, Daniel—is well structured, engaging, and hard to dislike."—Shawn Syms, *Foreword Reviews*

Praise for Kevin Hardcastle

"[*Debris*] has flesh and bone, soul and brain. It's a rare, rock-solid first book by ... a dexterous writer with unflinching vision. This book's gift is in constructing a museum of hard lives, letting us circle them like excavated marble statues, taking us close enough to see all their mutilation, power, and rough beauty."—Alix Hawley, *National Post*

"[*Debris*] has its own strong voice ... smoothly connected by uncompromising settings and Hardcastle's authentic, plain-spoken country-noir voice, the 11 stories collected here will appeal to fans of gritty, back-country crime fiction, even those who typically shun short stories."—*Booklist*

"Unflinching ... *Debris* is impressive for any writer, especially for a first collection ... Hardcastle comes close to a masterpiece."—*The Winnipeg Free Press*

"Each story is a fully realized world—as rich as it is bleak, the characters powerfully and carefully drawn ... *Debris* is a collection to savour."—*Quill & Quire*, starred review

"The stories are told with careful precision, free of authorial judgment, in prose that reminded me of the understated lyricism of later Thomas McGuane or of David Adams Richards ... [A] very fine collection, well-crafted and compelling."—*Malahat Review*

"Hardcastle manages heart-pumping scenes without ever coming off as trite, and his characters are always firmly grounded in the familiar—a fact which makes the carnage lurking off-stage all the more unnerving. *Debris* offers a fresh perspective on a familiar genre, and can be recommended for this very reason."—*Broken Pencil*

In the Cage

IN THE CAGE

KEVIN HARDCASTLE

A JOHN METCALF BOOK

BIBLIOASIS
WINDSOR, ONTARIO

FIRST EDITION

Library and Archives Canada Cataloguing in Publication

Hardcastle, Kevin, 1980-, author
    In the cage / Kevin Hardcastle.

Issued in print and electronic formats.
ISBN 978-1-77196-147-9 (softcover).--ISBN 978-1-77196-148-6 (ebook)

    I. Title.

PS8615.A68I5 2017   C813'.6   C2017-901941-4
                                              C2017-901942-2

Edited by John Metcalf
Copy-edited by Allana Amlin
Cover designed by Michel Vrana
Typeset by Chris Andrechek

Published with the generous assistance of the Canada Council for the Arts, which last year invested $153 million to bring the arts to Canadians throughout the country, and the financial support of the Government of Canada. Biblioasis also acknowledges the support of the Ontario Arts Council (OAC), an agency of the Government of Ontario, which last year funded 1,709 individual artists and 1,078 organizations in 204 communities across Ontario, for a total of $52.1 million, and the contribution of the Government of Ontario through the Ontario Book Publishing Tax Credit and the Ontario Media Development Corporation.

PRINTED AND BOUND IN CANADA

IN THE CAGE

PART ONE

The first time Daniel fought in the cage was on his twenty-seventh birthday. He had boxed as an amateur and went twenty-two and two with twenty knockouts. The losses were decisions, and he had only ever been hurt once in those fights but he never told anybody about it. He didn't like the boxing game and before he could be pushed to turn pro his trainer was sent to Fernbrook penitentiary for work he did with the local motorcycle club. He didn't come back. Daniel didn't go to the gym anymore and then he saw a Muay Thai fight on TV and he decided he was done with boxing. Within a year he had fought twelve kickboxing matches under North-American rules and won them all by knockout. He fought in Quebec and Alberta and on First Nations land and some of those fights weren't on his record and some were under Thai rules and the pathetic canvas matting of those rings were stained and stained again with men's blood.

In southern Alberta he found a gym that wasn't much more than a storage locker with floor mats, and there he learned Jiu-Jitsu from two white men who had learned a poor man's version from a half-Brazilian day labourer. When he went back to Ontario, Daniel found a true Brazilian gym with men of suspect lineage to players in Rio de Janeiro and Curitiba and they beat him bloody about the ears and twisted him to pulp and he dreamt about it every night, lying battered and aching in his one-room shithole apartment in the east end of the city. He didn't talk to his father anymore and he didn't go up north to the place he was born and grew up. His old man wanted him to come home and weld but the boy wanted no part of that life. He'd had offers to work in places remote and frozen without fight gyms but they were long withdrawn and Daniel cleaned the halls and toilets of his would-be alma mater and sometimes he shovelled snow out of entryways and laid salt on the pockmarked stone of the steps out front.

He turned twenty-seven in a cage near Fort McMurray. The man he fought had a huge, mutant head and cauliflowered ears and his nose buckled in at the bridge. At two hundred and four pounds Daniel gave up a lot of weight to the other man but he had no true manager and the fight had been re-classed as a catchweight bout and he would not see his money if he walked away. The only punch the big man threw was slipped and then that other man ate a one-two and fell and he was swarmed by Daniel and had his brow cleaved by elbow-strikes and his head bounced off the mat while he tried to get his forearms up.

Daniel fought in a legion hall in Lethbridge and there he left an American ex-wrestler turtled up against the cage with his rib broken from a knee and his left eye swollen shut. He fought in Red Deer and in Grande Prairie and the men he fought were younger and both lasted no more than a minute and when he got to his next fight at a cut-rate casino in Lloydminster the other fighter was not there. The promoter didn't want to pay Daniel but he did pay him and then Daniel sat in a motel room on his own and drank all of the unearned money away. He fought on a reserve outside of Vancouver and there he had his nose broken by an illegal headbutt that the referee didn't see and he gobbed blood and filth out of his mouth between rounds and his ear hurt where it had been torn under the lobe by the ridge of the other man's glove. Not a minute into the second round that man was prone and senseless from a left head kick and Daniel's shin stung as he walked the cage-perimeter with his hands in the air, his cornerman trying to plug his nostrils with gauze. He fought in Olympia and Portland and outdoors on a ranch in Montana, cowboys and rednecks sitting in wooden bleachers drinking beer as if they were watching high school football. He and another man went through the cage door in Lincoln, Nebraska and didn't know what to do when they got up on the cold concrete with the sparse crowd pulling away. In the cage again he dropped the man with a wild overhand right and the man had a lot of trouble coming around and Daniel was terrified. He went to a small town outside of Kansas City, Missouri that he couldn't remember and he had to sneak out of the back door of the community hall and he never fought that far south again. There were fights in Quebec now and he fought there often and won twice in televised fights. In Ontario there were no sanctioned fights but he fought on the Akwesasne and Rama reserves and then he went west.

At a backwater clinic outside of Medicine Hat a nurse's assistant with long red hair stitched his eyebrow and then put seventeen stitches through a cut on his shin. She asked him what he was doing with his life and he asked her the same. She was twenty-one years old and her family was American but she had been born on the Canadian side of the forty-ninth parallel under circumstances she didn't know or wouldn't tell. She had spent a few years in British Columbia with her older sister until that sister went home to tend to their sick father. She told Daniel that she had come to Alberta for the work, like everybody else, like him. He'd shied from the first stitch and she wouldn't let him get away with it. A man who got punched in the face for a pittance but didn't like needles. He had no fights in Medicine Hat again but he pulled his stitches and went back and then he started inventing new injuries and fantastical post-operative complaints. Before the first snowfall of that year he had fought twice more and they were married when the cold and bitter winter came and laid that country barren but for houselights burning in the black prairie night over wasted fields and empty roads.

They had a red-haired daughter in that bleak season. Over eight pounds and she kicked and wailed. If he thought he knew what love was, he was wrong. To be loved just for being alive. To be loved to the point of desperation for the little space that you took up. That was how he loved the girl and sometimes he could barely look at her because he didn't know what to do with it.

ONE

They drove through the cornfield with the sun rising and burning white in the sideview mirrors. The cruiser listed side to side like a dinghy at storm's onset, the tires sinking and then spinning free in the sucking mud. They had driven for a long while without speaking. The stalks had been shredded and strewn about and the car followed that wrecked path with five-foot walls of sagging, late-season corn at either door. Out they came into a clearing where a tornado might have touched down. That was where they found Daniel's truck.

The truck lay on its side with the passenger door sunk into the ground. There were cornstalks mangled through the grillplate and front fender and stuck up under the bent windshield wipers. Stalks were wrapped around the front and rear axle, twisted and pulled taut into a crude sort of rope, filthy and fraying. The windshield had been punched outward and hung down in a flap like the tongue of an old shoe. The cruiser stopped and Daniel got out and walked over to the wreck, his steel-toed boots churning the sodden ground and rising heavy with muck after each step. As he came closer to the exposed undercarriage he studied the way the truck had upended. It leaned hard toward the driver side and Daniel stepped wide of it and went on, walking around the part-crushed cab until he could see the truckbed. There he stopped.

Constable Smith was coming now and he was trying to keep his shoes on as he walked out into the clearing. He was hollering something but Daniel wasn't listening. The welding rig was gone. Daniel got down to one knee and ran his hand along the inside of the box, over the boltholes punched through the metal there. Daniel stood up and saw deep gauges in the bed where the welding unit had been ripped from its moorings. He reached out and clamped both hands around the edge of the box. His knucklejoints went white and then he let one hand drop and stood there with it dangling as he stared across the field. The outlying forest stood black and still. Mist clung ghostly to the firs.

Daniel gave the truck a little shove and felt it list slightly and come back. He went around to the other side and studied the undercarriage in silence. He reached up and spun the rear wheel. Hub toward the heavens. Daniel tilted his head back to see what was up there and when he did a flock of late-running geese flew past in an ever-shifting V, squawking as they went. In seconds they were smaller in the southern sky and after they were gone nothing else moved for a very long time.

The constable stood ten feet out from the truck and watched the man.

"Hey, don't stand by that thing," Smith said. "Don't get under it or anything in case it turns back over."

"I sort of wish it would," Daniel said.

"What?" the cop said.

Daniel didn't say anything else. He waited a few more seconds and then he made his way back to the other side of the wreck. He backed up a step and booted the top of the cab and the truck leaned hard and groaned and then started falling. When it fell it went all at once. The tires landed stiff in the ground and the vehicle did not buck but shuddered hard enough to loose a wheel well.

TWO

In the dark and pisswet alleyway, Daniel stood under one meagre light. A lonely bulb sticking sideways out of a socket in the moldy brick, glowing pale orange and humming high and quiet. Rain fell on it and hissed out of existence. He stood with both hands in his jacket pockets, staring blankly at the opposing alley wall not ten feet away. Four days past since they'd recovered his truck and he'd taken it to the mechanic to piece it back together hideous. He'd parked a block away and hoped the frame wouldn't take water in. Cars ran by at the near entrance and drubbed the gravel out of the shallow potholes there, sprayed rainwater on the sidewalk and set it sloshing back and forth in the holes to fill up again. The prepaid cellphone in his right hand started to whir and rattle. He took it out and as he looked at it a black van turned from the roadway and came bucking down the alley toward him. He put the phone in his pocket and hooked his thumbs in his beltleather. When the vehicle pulled up the side door was open and he got in and shut it behind him and the van went on down the alley into the waiting blackness.

They were in a crude cinderblock and sheetmetal warehouse about the size of a high-school gymnasium. Five men all told. A table with a duffel bag atop it, set up in the middle of the room. Little else in the place. Clayton sat at the table in a wooden chair with his arms crossed. Wiry man with wide shoulders and a narrow waist, clothes like an executive trying to dress casual. Short grey hair with no part and clean-shaven to the lined and aged skin of his cheeks and chin. A lone man sat opposite and smoked. A Francophone drug dealer named Asselin. Wallace King sat beside Clayton and he flicked through the bound billstacks and set the counted money aside. Clayton stared across the table at Asselin. The man exhaled too hard, snapped loose the ash from his cigarette even when there was none to drop. That man was not armed under his leather jacket but his minder at the door had a semi-automatic pistol slung in a holster with the clasp and thumbsnap loosed. Daniel stood on the other side of the metalframe doorway and he watched the table and the count and the man across from Clayton. And he watched the minder on the other side of the doorway, studied him sidelong.

"I know you," the minder said.

Daniel looked at him for a second. The minder wore leathers of his own but Daniel figured they'd had to slay a number of beeves to make a jacket wide enough to fit him. His skin had the boiled, pink hue of a man full with bought testosterone. Daniel didn't know the man's given name, only that they called him Lumpy, so called because he was lumpy with muscle.

"There's not much pistol work done inside that cage, is there?" said Lumpy.

"What the fuck are you talkin' for?" Daniel said.

Lumpy smiled and put his back to the block wall. Tried to draw himself up bigger.

At the table, Wallace King laid down the last bundle of cash and looked at Clayton. Nothing was said. Clayton nodded and reached across to Asselin and shook his hand hard and held it a few moments before letting go. The man dropped his smoke and crushed it underfoot as he stood up. His minder started walking to the table. Lumpy had gone a few steps before he realized Daniel wasn't beside him. He stopped and looked back. Daniel left his spot near the door and when he caught up with Lumpy they went the rest of the way across the room together. Clayton and Wallace were standing now. Wallace had swept the money into the bag and it hung heavy by the handlestraps in his right fist. The minder stood beside his boss and Lumpy and Daniel were opposite each other again with the table between them. Wallace started to hand the bag to Clayton and Clayton reached to take it but then his hand came back and there was a razor held there and it passed through Asselin's cheek and drew a line in his skin. All at once the line fattened and the skin separated and showed pink gums and white teeth for a moment before the blood ran.

Asselin staggered back from the table and his minder didn't see the cut right away but his hand started to move to his side. Daniel reared back and booted the edge of the table and it caught Lumpy high on his legs and his hand missed the gun. Then there was no table between them and Daniel hit Lumpy in the chin with a short right hand and as the man crumpled he took a left hook and another straight right and his eyes were rolled back to where the white twitched in taut ocular muscle. Daniel followed the minder down and grabbed the pistol even before Lumpy had settled limbstretched on the cold concrete floor. Daniel came back with the gun in his hand and turned to see Clayton talking to the man he'd cut, a revolver pulled from inside his jacket and pressed against Asselin's temple. Asselin was crouching and trying to hold his face together as blood slipped his fingers and ran his forearms and his shirtsleeves. Asselin bobbed up and down under the gun and blood danced the concrete and drew weird patterns as he hobbled by.

Daniel held Lumpy's gun and when he looked down at it he didn't even have his finger on the trigger. Wallace came over and Daniel turned at him quick. Wallace held up and reached out with one large and hairless hand.

"I'll take that, big guy," Wallace said.

Daniel gave up the pistol and Wallace handed him the duffel bag of cash. Wallace checked the chamber of the pistol and let the slide snap back and then he went over to where his boss had Asselin knelt down at gunpoint. Clayton was talking to the man and then suddenly Asselin's eyes were wide and he took his hand from his cheek and grabbed at his far shoulder and at the base of his neck. Muscles there gone rigid and severe through the skin. Then Asselin keeled.

Clayton lowered the gun and looked down at the man. He turned to Wallace and Wallace shrugged.

"What'd you do?" Wallace said.

"Nothing," Clayton said. "Well, nothing else."

Wallace kicked Asselin's boot. He did not move. Daniel dropped the duffel bag and hurried over. He knelt in the concrete beside Asselin. Put his hand near to the man's mouth and nose, leaned in close. The blood ran steady from the seam hewn through Asselin's face.

"Did you want to kill him?" Daniel said loud.

"Not really," Clayton said.

Daniel looked at Clayton and Wallace each.

"You fuckin' idiots," Daniel said.

He positioned himself over the man and put his ear to Asselin's mouth. After a few seconds he turned to face Asselin and made a ring over the man's lips with his thumb and forefinger and blew. The man's cheek split again and bubbled red.

"Motherfucker," Daniel said.

He did what he could to cover the wound and Asselin's mouth both and then he blew again. Daniel began compressions at Asselin's chest. He counted thirty and leaned in and listened once more. He breathed air into the man.

"Stop," Clayton said.

Daniel kept at it.

"What are we going to do if he comes around?" Clayton said. "Call the fucking ambulance?"

Daniel had nearly made his count but before he could Clayton stepped around Asselin and aimed his pistol at Lumpy. He shot Lumpy three times by his heart and put another bullet in his brain.

The van was parked on little more than a clay trail some twenty feet from the bay inlet. Jack Pine branches were bent against the vehicle panelling on the side nearest to the waters. A ramp had been built into the beach and over the low shieldrock. It led down to a ramshackle jetty that had no true owner but was built and rebuilt as needed. The three men sat quiet in the van and the blue digits on the dash climbed in minutes. Blackness otherwise. Not long and they could hear the distant growl of a small motor.

"That's him," Wallace said.

He got out of the truck with a garbage bag in his hand, weighted enough that it swung while he walked the ramp. Down and down to where the jetty left the beach. The inbound boat had one headlamp and it cut out sudden. The engine idled low. Wallace stood on the planking and waited. He knelt and reached for something. Another man got out in the shadow and started tying ropes to the dock-cleats. He stood full and they were talking. After a few seconds Wallace whistled loud enough to scare something clear from the brush beside the van.

Clayton backed down the ramp all the way to the end of the beach. Loose sands that covered the low end of the grade. They stopped again and Clayton pulled the emergency brake. The back double-doors came open and Wallace had his hands on the plastics that covered the smaller body.

"Aren't you going to get out and help him?" said Clayton.

Daniel shifted in the seat but he didn't go. The skin of his hands carried a red tint. He'd tried to wash at the warehouse but the place was a shell and there were no cleaning supplies. Ghost of the metallic taste of blood in his mouth that kept coming back.

"I don't believe I will," he said.

"No?" Clayton said.

"Ain't no way."

Clayton studied him some and then he got out. Swung the door shut. He walked around to the back and Wallace had already unpinned a metal trolley from its straps against the interior wall. He lifted it down to the jetty with some effort and then he reached back in and hauled the rolled-up man by winch-straps that held the plastics. One hand in either. He hefted the man and set him down hard on the trolley-bed. The second load had Clayton in the van on his haunches, pushing the thing clear. He got down to the dock again and he and Wallace managed to lower the dead man to the metal. Wallace started towing the trolley down the pier, the wheels clacking in the gaps. Clayton said his thanks to Daniel and followed Wallace down toward the boatman.

They watched the boat go out into the black with its cargo. Could hear it but small. From where they stood they could see small lights on the inland hillside. Distant glow of lamps way out on the big island. Clayton guessed where the ferry ran in the waters but he couldn't see enough to know for certain. He was a quarter-Mohawk by blood and his kinsmen had no active links to the First Nation out in the bay.

"When was the last time he got out there?" Clayton said.

"Dan?" Wallace said. "Don't know. Years ago."

"He was seeing that girl."

Wallace nodded.

"The family didn't like the idea of it. Tried to talk him out of it," Clayton said.

He spat from the jetty.

"That's one way to say it," Wallace said.

"He beat the one brother bloody. Stood off a few more until they got the better of him. They didn't let him off easy. He was lucky to get off the island."

"How d'you know all that?" Wallace said.

"Me and his old man picked him up at the ferry landing. Arthur wanted to go back over and kill somebody."

"That true his father had some Ojib blood?" Wallace said.

Clayton shrugged.

"He never looked into it that hard. He was always funny about it."

The men waited to see the boat lights turn on again. They didn't. Wallace started walking down the pier. Towed the trolley behind.

"If I remember right, somebody he knew put him on that ferry," Clayton said.

"Didn't think it was fair to see him killed." Wallace said.

Wallace came back to the van first and then Daniel did get out, took an end of the trolley and lifted it into the back by the interior bulblight. Sweat trailed the side of Wallace's head, his cheek and neck. Clayton was still down by the boat launch trying to see where it had gone. Daniel and Wallace sat the fender and the van sunk a half-foot on its suspension.

"You put a lot of trust in that man and his shitty boat," Daniel said.

"He's my cousin," Wallace said.

Daniel shook his head.

"They'd have a hard time keepin' the regular cops off the reserve if they find out there's corpses being planted there. Whatever you think."

"Thanks for lookin' out for us, man," Wallace said.

Daniel got off the truck. Looked to the waters and the dark. At the figure of the man stood out there on the warped planks of the jetty.

"I've about had it with all this shit," he said.

Wallace smiled a little. He said no more.

Daniel's truck crept into the driveway, gravel shifting under the heavy tires. No light shone in the cab. Wrinkles in the metal where the frame had been bent by the crash and bent back by a winch and harness while the truck sat anchored in a mechanic's lift. Daniel rolled the truck to a halt and put it in park and there he sat for the better part of an hour, his hands shaking above the steering wheel and his chest tight. Fog of his breath on the windshield. He'd pulled in at nearly five in the morning while the sky paled and he didn't move from his seat until a thin yellow strand grew slow at the horizon line. He made his hands into fists a few times and then he pulled the doorhandle. He had to shoulder the door open and the metal squealed and when he closed the door behind him he had to drive it shut with that same shoulder. Too loud. He looked at the house and waited for a light to come on. Nothing happened. Daniel stood with his hand on the battered truck, watched the world take shape. Highgrass fields and a thin, winding stream. The distant treeline. Nothing there that belonged to him.

He eased in through the front door and made it halfway to the fridge before he remembered his boots and went back and took them off. He crossed the room and took a beer from the fridge and his hand still trembled some but he got the cap in his palm and tore it loose. Tipped the bottle near upright at his lips and drank until there was nothing left but drops. Daniel set the bottle on the counter and his eyes watered. He felt like he might sneeze but he stopped it. Burped quiet against the back of his hand. He blinked until he could see the bottle clear again on the counter. Shook his head and tried to think where he might have whiskey. After a few seconds he went back to the fridge and got another beer and when he left out for the bedroom half an hour later there were five bottles lined up neat beside the toaster.

When he went into the room he could see Sarah on her back in their bed, her head to the side. Red hair fanned out over both sets of pillows. Her right hand lay palm up in the mattress-dent where his haunches came to rest every night. Daniel stared at her in the shallow light, at her small nose, freckles on either side that went sparse where they lined her dimpled cheeks. She wore a tank top that showed the ridges in her shoulders. Rude surgery scar for a torn rotator cuff. Slow swelling of her chest as she breathed. He leant against the doorway by his forearm with his chin at the crook of his elbow. She stirred and then her eyes opened. She blinked hard. Smiled at him.

"Hi," she said.

"Hey."

"What are you doing out there?"

"My shift ran late."

"I meant what are you doing standing all the way over there."

"That's a fair question," he said.

Sarah propped herself up on her forearms.

"You look like you got into it tonight," she said.

"Yeah?" he said.

"Yeah."

He looked down at his feet. Worksocks frayed and worn thin in patches. Quiet in the room. He looked back up at her.

"What happened out there?" she said.

Daniel kept looking at her.

"Just come here," Sarah said.

"I'm gonna get in the shower," Daniel said. "I got to wash this off me."

"Okay. Then after that get into this bed," she said, and threw the covers back. "But you gotta keep your filthy mitts to yourself."

"I can't make a promise like that," he said.

"I know."

She let herself drop to the mattress. Rubbed her eyes with both hands. Put her hands on the blanket at her belly. Daniel took his arm off the doorway but he didn't go into the room.

"Hey," he said soft.

"What?" she said.

"I gotta see the girl first."

Sarah had her eyes closed.

"I knew that too," she said.

Madelyn slept in a mess of blankets, pillows all about her. She'd managed to get the corner of the comforter up to her chin sometime in the night and wore the thing like a toga. She lay there with her arms and legs splayed out, skinny limbs in her wrinkled pajamas. She had lately started to outgrow her small bed. Daniel shook his head.

"Jesus, kid," he said.

He leant down to her and put his hand on her fore-head. Her skin very soft against the roughness of his palm. He smoothed her hair and saw the size of his hand next to her head, the swollen knuckles. Daniel put his right hand in his pocket and kissed her as gentle as he could on the top of her head and then got up and went out. Left the door part open. He loosed the door-handle and went down the hall with his head hung low.

He'd a dream that he had many times before. That he always remembered. A cage with the fencing painted black and the crowd back beyond the cage. Sound of so many people talking. He was fighting a man far bigger but he did not fear it. On the matting he moved well and he took the centre and they traded. But there the man was fast and Daniel's punches were slow, like they were moving through waters. He kept at it and then his right eye went black. He was over by the cage wall. The outside leg knelt in the narrow ditch between the mat and the fencework. He was trying to cover but his arm wouldn't come up. By the one good eye he saw two men at ringside. The man that looked like Daniel pointed. His other eye quit. He could hear his heart and his breathing. Heavy thud of bonejoints finding his face and sideribs.

When Daniel woke up he saw the girl sitting cross-legged at the foot of the bed. He'd taken her arm sudden through the sheet. It didn't seem to bother her.

"Hey," Daniel said, and let go.

"You okay, dad?"

"How long you been sittin' there?"

She shrugged. Daniel coughed and ran one hand through his short hair. Pushed himself up so that he was leaning against the headboard. He'd no shirt on and the girl was studying the shape of him.

"You slept a long time," Madelyn said.

"Yeah?" he said.

"Yes."

"I'll remind you about saying that when you start workin' for a livin' and Saturday rolls around."

Madelyn sat there quiet for a time. She had her hair tied back loose and wore basketball shorts and a Raptors T-shirt. Athletic build in the making. She was barely twelve but by her eyes she looked older. Her nose twitched.

"Jeez dad, you're ripe," she said.

Daniel turned to her slow. She mimicked him.

"That's about how I feel," he said.

"What?" she said.

"Nothing," he said.

Daniel sat up full in the bed. He looked for his shirt and saw it on the near floor. The girl reached down for it and handed it to him.

"Well, it's okay," the girl said.

"Thank you for saying so."

"Mom said don't wake you up."

"You didn't."

"You were saying weird things and moving around. Did you have a bad dream?"

Daniel thought on it.

"I don't remember," he said, and then he threw the covers off. "Let's get up outta here and see what's happening."

"Okay," she said.

He pulled the shirt on and stood up beside the bed and Madelyn cleared out toward the door. When Daniel got there he punched her shoulder light with his left hand and followed her out. She stopped short and planted her feet. Daniel shoved her some and she took hold of the framing. Held on as long as she could. When she came unmoored she had to jog a few steps to stop from falling.

Sarah sat at the kitchen table reading the paper, a can of Diet Coke in her hand. When she saw them she got up and went over to the oven and opened it.

"Sit," she said.

Daniel did as she said. So did the girl. She ran her hair back behind her ears and took a sip from the can in Sarah's spot.

"Madelyn, you already ate your breakfast," Sarah said. "You should go back out and practice. I'll be there in a minute."

"It's alright," Daniel said.

Sarah took a plate of bacon and sausage out of the oven and then went to the microwave and turned it on and then started putting the meat on a cool plate. When she was done she went to the toaster and pushed the lever and then she waited for the chime from the microwave and heard it and then took the eggs out, steam rising from the bowl. She forked out a mouthful and tried them and then she scraped the rest out onto the plate. Brought it to him.

"Let me know if they're any good."

"Yes ma'am," he said.

She went back to the counter for the toast. Carried it over on a plate. Daniel took a knife up and spread the butter on thick. Madelyn watched him.

"That's an awful lot," she said.

"I'm about to hear that again from her, so just take it easy."

Sarah got him a mug from the cupboard and poured his coffee. Handed it to him.

"I didn't think I'd sleep like that," Daniel said. "What time is it?"

"It's not that late," Sarah said. "Now eat."

Sarah settled at the table and took up the paper again and read at it. Once in a while she'd look up over the page to him. Madelyn poured juice into a glass and read the print on the back of the paper. Reports of a warehouse fire in the city that spread to bordering soyfields and still burned wild when the presses ran. Sarah hadn't seen it. Soon enough she quit reading and set the paper down.

"Come on," she said to Madelyn.

Sarah got up and went through to the bedroom and came back in sweats. Running shoes in her hand. Madelyn left her father at the table and found her beat-up shoes in the entryway, pulled them on with the laces still tied. Sarah made a noise at her but left it at that. They went outside and let the door close. Sound of a basketball on the packed gravel. Daniel had made Madelyn a backboard out of plywood and fixed a rim to it firm, bracketed the entire ugly thing to the lip of the roof. He sat there eating and could see them both through the kitchen window. Madelyn put up free throws with an awkward kind of shot where she catapulted the ball from back over her right shoulder. More often than not Daniel heard just net or the back-iron of the rim as she sunk buckets. Sarah caught the ball or tracked it down on the misses and fired it back to the girl. Daniel cleared his throat and put his head down while he ate. The knife and fork shook some in his hands and he studied that for a second while he listened to the sound of sneakers shifting grit.

THREE

Daniel waited in the driveway and studied the truck. There were slight gaps where the windshield didn't fit snug and they could be seen from ten feet away. The bed itself had come loose near the cab and had been welded back to the chassis. The brake lights simply didn't work anymore. But Daniel had the papers from the mechanic for the safety, paid for with a bottle of whiskey and an hour in the mechanic's shop sipping it from the bottle. He spat on the gravel and then went over to the truck and checked the box again, the clamp marks where his livelihood had recently been bracketed to the metal. Daniel couldn't even pretend that he'd never lost the thing as the rear-end of the truck had been raised to account for the weight and without the welding unit the tail-end of the vehicle jacked skyward as if he were racing it at some kind of demented backwoods drag circuit.

He wiped sweat from above his ears. His shirtback clung to him. They'd left the ball in the bed of the truck so he fished it out, turned around and started back toward the house. Stopped halfway and looked up at the pale blue sky. Tendrils of white trailing one lone cloud. He bounced the ball on the driveway with both hands.

When Daniel heard the front door open he snapped out of it and cleared his throat. He palmed the ball in his right hand and held it out at his side. Madelyn came out to the drive and tried to snatch the ball away. Daniel faked and then held it high enough above his head that she couldn't reach it. The kid told him to shoot. He looked to the net and tried to take a shot and it was disgraceful. All the mechanics of it were wrong. The ball missed the rim entire and clipped the one edge of the backboard and ricocheted to the side.

"Jesus," he said.

Madelyn was laughing as she passed him for the truck. Daniel went into his pocket quick, got her hand as she passed and put a ten-dollar bill in it. She went by without a word and without looking at what she got and stuck that hand in her jeans pocket. Madelyn climbed the back fender and swung her legs over one at a time. She sat on the box and waited, stared off down the county road.

Sarah left the house with the keys hung from a fore-knuckle on her right hand. She blew a loose strand of hair out of her eyes and looked at Daniel.

"She'll have had enough before you've even got there," Daniel said.

"I know it," she said.

"I'd come along, but I gotta see that man out in the hills."

"You think he's the one who took the truck."

"I'll know before long."

"You got wheels?"

"Gotta walk down to Murray's after. He says he'll lend me his car."

Sarah let out a little grunt and then leaned in and put her arms around him and kissed him on the neck.

She whispered in his ear and the fine hairs of it stood up. She unhooked her arms from around his neck. Got into the truck and shut the door and rolled the window down.

"You ready, kiddo," she called.

Madelyn got down from the box and waved over top of it to Daniel.

"See you after," he said.

He went to Sarah's door and waited for her to clear the frame. She tried to pull it shut but it wouldn't close snug until he leaned hard against it with his shoulder. He gave it another dig and then he looked up at his wife and tried to smile but couldn't get it right. He backed up to let them go and stared down the driveway for traffic though there was none. Never was.

"Hey," Sarah called.

He turned.

"We'll be back soon. Don't wreck the place."

"No promises," he said.

Daniel was about to start his walk for the house but Madelyn called for him.

"Dad," she said. "You're bleeding."

She had her hand up and was pointing at the knuckle side. He lifted his own and saw a band-aid worked loose from his one finger. Wander of red down the length of the digit.

"It's okay," he said. "Just a scratch."

The girl sat back. The truck rolled down the grade and he'd covered his one hand in the other as they left out. Sarah had an arm behind Madelyn's seat and was looking over her shoulder to the road. The girl had her eyes on him yet. He waited until they were reversed into the lane and then he made for the house. He heard the transmission gear up to second but he did not see them go.

Daniel showered and he stood in the bedroom for some time before he dropped the towel and let the air at his nethers. He found underwear in the drawer but no jeans. So he went to search them out wearing an old pair of cargo shorts. Found himself in the basement looking for the light switch. He'd set up a heavy bag there with duct tape covering the dried and cracking leather. The tape had worn out and been retaped and it wound over itself now, layered crooked throughout. Daniel walked by the bag like it wasn't there and found his jeans in the dryer and made for the stairwell. When he passed the bag again he pawed at it with his left hand and the jeans slipped off his shoulder. He put them down and threw another light jab and then a hard jab and felt the heft of the bag under his raw knuckles and then he threw a one-two and stung the bag with a straight right and sent it spiralling counter-clockwise. Spackling of blood on the old tape. He shook his right hand out and looked at the bruising there, the little tears in the skin. He stopped the bag and held it still. He backed up and threw a half-assed one-two and then whipped his right leg wide and drilled the leather with his shinbone. Sound like a nail being hammered in the hollows of the place. Daniel felt off-balance some, so he reset and then threw another right round kick. Turned his hips better. The support beam where the bag had been bolted shuddered and sent rumblings through the house. He stutter-stepped to throw a high left kick and rotated hard on the ball of his right foot and there his shinbone dug deep where a man's head might be. Daniel finished the rotation with his hips and shoulders facing right and his leg came back quick and he stood at the ready again. He drilled the bag with a few more low kicks and they felt better and better and his hairless shins had gone red but they didn't sting enough to bother him. Weird sensation in the skin, atop nerve-endings he'd long quieted in training rooms and in the cage.

Daniel took up his jeans and shut off the light and went up the cellar stairs in pure blackness. Then he was out in the lit corridor. He shut the door behind him and wiped a line of sweat from his forehead. He went into the kitchen and sat in his shorts at the table and looked around the small house. There were fissures in the ceiling plaster and wind whistled through the sideyard door and the core-rotten window frames above the sink. The stove had been old when it was put in fifteen years ago and Sarah washed her dishes by hand in hard country water that had to run for a few minutes before the brown-red tinge of rust and seepage cleared out of the stream. He studied the old fridge with its lever-handle and yellowing corners and then he noticed that the fridge magnets held nothing there except for a few handwritten notes. No envelopes for their bills. Daniel looked around for just a minute more and then he got up from the chair. Flung his jeans onto the living room couch as he went by. A few seconds later he came past the other way wearing a sweatshirt and his sneakers and he left out through the kitchen with the screen door swinging wild and slapping back against the jamb.

Daniel ran over uneven ground with knots of hard dirt and tallgrass and he heard his heartbeat up in his ears. He went up a gradual rise and passed a stand of elms. Near them a weather-worn cross, stabbed into the earth. He'd not lived there long enough to know who or what lay under that ground but he thought about it long after he passed. He made his way out toward the treeline and it did not come quickly and when he got there his chest ached. He slowed and stopped long enough to grab hold of the low-hung limb of a fir and his hand came back sticky with gum. Daniel was about to turn and make his way back but in the shadow at the forest-edge he saw something move behind the tree columns. A shape there. A second later it was gone and he didn't know if it was an animal or just a trick of the brain. He took one step onto needle-strewn soil that rarely felt sun and that one step was enough to turn him around.

Daniel found his pace on the open field and headed home, left a trail of little dustclouds to settle in the grasses. The house that he went to sat lonely, penned in by dirt road and fields and the forest beyond. The kitchen side door swung free, as he'd left it. Moved on spent hinges by a chill easterly wind.

FOUR

Sarah took Madelyn into town through a series of winding concession roads. They came to a spot where the lanes dropped into a deep valley and Sarah didn't slow. They went down into the dale and Madelyn had her right arm braced in the window frame. The trees on either side of the road were naked now but in other seasons the limbs of those trees would be so thick with foliage that they'd bend almost double and set the valley in shadow. Branches sometimes fell down onto the road in wild summer storms and in the winter ice and snow would build in the drop and send drivers sideways into the bracken at the road-edge or over wind-hewn snowbanks into frozen marshland. Madelyn had been likewise warned about that deep valley when she was younger, to not play there with her friend that lived on one of the bordering farms. Daniel and Sarah told her that it was dangerous. The schoolchildren who lived on those farms told her it was full with ghosts for all the travellers killed there. Madelyn knew every copse and hollow.

In the town they drove from place to place. The truck sat in parking lots outside of rectangular buildings of painted brick. Worn-out flags flew the metal poles out front. Later yet, the truck sat crooked at curbside in front of banks and hockshops. Sarah went into those buildings with papers in her hands and came back with more papers and she propped a ledger against the dashboard and wrote in columns there and then put the papers away and then they went somewhere else. Madelyn waited inside of the truck and listened to music on the radio or slouched in the seat and fiddled with dials and levers. Popped the door-latches and then slapped them back down again. She read for a time from a book she'd brought. Kept her head low when she saw anyone she knew.

At one enormous corner building Sarah parked the truck and got her papers in order. It stood tall enough to shade half of the block. Built of heavy brownstone, windows framed in oak. Madelyn set the book down.

"You want to come in here?" Sarah said. "Take a look around."

Madelyn nodded and Sarah waved her out on her side and they both got out of the passenger-side door. They went across the sidewalk and up the rock steps, each wide enough to lay down on. Madelyn followed Sarah through the open doorway onto battered planking that creaked under their weight. The main floor was one massive room with a cathedral ceiling and row after row of shelves. All manner of bizarre and indescribable things set alongside cheap trinkets and items broken and obsolete. There were tarnished lampstands and light fixtures beside novelty coffee mugs and ashtrays. Old stereo equipment and speakers. Packaged popguns and rudimentary toy trucks and cars. Boxes of action figures with arms missing and teeth marks in the plastics. Ceramic plaques with prayers etched on them. Ships in bottles. An entire suit of armor standing upright in the aisle. They walked down the one side of the store and passed a series of glassed-in countertop displays of baseball cards and comic books. They came to a cash register where nobody stood and Sarah rang a bell and waited. Hocked jewellery close by, necklaces laid out on doilies and wedding rings fixed into the slots of a velour cushion. Madelyn had already started to wander. A woman came out from the back room and she had white hair and her glasses were too big for her head. She stepped small and quick, blinking all the while to better see who was there at the counter.

Sarah spoke to the clerk for some time and the old woman nodded and then went to the back room and there was some commotion and something clattered to the floor and the woman could be heard cursing soft from somewhere in there. Madelyn had gone down the length of the shelf opposite the counter. Rows of porcelain dolls stood there, some near three feet tall. All were dressed in their finery and some had dolls of their own and they were glass-eyed and curly haired and wore shiny little shoes with metal clasps. Madelyn reached out slow and touched one of them on the cheek and then pulled her hand back. She looked down at her finger and then after a moment she reached out again and touched the doll's dead glass eye.

When they left the store Madelyn held a paper bag in her hand, the open end folded over on itself. They got in the truck and Sarah scribbled in her ledger one more time and then closed the book and slid it onto the dash with the pen clasped to its cover. Then she turned to Madelyn.

"Okay," she said. "Now, what do you want to do? You want to go down to the docks, get some fries?"

Madelyn had the little bag held tight against her hip.

"Maddy?"

Madelyn looked up.

"What'd you get?"

The girl took the bag up and handed it over. Sarah opened it. Reached in and came out with a small folding knife. Handle of real wood. It looked like a toy but when she flicked the blade straight it was good steel.

"You aren't gonna make me take it back, are you?" said the girl.

Sarah closed the knife over. Put it back in the bag and set the bag on the dash.

"That's a conversation we're gonna have later," Sarah said.

They'd reached the northern limits of the town and met the two-lane highway that began there and led west and then south toward the city. They were to cross straight through and head home. Instead, Sarah took the truck slow through the intersection and then turned east. A lone man on a chopper passed them going the other way and he wore his leather kutte and club colours. After that there were no more vehicles travelling that barren stretch. The road hadn't been assumed by the county and it ran through marshland and granite bluffs and over a narrow concrete bridge settled in swamp that led to places remote and sparely populated.

"Do those bikers live out here?" Madelyn said.

Sarah didn't look at her.

"There's good people here. Good and bad. Like everywhere else."

By and by they found a wider carriage road with men repaving the lanes section by section. They passed a sign that marked Wahta Mohawk territory. The men stood by and watched the truck go. Slow on that winding throughway with forest on either side. Sarah let off the gas for a stretch, observed the rusted and part-hidden street signs until they neared a break in the treeline. No marker for that road. There she turned and drove the truck hard over buckled asphalt. A quarter-mile in and they were travelling on nothing more than dirt and packed clay.

Sarah parked the truck at the side of the road and told Madelyn to stay put. She got out. There was a steel security gate between two lengths of stone-laid wall with no visible end, lines of razor wire bracketed to the flat top slabs. An intercom system had been built into the stone beside the gate. Sarah looked up higher and then searched the near trees. Sure enough she saw the glint from the lens of a small security camera set there to watch the road. She walked up and pushed the call button on the intercom. Nobody answered so she hit it again. After that she just pushed the talk button and went at it.

"Anybody home?" she said. "I need to talk to Clayton."

She let go and looked over at the truck. Madelyn had turned to kneel on the seat. Watched Sarah through the back-glass of the cab. Sarah eyeballed the gate and the camera for a minute more. Then she started back toward the truck. She'd not made it three feet before the intercom crackled.

"Who's there?" the intercom said.

Sarah took a deep breath and then turned and went back to the gate. She pushed the button.

"You know who it is," she said. "You can see me, Clayton."

She backed up some and waved at the camera. The intercom clicked again.

"Alright. Come in," Clayton said.

The gate unlocked and started retracting into the actual stone of the wall where the intercom was set.

She pulled up on the open lot beside three other cars and a custom-built two-ton truck with a gunrack fixed to the cab's back window. Three sets of levered hooks but they held nothing. She had her fingers on the door-handle awhile before she got out.

"I won't be long," she said. "You don't get out of this truck for any reason."

Madelyn nodded.

"Let me hear it."

"Okay," she said.

Sarah laid a palm on the top of Madelyn's head.

"Promise me."

"I promise," she said. "Jesus."

Sarah got out of the truck and walked across the lot toward the house. Two stories of brick and timber with a narrow front porch, enough space to stand or sit between the outer walls and the wooden railing that ran the length of the decking. And there a man did sit, watching her with his feet flat to the planking and his hands in his lap. He wore jeans and boots and a brown leather jacket and he had scars on his face that could be seen plain. Still, he had a handsomeness to him. Light brown skin. Black, black eyes. Hair cropped to stubble.

"Hey, Wallace," she said.

"Hey," he said. "Been awhile."

Sarah had first met Wallace King when Daniel moved their family up north from the city, to Daniel's father house. Wallace was born and raised on the island reserve and during high school he billeted with Arthur and Daniel through the winters, instead of taking the ferry to the mainland and riding another hour to school by bus. That was nearly twenty-five years ago. When Sarah met Wallace he had a wife and twin sons on the island. When he'd made enough money he moved them into the town of Marston, on the south side. The family still lived in that house but Wallace hadn't for years.

Sarah got to the steps and stopped there.

"Clayton said I could come down. I just need to talk to him a minute," she said.

Wallace nodded.

"He's up in the office."

She walked the steps and Wallace watched her climb. Sarah turned at the door. She was looking out to the front lot. Wallace squinted and leaned forward a little and then sat back.

"She looks like you."

"That's what I hear," Sarah said. "Your boys alright?"

"The boys are good. Smart."

Sarah smiled.

"I'll keep an eye on her," Wallace said.

Sarah went onto the porch and opened the screen door. Behind that a steel security door and it was wide open. The main floor of the house had two large rooms, one of them furnished full with bunks against the wall, what looked like a bathroom entrance. There was no kitchen. Sarah took a step inside.

"Where the other guys at?" she said. "The ones those cars belong to."

Wallace studied her.

"They're around here somewheres," he said.

He nodded toward the house.

"Go on in," he said.

So she went.

Clayton sat with his hands clasped together atop the desk. He read figures in a ledger. When Sarah came in he leaned back and closed the ledger and pushed it aside and then he motioned to the chair on the other side of the desk.

"You need a drink?" he said. "I don't know what I've got. Don't get too many visitors out here."

"It's okay," she said. "I'm not staying long."

He raised his eyebrows, set his hands on his thighs. Even at rest in the house he wore a white dress shirt tucked into dark-blue jeans, not a wrinkle in the fabric.

"Shoot," he said.

"What did you do to him last night?" she said.

"Pardon?"

"What did you make him do?"

"I can't make him do anything he doesn't care to," Clayton said.

"You've known Daniel almost his whole life," Sarah said. "And Wallace, I don't know?"

"He was about thirteen."

"If Dan was your son would you let him be involved in this shit?"

Clayton thought on it some. Shrugged at her.

"He's not."

Sarah stared at him a long time. He didn't speak and he didn't speak and then reached for a drawer in the desk. Came back with an envelope and dropped it on the desk before her. She didn't have to open it to know what it was. Or to guess how much you could fit in an envelope like that.

Sarah shook her head once.

"I don't need your fuckin' charity," she said. "I just need him to come home in one piece.

"He's good at this, Sarah. You should just let him work."

She stood and took her purse up from the chair. She looked around the room. Old hunting rifles hung in brackets on the one wall. Furniture made from great chunks of driftwood dredged from the bay. Paintings that she knew even he could not afford. Two framed diplomas on the wall nearest to the desk, plain to read from either side. The one from a polytechnic criminology program and the other a certification for risk management. There were no photographs on the wall or the desk and Sarah found that strange. Clayton had brothers and cousins in the region. Some of whom she knew him to be close enough to. He'd been married young to a full-blood Mohawk woman but she'd been gone some twenty years. Killed in her sleep by an aneurysm. No trace of her anywhere.

"Not long and we'll have enough money," Sarah said.

"From working with the geriatrics, with the pills and pisspails?"

"I got plans," she said.

Clayton said okay. He still hadn't reached for the envelope.

"He's got a line on how to get the truck rig back," she said. "It doesn't matter."

"You and I both know that he can't afford a new rig."

"It ain't the new rig. He knows the fella who took it."

Clayton sat up straighter in the chair. He tried to pretend he hadn't.

"How's that?" he said.

"You don't think he's got people who'll tell him shit he wants to know? Better than that. People like him. Some'll talk to him even without threat or coercion. Can you imagine?"

Clayton settled some.

"Well, good," he said.

Sarah went to the door. Opened it and held the knob but didn't go.

"The old man would've killed you over this shit. Had he lived to see it. You know that, right?" she said.

Clayton nodded.

"Maybe," he said.

Sarah closed the door behind her and walked the hall. Kept her eyes on the office door. She had to watch her feet as she stepped quick down the winding staircase.

When Sarah came out of the house Wallace's chair was empty. She could see him standing out in the middle of the lot, watching her truck. Three men were getting into a black sedan. The driver was standing between his car and her truck, talking to Madelyn through the window. He had very blonde hair and an odd way about him. He was handling something as he spoke with the girl. Sarah crossed the lot to Wallace.

"Everything good?" he said.

"Yeah," she said, but she'd not take her eyes off the blonde man.

"It's okay," Wallace said. "He's Clayton's nephew."

Someone called to the driver from inside the car and he turned and spoke at them. He looked back to Madelyn and handed her the thing in his hand. It was the knife she'd bought, drawn full with the hilt toward the girl. Madelyn folded the blade while he watched and he said something else before he got into the car and fired the engine.

"Jesus H. fucking Christ," Sarah said.

Wallace looked to her.

"Thanks, Wallace," she said.

"No problem," he said.

She found the keys and started for the truck. Wallace walked her over.

"Why is it that the main part of that house is all upstairs?" she said as they went. "All the living rooms and the kitchen and everything."

"Clayton's idea," Wallace said. "He says it's a lot easier just to defend a staircase."

Sarah asked no more. She left Wallace at the edge of the lot and he waited while she brought the truck around to leave. Sarah waved and Wallace raised a hand. She drove up the grade and left the grounds with her daughter and long after they were gone the man yet stood there, watching the pass while the daylight crept out.

FIVE

Daniel walked the perimeter of the place with his eyes on the house. Nothing stirred and the drapes were down in the windows of the oddly shaped bungalow. The side panels were stained wood but they'd long lost their colour and begun to curl. Some had fallen. The house was penned in by woods on all sides save for a winding drive that led down to the forest road. Daniel could see clear to distant baywater through a patchy section of the treeline. There were snowmobiles dismantled in the yard and rusting to nought on the tall-grass. Old tow-trailers piled somehow in one corner of the grounds. A makeshift service mechanic's garage attached to the main part of the house, a sign there that said what they can't fix can't be fixed. The garage door had been pulled shut and bolted. No vehicles in the driveway that led to it.

Near a busted tree stump Daniel got to his haunches with a good sightline to the back windows of the house. The decking built there. He waited there long enough to know that if anyone was home they were laid low or sleeping. Then he trod the yard toward the house, light as he could go. He kept an eye on his feet, wary of traps that might've been planted there, intentionally or not. Near to the deck there was another big stump with a small woodpile aside it and an axe stuck out of the top of the thing. Daniel walked over to it and freed the axe. Felt the heft of it by one hand. He carried it off and climbed the steps slow.

Through little gaps in the curtain he could see some of the house. Living room of antiquated furniture and old heirlooms and photographs, all kept immaculate. No cans or clutter anywhere in the place. He took hold of the sliding-door handle by two fingers and pulled small. It shifted. He stood there a minute and listened to the house. Then he slid the door open and moved through the curtains.

Daniel stood in the dim main room with the axe hung low at his side. He listened and he listened. Scent of dust and dry timber, faint chemical smell that he couldn't identify. There was a TV in the one corner of the room and a stereo system on the wall to the side of it. All of it turned off, as well as the lamps and ceiling lights. He went through to the kitchen and saw a dish-rack empty and bone dry on the sink counter. No kettles or coffee pots. Room by room he walked the house and a strangeness built in him as he went. Clothes hung in the bedroom on a pole fixed into a cutaway in the one wall, a gap in the middle with just empty hangers there. No sign of the man anywhere and Daniel made his way through the house again to be sure. The garage wouldn't even tell him anything, with the tools racked and some beside snowmobiles and cars, and no way to tell if they were waiting there or left for good. He couldn't even guess if a vehicle was missing as he'd no way of knowing how many were there to start.

On his way out he stopped again in the kitchen and looked through cupboards and drawers. The fridge was near empty when he opened it, save for a couple bottles of beer and some condiments, freezer full with vacuum-packed meats. Daniel took one of the beers and sat the counter with the axe laid over the sink basins. He turned the cap and drank. When he left the place he closed the glass sliding door over and then the screen door. Down in the yard he raised the axe and drove it back into the stump where he'd found it. He turned to the house again and examined the place. Daniel couldn't remember opening the screen door so he went up and started sliding it back. Halfway he stopped and leant close, knelt on the decklumber. There was a clean slit through the screenmesh long enough for him to get his hand through and feel the simple latch on the other side. Daniel cleared his hand and turned quick to the yard. Bird cries in the deep wood. After awhile he slid the screen door full open and left the place by a foot trail that led down to the valley and the town proper.

SIX

Daniel hung up the phone and set the receiver down on his kitchen table. He went back outside to the front steps and sat down on the cold concrete and stared out at the dirt road to their house. Old telegraph lines were strung high above, swaying some in the twilight. Frantic shape of a bat flying, hunting mosquitos. A near-full bottle of beer sat on the step beside Daniel and he picked it up and poured it out on the grass. He leaned back with his palms on the stone beside him and there he waited until he saw a speck of light appear way out in the blackness. He watched that light swell and split into two and come down the road twinned, brighter and brighter as they neared.

When the truck pulled into the driveway, Daniel sat there for another few seconds and then he stood up and brushed the grit off of his jeans. The driver door popped and Sarah shoved it open and got out and slung the straps of her purse up over her shoulder. The girl got out on the other side and swatted the door closed. Hustled on toward the house with grocery bags dangling from either hand. She passed without a word and went in. Daniel met his wife at the truck and Sarah handed him one bag and he kept his hand out for more but she'd not give him anything. She reached into the cab again and took out three grocery bags and shoved the door shut with her hip.

"How was it?" he said.

"Long," she said.

Daniel nodded toward the house.

"What's her malfunction?" he said.

"Where to start," Sarah said. "You been home awhile?"

"Yeah," he said. "I was just sitting out."

"I didn't know we'd be gone so long. It got dark in a hurry."

"That's alright," he said.

"How'd it go out in the hills?"

Daniel shook his head no. He reached down and took hold of the bags she had with his free hand. Lifted them and tugged. Finally she gave them up and followed him to the house. She went by him to get the door but she didn't open it.

"What's the matter?" she said.

"I don't know yet," he said. "Probably nothin'."

She looked him up and down.

"There's food in here," he said. "I don't know how good it is, and I know for sure it ain't hot. But you could probably eat it."

"I'll be the judge of that," she said, and pulled the door open. He lingered.

"When d'you work at?" he said.

She kneed him in the asscheek and there he did move. The screen door swung and latched.

"Too soon," she said. "But we've got some time."

She kissed him at his chin and walked through to the kitchen. Flicked the lights on full and started moving plates about. Madelyn was in there unloading the bags she'd carried. Daniel took one last look at the outer dark and then he followed them inside.

At midnight Daniel sat out on the step again. Sarah had taken the truck hours before and Madelyn had fallen asleep atop her covers with her clothes on and her little TV flickering in the corner of the room. He'd looked in on her three times while he waited. When the car pulled into his driveway he held his index finger up to his lips. The driver nodded. Daniel stood and stepped back into the house.

He came out a few seconds later with his jacket on and the driver of the car got out careful and left the door open.

"Hey Murr," Daniel said and shook the man's hand. "Thanks for comin' by."

"No worries," the man said.

"I know it's twice in one day, but I can't have those motherfuckers drivin' out to the house."

"No way," Murray said. "I get it."

The man was in his late fifties and stood about five-foot-eight with thick, salt and pepper hair that could have used a cut some weeks ago. Worn-out jeans and boots on him, button-up plaids over his wide shoulders. Rough brown skin through his cheeks and chin though he'd nothing to shave but the moustache that grew thin at his upper lip.

"There's a full tank in that old bastard," he said.

Daniel nodded. He took a long look at the black Monte Carlo, idling on the drive.

"Door's open," Daniel said. "And you know the girl won't wake up to the TV or anything."

"What do you want me to tell her if she wakes up?"

"Just tell her I'll be back shortly. And don't take any shit."

"And what about your old lady? What does she know?"

Daniel took the keys from Murray.

"That's a tomorrow problem," he said. "Today ain't over yet."

Murray clapped Daniel on the shoulder hard and then started for the house. Daniel was getting into the car when Murray came tip-toeing back, pointing at something in the car. A six-pack of tallboys were stood on the passenger seat leather. Daniel grabbed it by the rings and handed it over.

"Shit," Murray said. "Almost blew the whole deal before it got started."

"I got beer in there," Daniel said.

"Well, you might not later."

Daniel closed the door and Murray pushed it snug. He waited there a second with his thumbs hooked under the top of the window frame, fingers flat to the roof.

"Be careful, bud," Murray said, then he put his hand out again and Daniel took it. The old man seemed like he might pulp Daniel's fingers. Concern in his dark eyes.

"I'll be back in a couple hours," Daniel said.

Murray nodded and let go. He went toward the house and up the steps. Daniel let the gearshift down and backed out of the drive as slow as he could. He waited there in the lane until he saw the door of his house close over and then he crept the car down the road. Seconds gone and he could see the glow of the porch lamp but small in his rearview mirror. There he thumped the gas pedal and the tires threw broken chips of brittle tarmac as he went townward through cold and lightless country.

They were waiting for him this time. Wallace stood beside the windowless black van, sat crooked on an empty concrete lot. Daniel had parked the car a block away and came over on foot. No vehicles passed on the bordering streets and the area was poorly lit. Grid of industrial plazas and storage lockers and low-rent warehouses guarded only by dogs and decoy cameras. They were at the western limits of a suburban boomtown between the northern counties and the city proper, a part of the town that development had skipped over or forgot outright. The lights of the town carpeted a mountain-rise to the east. To the west there were abandoned train tracks aside a rude, skeletal wood and further lay swamp and wildgrass and nothingness.

Daniel stepped light and Wallace didn't see him until he'd got within twenty feet of the van. Wallace's hand went into his coat for a second and then came back out. He shook his head, leaned down and put his hands on his knees. When he stood up again Daniel could see the pistols under his jacket, Kevlar strapped loose to his chest over a black T-shirt. The van's side door had been left open a crack and now Wallace slid it gentle to the side.

Clayton sat on his haunches with two other men that Daniel had seen before and one that he hadn't. The two men he knew were Mike Moreau and Troy Armstrong, thieves and gun thugs that Clayton hired regular. They had tactical shotguns resting across their knees. Each of them held the pistol grip with their index fingers pressed flat against the trigger guard. The man that Daniel didn't know had short blonde hair and a scar that ran the length of his scalp and trailed off into his left eyebrow. Wiry man and broad under his bandit blacks and flak jacket. Built much like Clayton, but on a plainly larger frame. His eyes were so pale that they did not seem real. That man had his back against the barrier between the front and rear of the van, his legs laid out full, one crossed one over the other at the ankle. Combat boots under black cargo pants. He stared at Daniel long enough that the other men shuffled in their gear. When Clayton started speaking the man quit it and looked out vacantly at the streets and lots beyond.

"You're late," Clayton said.

Daniel looked at each man again. Clayton had pistols slung in the open over his shirt.

"Why you all got the fucking Kevlar on?" he said.

"Just get in," Clayton said.

Daniel glanced back over his shoulder to where he had parked the car. Smell of burnt rubber in the air. Distant woodsmoke. He climbed up. Wallace shut the door and Daniel took a seat against the divider beside the pale-eyed man. He sat with his forearms over top of his knees and felt the van sink some as Wallace got into the front seat. There came the sound of the driver door pulled shut and the engine firing and then they were travelling.

"I thought you said we were just goin' to talk to this dude?" Daniel said.

Clayton checked the chamber of his right-hand pistol and he didn't look up.

"Is that what I said?"

"Well you didn't say we were gonna fuckin' storm a beachhead."

Still Clayton examined the gun. He holstered it and leaned back. Laced his hands together in his lap.

"This shiftless crew of degenerates boosted a vehicle that I owned and a trunk full of weed and oxy," Clayton said. "And in doing it they took a tire iron to the fellow who was driving. This kid, Jimmy Maher."

"I know the guy," Daniel said.

"Well they split his fucking head open and left him there against the curb, where he very nearly drowned, laying up against the mouth of a sewer drain."

Daniel cleared his throat. Turned his neck so that it cracked.

"He alright?"

"Yeah, he's wonderful," Clayton said, and set to unfastening and refastening the Velcro straps on his vest. "He isn't dead, if that's what you mean. And it took a while to make sure of that."

The van banked around a wide turn and the men braced themselves where they sat. They ran straight again and faster now on smooth road.

"This young biker that robbed you, name's Dubeau, ain't it?" Daniel said.

"Yes."

"He's a relation to a big man in the club, charter original."

"I know who he is."

"You can't go hard at that guy. They will fuck you where you live."

Clayton said no more. After a while he sat forward and got the attention of the shotgunner Armstrong. He beckoned with his forefinger and Armstrong reached down to his side and pulled a semi-automatic pistol. Clayton took it from him by the barrel and then leaned forward, held the butt-end of the pistol out to Daniel.

Daniel just sat there until Clayton's hand dropped. The pale-eyed man kept weighing him up from the side but Daniel wouldn't acknowledge him. Clayton gave the pistol back and it was tucked down into the space between Moreau and Armstrong. They'd all gone solemn. Soon enough the van slowed and went along at a creep. Armstrong reached back down to where he'd pulled the gun and came back with two hockey masks. They set about putting them on and each of the masks were painted to look like a skull. Shaded in greys to show ridges of bone. Clayton pointed to each man and told him to take the fucking things off. Moreau and Armstrong looked at each other and fretfully started to pull their masks. It bothered Daniel that Clayton was so sure they'd not need them.

"How about you let me talk to this guy before you start layin' people out," Daniel said.

Clayton looked out through a narrow slit at one of the rear doors. He closed one eyelid to better see and then he turned.

"That's why you're here."

"Something in the water up this way," said the pale-eyed man.

Daniel did turn then. The blonde man was smiling a little and again he stared. Something sickly there in the pallid deep. He shifted slight and the shortened stock of a double-barrel shotgun stuck out from his far side. The barrels had likewise been sawn short and the man moved again and the gun was gone into his coat. Daniel looked back at Clayton.

"You got any more Kevlar?" he said.

"What you need it for if you're just talking?" the pale-eyed man said.

Daniel pointed at the man.

"Who in the fuck is this guy?" Daniel said.

"My nephew," Clayton said. "Come back from the states to put in work."

"You got a name for him?" Daniel said.

"Tarbell," Clayton said. "Aaron Tarbell."

"Never heard of him," Daniel said.

He settled and breathed calm. The van slowed and slowed and then it stopped. Wallace got out and shut his door and left the keys rattling in the ignition. He came around to the panel door and slid it open and Daniel's feet were the first on the ground. He walked the dirt and stone, unarmed and unarmoured, and he did not slow nor wait to hear if they were trailing him.

Three men sat on their choppers outside a four-car garage with Dubeau Motors bolted above the hangar. Two of them were tall with long hair and they were father and son, both named Lennox Merritt. Blonde hair on Merritt Jr. and Merritt Sr. gone mostly grey. Nearer sat Billy-Jo Contois, lean and shirtless under his kutte, a number of crooked scars tattooed over on his arms and torso. Their bikes faced the building, a great brick-built monster with a tired metal awning running the length of the shop. There were picnic tables sat out front and a charcoal grill with smoke spilling out from its sides. Dubeau came out from the garage with a beer in his hand and he settled straddle-legged on his pan-head. Patches on his kutte with the top rocker plainly visible. He drank at the beer while the other three men chattered and cursed and then set to laughing. Even sunk low on the bike he was far taller than the other men. Dubeau saw Daniel coming and he sat up straight. When he saw Clayton and the blonde man he stood.

"Sit down, man," Daniel said. "It's alright."

The other three bikers shut up but Contois' hand went to his waist.

"Do not fucking draw any pistols," Daniel said to him. "Don't you fuckin' do it."

The hand kept creeping.

"B.J." Dubeau hollered. "Knock that shit off."

The man let it fall.

"What's up, fellas?" Dubeau said. "Don't see you all out here much."

Dubeau pointed past them.

"I don't know you," he said to Clayton's nephew.

Tarbell took a step and started to say something.

"Shut the fuck up," Daniel said. Tarbell froze and looked to Clayton but Clayton would only eyeball the bikers. Dubeau just sat there.

"You know what you done," Daniel said. "You all jacked that car and put a kid in the hospital. I'm gues-sin' you didn't know who he worked for. But you gotta give up what you took or hand over what it was worth."

Dubeau nodded.

"I already got this talk at church, from the big men," he said. "We knew you'd be comin' for it."

"What else did they say?"

"Said give it to you."

Dubeau got up and the bike rose on its springs. He downed his beer and scratched at his chest and lifted his left leg clear over the bike. He stood about six-foot-five and had wide shoulders and nearly no neck and short black hair slicked to one side. He pitched the beer can into an oil drum a few feet away from the grill and then he started for the garage.

"Hold on," Daniel said. "I'm comin' in there with you."

"Okay," Dubeau said.

Clayton told Daniel to go on but Daniel had already started walking over to Dubeau. The other bikers watched them go. Dubeau led the way into the building through the open hangar.

"I heard you were about done with this shit," Dubeau said.

"I'm here, ain't I?"

They walked through the shop, past countless parts and filthy utility shelving and an ancient hydraulic lift. Daniel kept his eyes on Dubeau's back and on the biker's hands. When they got to the dim back room Daniel stopped in the doorway. He inventoried the place quick while Dubeau retrieved a large duffel bag. Hefted it out to the shop floor so that the insides of the bag could be seen under the ceiling fluorescents.

Daniel didn't check it. He just nodded and took up the straps. Waved Dubeau by and followed him back out toward the front of the shop.

They were not five feet out into the lot before the shotgun bellowed. Daniel sunk to his haunches and went sideways toward the building. Streak of muzzle-fire against the black. Dubeau spun forty-five degrees and as he turned there were pieces of him flung out in the open air. One part of the man flew skewered with rib-bone. His leather kutte had been shot to ribbons on one side and stuck wet to the man. He sat on the tarmac with his right leg bent at the knee and his left leg straight out. Sat funny like that for just a second before his weight carried him over and put him face-down to the asphalt. Metals were ringing in the shop. Out in the darkness the concussions echoed and came back to them over miles of hard and mottled field.

Daniel managed to get up by the garage wall and as he stood so did the Merritts, father and son. They were looking at Clayton and Tarbell, his double-barrel shotgun held low with the sawn muzzles leaking smoke and vapour. The Merritts were barely upright when Moreau and Armstrong showed at the other side of the lot and opened up on them. They'd both circled around the building and waited and now they came forward deliberate. The biker Contois had drawn his pistol sitting and fired twice but missed and he took shot to the neck and chest and slumped to the bike and somehow as he folded he fired one more round into his own leg, just below the hip. His jeans began to turn maroon. Moreau and Armstrong did not let up and spent shotgun shells were spat clear and new shells racked and the Merritt's were blown backward through their motorcycles and landed dead or dying, crumpled strange near the outer brick wall of the shop. The barbeque took shot and went over slow, puked up a mess of seared meat and lit coals when it hit ground.

When the firing stopped, Daniel climbed back to his feet near to the building and stood with his hands up and out. High, steady tone in his right ear and . all over his jacket. He looked at the shotgunners and the killed bikers. Dubeau had bled out with his right leg bent up under him and his mouth open, eyes wide and staring blind to the west. The bikes dripped red and Merritt Sr's had fallen on him after he'd gone over it. Daniel took a step forward to check on the younger Merritt, laid out beside his bike with all his fluids spilled to the asphalt. He'd known that man most of his life.

Daniel stared into the hangar by the thin inner light. He counted steps from the doorway to the spot where Dubeau fell. Figured on how close he'd been when the man was hit. He put a hand to the near chopper's handlebars and gripped it hard as he could. Took hold of the affixed mirror and wrenched it from its moorings. Then he turned and walked toward Clayton with his eyes cold on Clayton's nephew. Tarbell had been observing his work and he didn't look up until Daniel was nearly on top of him and even then he seemed not to know what he was looking at. The shotgun rose like he were using it to wave and Daniel pushed it aside with the outside heel of his right hand and cracked the man hard at the cheek with a left hook. Turned over full with most of his weight behind it. Tarbell let go of the gun as he fell and it clattered to the ground. Daniel kicked it wide and went on. An angry red line had been drawn high in the felled man's cheek and as he tried to crab his way backward the cut opened up and the blood came fast and ran the underside of Tarbell's face. Daniel stopped and waited and Tarbell got to one knee all at once and his hand was already reaching inside of his jacket. Daniel beat him to it and yanked the pistol loose and then got hold of the blonde by his shirtcloth and drove the butt into the bridge of the man's nose. Tarbell would have dropped again but Daniel held him up and hit him clean between his rolled-back eyes before Clayton and his two hired-men wrapped Daniel up and wrested the pistol from his hand and dragged him clear.

They left the city limits by the narrow highway to the north. Daniel following the van in the borrowed car. Soon the van pulled off of the highway entirely, went down into a gravel gulley beneath an unfinished overpass with the rebar exposed. Tarp tied over the length of it and rippling in the wind while one loose corner slapped hard against the formed concrete. Daniel would not follow them down. He'd parked on the soft shoulder and waited until they started flashing the lights. His phone vibrated inside his coat.

"If you think I'm goin' down there you are out of your fuckin' minds," he said, and hung up.

They waited yet in the construction site. Daniel put his knuckles hard to the horn and kept at it until the van's running lights came on and it started to climb back up the grade.

He followed the van at a distance until they reached Marston. Already he guessed where they were going.

They came into the town by some grim county roads and had one set of traffic lights to hold them up. Daniel was back behind them in the lane a good deal though there was no one else between the two vehicles. As they waited for the lights to turn, a slick new police cruiser passed Daniel in the next lane and pulled up beside the van. Painted grey and black to better hide it on the sideroads and cutaways. Daniel saw the silhouette of just one head moving about in the driver seat.

"Don't you fuckin' dare," he said.

They were like that for minutes and then the light turned. The cruiser peeled off to the right and turned down the crossroad, no signal before he went. The van rode through the intersection slow and Daniel kept pace.

Just inside town limits they took a road that led them down a modest line of shops and apartments, a good number of them vacant or for sale. There were just a handful of cars parked spare along the length of the street. The streetlamps were few and not all were on. Dark among the buildings was an old corner tavern that Clayton owned in principle if not in name and it had been closed for perhaps two hours when the van took the curbside out front. Daniel slowed and put the car in reverse and wheeled backward so that he was sidelong to the building on the cross street. From where he stopped he could see a fire exit and a door that he knew opened by pushbar on the other side.

Wallace got out of the van and walked the pavement toward Daniel. All Daniel had for arms was an old, weighty cudgel that Murray kept between the seats. He watched Wallace come close and got out from the car empty-handed.

"You'd better keep him in the van," Daniel said.

"I know," Wallace said.

Daniel had his thumbs hung in his belt and his fists pressed to his thighs. He stood square to Wallace until the big man settled and crossed his arms and rested his ass to the hood of the Monte Carlo.

"Who the fuck even has a gun like that?" Daniel said.

Wallace shook his head. He couldn't say.

Clayton had his pistols on the table and his hands in plain view, one flat to the hardwood and the other holding a glass of whiskey. There were stacks of bills set in rows by Wallace as he tallied them up. They'd taken their dope back and whatever else they'd found at the garage. Daniel sat opposite and upright and he seemed not to even blink. Clayton kept telling him to simmer down but Daniel almost had a frequency as he waited in the chair.

Wallace called out the count to Clayton and Clayton said okay and took five short-stacked bundles and set them on the table in-between he and Daniel.

"If you stay on," he said.

"It ain't about the money," Daniel said, to the both of them. "The MC is gonna bury every last one of us."

Clayton didn't seem moved by the idea. Nor Wallace.

"They work for the same people I do," said Clayton. "Those in the club that want to be part of what's coming knew they'd have to burn some deadwood."

"I don't believe that. There's gonna be blowback."

"You still don't understand, do you, son?" Clayton said. "Things are changed."

Someone knocked at the bolted security door to Clayton's office. Clayton drank at the whiskey. He didn't turn to see. Wallace went to the door and looked through the lens and unbolted it long enough to talk to the man on the other side. He shut the door and locked it again.

"His nose ain't broke," Wallace said.

"Good enough," Clayton said.

Wallace went to the bar and came back with the whiskey bottle. He set it down in front of Daniel aside his empty glass. Daniel drank right from the bottle and stood it near to the money.

"You gotta cut that kid loose," Daniel said.

Clayton thought on it.

"He'll do the things that other men won't do," Clayton said.

"He's awful blonde to be working out at your place up the highway. They ain't gonna tolerate the likes of him for long."

"He's got Mohawk blood. I can prove his line, whether they know the man or not," Clayton said. "Doesn't matter what he looks like. In fact, it's a little more than useful, his looking the way he does. How often do you see the cops pull over a clean-cut white boy?"

Daniel stood and drank once more. He wiped at his mouth with the back of his hand and told Wallace to get the door for him. Wallace wouldn't move until Clayton said okay and that aggravated Daniel more than he could hide. Clayton stood then and took up a bound stack of bills and pitched it sidearm and it caught Daniel high on his shoulder and fell to his side. Daniel turned sudden and swatted late at where the money hit and then saw it on the ground.

"What the fuck?" he said.

"In all the years I've known you, you've been too scared to commit all the way," Clayton said. "Do it now and you will have more money than you knew there was."

Daniel dipped low enough to snag the bundle of cash in his right hand. He whipped it back at Clayton but too hard and it flew wide and missed Clayton by feet. He turned casual after it passed to see where it ended up.

"I ain't like this psycho you dredged up," Daniel said. "Hell, I ain't even like Wallace."

"You are," Clayton said. "I know better than anybody."

Wallace had taken to leaning against the wall near to the door. Daniel looked him up and down. Then he took hold of the door latch and pulled, standing so that he could still see both men in the office. Clayton had left his seat and came around and sat the edge of the table.

"The money ain't everything," Daniel said, and started to leave the room.

"That's what Sarah said too," Clayton said.

Daniel stopped leaving.

"What?"

"When she came out to see me up at the house the other day," Clayton said. "She didn't tell you?"

"How would you like to be dead?" Daniel said.

Wallace took a step. Clayton held his hand out no.

"Just think on the work," Clayton said.

"All I do is think on it."

Clayton pushed himself up and walked across the room to Daniel, put a hand on Daniel's shoulder. Daniel let him.

"You quit on me now, you are not ever coming back," Clayton said.

Daniel waited for the hand to drop and then he cleared the threshhold and pulled the steel door shut. The main front room of the bar was barely lit and the gunmen Moreau and Armstrong were drinking slow on a benchseat at the wall, facing the back office and the barroom proper. They looked up at him at the same time. Daniel did not go by them. Instead he turned and walked a long corridor past the kitchen and the washrooms and left the place by the fire exit. A siren wailed for the few seconds it took him to clear the exit and shove the door back, carried down the village streets. It had gone cold outside and dew covered the Monte Carlo and he could smell it in the grasses. He got into the car and drove the empty streets fast toward home.

SEVEN

Sarah stood in front of the glass doors of the retirement home and read from her book under yellow spotlight. She'd blocked the entryway with a chair so that the inner door did not close properly and if she were buzzed or there were signals sounded at the front desk she'd still hear. Out in the lot were few vehicles. Daniel's battered truck amongst them. Some belonged to residents but were never driven. Boats with paint that shone and low mileage and benchseats in the front. More than one of those cars were old enough they had to be retrofitted with seatbelts.

The building and the parking lot was built on a rise and Sarah could see almost the entire length of the main road in either direction. In her half-hour out front she saw a total of three cars pass by in the street, two of them side by side and racing wild toward the bottom end of town. The grounds beside the nursing home were little more than mowed turf and withered flower gardens. Long run of wire fencework that made up the rear boundary line. Thereafter a descending hill of rock and weed and wildflowers. The grade fell steady for a half-mile before it levelled and gave way to highgrass marsh and then lakewater.

Sarah heard crickets fiddling and the rustling of trees. She finished her chapter and pitched the book into a nearby ashtray-topped trashcan and there she left it as she pulled the chair free and went inside.

She walked the halls and looked at her watch. Sung quiet to herself and where she ran out of words or songs she made up her own, notes left late to hang in the re-circulated air. She passed many closed doors with dim light or pure black in the gap below but often she passed open doors with whatever darkness or lamp-glow laid plain for her along with whistles, whimpers or snores from within. The difficult shifting of bod-ies. Sarah looked in on everyone and she listened for sounds that she knew and she listened harder for those that she might not have heard before.

Sarah turned the corner and there she saw a rectan-gle of light bleeding out over the hallway carpet. She held up for a moment and then she walked across it and leaned against the doorframe with her hands in her scrub pockets. Inside the room an old man sat in an armchair with a bottle of beer in his hand. Small table-stand in front of him. Across the room the TV played but the sound had been turned down and the man had angled his chair toward his window, the curtains drawn and billowing soft by the cool night air. He sat in his slacks and his T-shirt with his heavy chest raising the cotton and white hair sticking out from his shirt-collar. He had thick, silver hair on his head and it had been combed and combed to keep a part but still would not behave. The man's nose was large and run through with an old scar at the bridge, wide jaw below. Parts of him had gone softer with age but his frame was huge and his limbs long and the forearms thick and heavy with cordmuscle. The bottle was small in his great, knobbled fingers as he drank at it. The man paid no mind to the door, tiny speaker-buds in his ears and the wire running to a stereo on the tabletop beside him.

"Hey there, Mr. Bradshaw," Sarah called out.

The man seemed not to hear her. She didn't fret.

"John," she called. "The police are here. They say they got a warrant out on you."

The man sipped the beer again. He wiggled the earphone in his left ear and set his hand back down on the chair arm.

"There's a bunch of naked ladies come to see you," Sarah said. "They say they just want your autograph."

The beer paused on its way up.

"You'd better send them on in," he said. Then he finished his drink before turning and setting the empty bottle on the bedside table and pushing a button on the stereo. He straightened up in the chair again and took the earphones out.

"Hello," John said.

"Hey," she said. "How are you?"

"Well," he said. "I was just takin' the air."

"Okay."

The old man reached down and rummaged around in a trashcan. Ice rattled against the metals. His hand came up with two bottles pinched at the neck between his foreknuckles. He set the bottles down on the small table before him. There was an empty chair on the other side of the little tablestand and he waved at it.

She stood in the doorway yet and leaned back to scout the long, dim corridor. She looked back into the room. The old man hadn't moved nor changed his expression. She blew a loose strand of hair out of her eyes and then got up off the doorframe and went inside.

"You know you ain't supposed to bring beer in from the dining hall. Don't you?"

"Oh yeah?" he said.

"I think we might have gone over that rule before."

"First I ever heard of it."

Sarah settled hard in the chair. John took one of the bottles and his palm just passed over it for a moment but the cap had been twisted off and now sat somewhere in his cupped hand. He slid the bottle over to her across two feet of tabletop and then he uncapped his own and held it out. They clinked bottles across the table and drank. He pulled deep. Sarah took a long gulp of her own and rested and then sipped again.

The old man studied her.

"They workin' you hard in here?"

"It's the same as ever."

"By the looks of you I would say that it's a pretty rough beat."

"Thanks a lot," she said.

The old man took a swig and leaned back. He gripped the edge of his chair with his free hand. Sarah squinted her eyes at him as if she were trying to see something far away. Then she took another drink. She glanced over at the door. Nobody.

"It's as tough as you want it to be I guess," she said. "Depending on what you put into it."

The old man nodded.

"I figured as much. Some of these nurses don't seem too hard done by at the end of their day."

"They're not nurses," Sarah said.

"What's that?"

"I said they're not nurses."

"You're a nurse aren't ya?"

"Not yet."

The old man grunted.

"In that case I want a decrease in my rent."

Sarah smiled.

"I'll see what I can do."

"And don't give me no shit about the beer either. Or say nothing to the bigwigs."

"Never do."

The old man paused.

"I know," he said.

The big man put his bottle down empty. He reached into the trashcan and as he was pulling another he looked at Sarah and she showed her half-full bottle to him. The man brought the one bottle up and its cap had been twisted loose by the time it cleared the table. He took a swig and set the full bottle down beside the spent one.

"What d'you do with the empties, John?" she said. "I never find them in here and I never heard any of the other girls chirp about it."

"Ah," he said. "I just pitch 'em out the window. I imagine they roll clear to the water."

Sarah shook her head. She took another sip and stared out at the night through the thin curtain-cloth. Pale lamplight shone soft over the woodland grounds from lightpoles that had been sunk long years before Sarah was born.

"It's hard to look at you sometimes," he said. "You know that?"

"You've said it."

"She'd have got any older than she did I think she'd look like you."

Sarah tried to smile but had a hard time with it.

"Don't think you got all this time set aside for you later on. There's nothin' guaranteed," John said.

"Wouldn't dare."

Sarah sat up and reached across the table. He was looking toward the woods again. His fingers let go of the chair arm and hung there and then grabbed it again. After a few seconds his hand came up and covered the all of Sarah's hand.

"Are you alright?" she said to him.

"I'm fine," he said. "It's nothing new. I got plenty to drink, and it's a nice night. I got some good company."

He took his hand back but he'd not look at her again.

"Nights like this I dream of being on the boat. Back east. About the whales where they run off the coast. I wake up I can still smell saltwater and gotta feel my face to see it ain't chapped from the cold."

They were quiet for some minutes. John had not drunk at his beer since he'd brought it up and now Sarah reached over and stole it out of his hand and swigged. He smiled big before he took the bottle back. The old man drank and wiped the corners of his mouth with his forearm, settled with the beer in his lap.

"So where are all the fuckin' ladies you promised me?" he said.

Sarah laughed and the more he waited calm for the answer the more she kept at it.

In the small hours of morning Sarah sat alone at the attendant's desk on the ground floor. She'd gotten very few calls throughout her shift and none were serious. Lost pills and trips to the bathroom. General confusion in the night. Sarah read from a new book until her eyelids started to drop and when her head nodded she kneaded her cheeks with her palms and then she got up and went to the little hallway kitchen to fetch more coffee. As she stood beside the percolator she felt strange and turned in time to see the tail of a nightgown passing the doorframe. She left the coffee dripping to the pot and went out.

An old lady in her eighties stood near the outer door.

"Hey, Mrs. Robitaille," Sarah said.

The woman kept at it.

"What's going on?" Sarah said. "It's pretty late to be taking a walk."

The lady pressed her lips together hard. She would not quit the handle.

"I'm following that man who left his room," she said. "I woke up and I saw him and I started to follow him."

Sarah stared down at the hunchbacked woman. Thin white hair and creases of skin at her neck. Blue mapwork of veins on her wasted hands. Whatever else, the woman's eyes were resolute. Sarah put her hand on Mrs. Robitaille's shoulder.

"Who was the man?" Sarah said.

Through doorglass the old woman checked the outer lot. She gave the door one more shove and then looked up at Sarah.

"It was that big man. He just up and went like nobody's business. Not a hitch in his step. I think he must be feeling better."

Sarah stood up straight and likewise scoped the grounds. No one was out there. She tried to think if she'd dozed and lost time at the desk but the door buzzer would have woke her. It had never gone off and there were no blinking lights on the desktop panel.

"It's cold out there," the old woman said. "And he didn't even have his jacket."

Sarah watched the old woman put her head against the pillow and all but instantly fall back into sleep. She waited for a moment longer until she heard the woman's lips whistle. She went out and shut the door soft. Let the doorhandle turn until the latch slid soundless into the strike. Sarah walked down the hall to the next room and saw the door open. Just slightly. Strip of flickering light through the gap. She put her hand on the door.

The TV played silent and flashed shallow light against the far wall and over the length of the man's bed. The room had gone very cool. Early morning chill that crept the open windows, tickled the curtains. Atop the bed lay a huge round of covers. The old man's head rested low in the valley that its weight had made in the pillows. Sarah walked over to the far side of the bed and went to shut the windows. She stopped and turned.

When she pressed her fingertips into the soft underside of his jaw the skin was cold. She pressed harder and then she leaned down and put her ear and cheek beside his part-open mouth. Sarah found his wrist under the blanket and grabbed it and soon she let it go. She took his face in her hands and rubbed at his bluing cheek with her thumb. She stepped away.

Sarah sat beside him in the bed with her hands on her knees. She took deep breaths until she could stand up again. When she stood she couldn't see and she sat back down. She wiped at her eyes and there she saw a lonely bottle neck-deep in the icewater of the metal trashcan. She pushed her hair back behind her ear and sniffled hard and then leant down and got hold of the bottle. She brought the beer up and let it wet her smock. Then she gripped the cap and turned it loose and took a long drink. She tried to look down at John but she couldn't so she got up out of the bed and sat in the chair where he'd been some hours before.

The wind came harder now and the thin drapes blew up against Sarah's chair and goosepimples rose at her pale neck. She drank slow by the flickering of the television and soon she shut it off. Empty bottle in her hand. The room would not darken. Morning rose up over the outlying water and through the tree-columns. Birds spoke and half-naked branches shook their leaves.

EIGHT

The Monte Carlo backed out of the drive and cut into the road. Dust spun up in the lane and hung there. Daniel stood on the step with a beer in his hand and the cold in his bones. Murray had asked him nothing and he'd offered nothing. Light frost covered the grass but it had come late in the night and took but minutes to melt as the sun rose and spilled yellow through the far trees. He went inside with the bottle and sat on the couch. He finished the beer and got another and went down to the cellar.

He heard her before he saw her. The boards speaking soft as she came down. Daniel wore just shorts and he had clothes soaking in the laundry sink beside an old washboard. Steam rising from the water.

"Dad," she said.

He did not look up again.

"Are you alright?

"Yeah," he said. "Now go back to sleep."

He could hear the truck climbing the drive. The engine quit and the door opened and shut. Daniel's pulse gained pace a little and he tried to settle it. Keys jangled and the doorknob turned. When Sarah saw him there on the couch she froze up. He sat in his gitch on the edge of the couch cushions. Bottles stood up empty all over the coffee table. He'd been watching a nature documentary about wolverines with the sound almost too low to hear.

"What are you doing?"

"Hey, Sarah," he said.

"How is the kid?"

"She's fine," he said.

Sarah hooked up her keys in the entryway and went into the kitchen and set her purse on the table. A few seconds later she came back with two beers and sat beside her husband in her scrubs. She started to lean into him but then she stood up and pulled the scrub-top clear over her head with both hands and pulled at her wrinkled T-shirt by the hem. She tossed the garment into the middle of the floor and then took her pants down and tossed them as well and sat down again in her underwear. Daniel reached over to the end of the couch and picked up the blanket he'd left for Murray and he held it out to her. She bit at the nails of her left hand and looked at the blanket. Soon she took it from him and shook it out and laid it over his bare legs and feet and then over hers.

"You've not slept a minute," she said.

Sarah grabbed up the beer bottles from the table one at a time. Uncapped the first and gave it to him and then opened her own. She put an arm around him, rubbed at the cold skin of his back.

"I think Clayton got us into something we can't get out of, no matter what the motherfucker thinks," Daniel said.

He told her the all of what happened and she listened with her heart beating hard against him. She drank the beer in gulps and set it down and put her head in her hands.

"I should never have gone out there to talk to that son of a bitch," she said.

"It wouldn't have made a difference whether you went out there or not. He would've called me anyways."

Sarah got up and went out of the room. Daniel started to stand but she was already coming back with more beer. He sat again and she settled back in beside him.

"You need to stay away from him now," she said. "You understand me?"

Daniel just stared at the TV. She took him by the chin.

"Whatever problems we got, they won't be fixed that way," she said. "Not anymore."

"It all just sort of got away from me," he said. "I didn't see it coming."

"It's different now from when you started working for him," Sarah said. "You'll get yourselves killed, the way this is going. I could tell from talking to Clayton."

Daniel nodded once.

"I know I don't want to end up like him," he said.

"Good," Sarah said, and she took his face whole and kissed him. Daniel kissed her back but that was all.

She blinked hard and then she swung her feet up so that her legs rested atop his legs while she lay back against the far couch-arm. He put his forearms over her ankles and held her gentle at the calf by his heavy fingers.

"Somebody died tonight at the home," she said. "And I was with him not long before. No sign of it at all."

"I'm sorry," Daniel said.

"I liked him very much."

Sarah drank at her beer and set it on the floor. She put her hands on her chest and they rose and fell slow. She told him about the old lady who'd gone looking for the dead man.

"You see anything?" Daniel said.

"I don't know. It was late and I didn't know what was happening anymore."

There were stirrings in the girl's bedroom partway down the hall. Sarah sat up again. They both waited quiet to see if the girl was awake. Nothing more. Sarah took up Daniel's hands so that she could better what he'd had to do with them. They would not rest.

"What are you thinking about right now?" she said.

"Those men I helped kill gave up no ghosts. Not that I could see."

She kept on studying him but he'd say no more. He seemed to take a chill. He shuddered against her and she gathered him up tight. When he'd settled Sarah kissed him and pressed his head to her heart. Then she loosed him and pushed him down so that he lay back full on the couch. She rested atop him and held him until he slept. She didn't sleep for a long time and then finally she did. Sunlight speckled her long pale legs and the scarred musculature of his arm where it rested low. Shadow on their sleeping faces.

PART TWO

He fought nearly thirty fights all told. He lost two by decision and he was never knocked down in the cage. There were few gyms to train at but more fights to be had out west and he drove sometimes hours in a day to have boxers try to kill him in sparring and to have wrestlers smash him into worn floormatting and against padded cinderblock walls where he would battle to get back on his feet. He broke fingers and toes and had a maxillary fracture that made him spit blood for a month, gobs of maroon clot, red-streaked phlegm. When he touched his eyeball his front teeth hurt. Daniel didn't know if it would heal but it did and he sparred again at gyms by the edges of cities and in most places the men eventually wouldn't spar with him anymore. His elbows were chipped and the nerve-endings in his shins had long stopped complaining. He took less and less damage and his once-broken nose stayed straight, so rarely did it take a clean shot.

Sarah stayed home with the baby and then she went back to work and Daniel spent as much time at home as he could. Sarah had friends and they watched the child sometimes. When he would take the baby from them they always seemed not to want to give her up. They'd cringe as he picked her up, as if he would crush her head in his monstrous hands. They had never shook the hand of a fighter and they were always taken aback by the careful way he took their grip in his ruined fingers.

The man he fought next had been trained in northern California and he had heavy hands and caught Daniel but he didn't drop him. Late in the third round Daniel hit the man with an uppercut and a combination of hooks and the man dropped and then shot back up and tried to tackle Daniel. He stuffed the man's takedown and could feel that the man was not right and he got him into the Thai clinch and threw knees to the man's belly and ribs and when the man dropped his hands he took a hard knee to the mouth and the fight was over. Daniel went back to his corner trailing blood on the canvas. The cutman came over to him quickly and went to work on his eye. In the final exchange he had taken a headbutt to the ridge of brow above his right eye but he hadn't felt it. The doctor came over after they had raised the other fighter and set him on his stool and the doctor looked at Daniel and asked him questions and then he left. Daniel put his hands in the air and hugged his cornermen and then he went to the hospital to have his eyebrow stitched back together.

That spring they moved east. The prairies were not his home and Sarah wanted to see water and the plains winter got longer and harder every year. Daniel knew people in the east and there were fights aplenty there now and he needed only a win or two more to get the call for bigger shows and more money and the right to quit when the time came. They settled just south of the city and were to move into the city proper when he earned enough. Daniel saved his winnings and put a deposit on a small semi-detached house in the far west end.

In the last week of training camp for a televised fight Daniel's right eye stopped working. He saw sudden flashes of lightning and objects floating that he tried to swat at first before he realized they weren't there. He knew he had not been concussed. They took him to the doctor and the doctor studied the eye and told him that he had a detached retina. Before the end of that week they performed surgery to seal the retinal tears and Daniel didn't fight and his opponent was submitted by a replacement fighter.

He had fought twenty-nine men and knew he would never fight a thirtieth. When he healed he hit pads and haunted the gym and helped train young fighters. He got there less and less and then one day he left with his gear and they never saw him there again. There was no work for the man and he lost the deposit on the little house. In July of that year Daniel got into a car with his wife and his child and they went north to the town where he was born, to the house where he grew up and where his father had lived his whole life.

NINE

Daniel spent late autumn welding aluminum bleachers. By the time snow began to fall he'd been farmed out to cut apart the carriages of buses and vans and make structural welds to hold the new vehicles together. Daniel worked on finish carpentry and he upholstered vehicles and installed plumbing and fixtures. His welds were all sound and he had a reputation for his skill in it. The company was scraping up work for him as a favour and he took whatever work they found.

He'd come home with marks on his arms and wrists where hot metals burned holes through his heavy jacket or went into his sleeves. Sometimes he'd come in late with the skin of his neck sootblacked where his helmet and visor couldn't protect it. Sarah and Madelyn waited for him if he were late for dinner. Or sometimes Sarah would let Madelyn eat in front of the TV and she would wait for him. Other times Sarah worked and Madelyn went down the road to Murray's house where he and his wife near spoiled her for everyone else. On those nights Daniel came home to an empty house and sat there filthy on the couch and drank beer. He microwaved his dinner or forgot entirely after a half-dozen drinks. When Sarah worked the graveyard shift Daniel made sure Madelyn went to bed and then he sat out on the deck in the cold night that told of coming winter and he watched the starlit sky. He was exhausted and tried to turn in early on those nights but he couldn't sleep without his wife beside him. If he did sleep it was the shallow kind that comes behind drink, and in the morning to follow he often felt like he hadn't slept at all.

Snow fell on the first Friday in December while Daniel stood on the roof of their house with a borrowed power-washer, blasting clumps of rotten leaves from the eaves-trough. He'd finished his shift not long before sundown and had the powerwashing rig set up in the back of his truck. Sarah hadn't come back from work yet. Madelyn was at a friend's after school and had plans to stay the night. He'd climbed a ladder and got onto the roof with the gun in his hand at the end of the long hoseline. There he stood in the grey evening, truck-radio blasting over the high growl of the washer-engine, white flakes falling heavy to the shingles where he'd set his feet.

He was still up there when Sarah got out of her co-worker's car and walked up the driveway. He couldn't see her plain until she was right under the house. White in her hair and her coatshoulders already wet.

"Just what in the hell are you doing up there?" she said.

He blasted a pocket of mulch out of the corner troughing and they watched it fly into the yard.

"You think you could grab me a beer and toss it up," he said.

"How about you just get down before you break your neck?"

Daniel squatted at the edge of the roof so that she could see him and the washergun.

"You gonna have a shower inside, or you just want to get it over with here and now?" he said.

She put her hands to her hips, didn't move a step.

"You'd live the rest of your days on that roof," she said.

"I'll be down in a minute," he said.

Sarah went up the steps and into the house and closed only the screen door behind her. Interior light shone to the wet decking. Daniel went back to the place he'd been. He opened up on the last segment of eavestrough, aimed into the metal half-pipe until the backlogged leaves were flung clear or washed out through the drainpipe to the yard below. Then he stopped and stared up at the moon-less sky. The snow fell hard. He raised the gun vertical and a jet of water tore up toward the heavens.

They ate supper together and afterward Sarah showered while he changed out of his wet jeans and sweatshirt. When she went into the living room he was sitting on the couch, working the cork out of a bottle of wine. Two glasses on the table. She passed behind and got her arms around his shoulders.

"What's this?" she said.

"Neither of us have got to work tomorrow, and the kid took off."

"Almost unbelievable," Sarah said.

She came around the end of the couch and sat with him. He poured the tumblers nearly full and handed the one to her. Sarah sipped the wine and Daniel downed a mouthful. He'd put an old CD of hers into the crappy stereo that rested on a table across the room. It played Bruce Springsteen for a time and then a bunch of Nirvana tracks. There seemed to be no clear design to it.

"You didn't say much about work," Sarah said.

"There's nothin' worth saying," he said. "They got me on all the shit jobs."

Sarah asked no more about it. They sat drinking and listening to the tunes until the CD started skipping and stammering out the same line of *In Bloom* over and over. Sarah took up a pillow and chucked it across the room. It clipped the speaker and the song kept on and ended. Queen started playing. Sarah took and drink and swayed a little to the melody.

"Murray and Ella asked us down the road to their place if you want to go," Daniel said.

Sarah brushed her hair back behind her ear, straightened the hem of her dress.

"Yeah, we should head down for a drink," she said.

"They'd be pretty happy to have us by the sound of it."

"Okay," she said. "But we'll go in a little while."

"Sure," he said.

She lifted her bare feet and pulled her knees up under her so that she was looking at him right in the eye. She took a big drink, emptied the glass and set it down. She flicked at his glass with her fingernail. It rang small. Daniel smiled and drank the wine. Sarah took the glass from him and turned and set it behind her on the table. When she turned back she had her chest up against his shoulder. She shifted her knee over his legs and got on top of him.

"Okay," he said.

She kissed him and he got hold of her firm by her lower back. She held him close and then bit at his neck and his ear and leaned back with his face in her hands. He dropped his hand down under her skirt and grabbed her bare ass. She shifted and then took the whole dress off over her head and let it drop. She stared down with her dark eyes. Cheeks gone very red. He stared back at her and he could barely gather air fast enough to breathe.

TEN

Come Christmas that year and they didn't suffer as they thought they might. They spent little on themselves and wanted little to begin with. Madelyn wanted less than she should have and they got her more. They had a Christmas tree that Daniel had cut from the outlying woods. That he'd brought down with a shortaxe and hauled across the fieldsnow on a wooden sled. They had turkey and wine and heat and electricity. And they had two days together without work. Those hours were sweet and they went quick and then Sarah had to go back to the nursing home in the evening on Boxing Day. Daniel lay in bed alone and slept thin, meagre sleep and then the morning showed. He waited by the door in his steel-toes and coveralls while his wife pulled into the driveway and got out of the truck. Left it running. He kissed her as she passed by and handed him the keys. Then he got into the vehicle and drove it back down the road over deep ruts of sand-spackled ice.

He pulled into the jobsite and saw few other trucks on the lot. The office was no more than a line of joined trailers sitting on blocks in the hard earth. Daniel got out and went up the makeshift stairs and knocked on the office door. The site foreman came out from behind his desk and unlatched the door without looking. Daniel went in and watched the man go back to his desk.

"We got you on that steel fencing today," he said.

"Alright. Where the other guys at?" Daniel said. "They call in hungover?"

The site-boss smiled crooked. He took off his glasses and let them hang around his neck by the tether.

"We gave a few extra days off to the more senior guys," the site-boss said. "They got projects coming up in the new year. So they could afford a day or two extra. Give that work up to some of the newer fellas like yourself."

Daniel put his hands in his pockets and looked down at his boots. Back at the boss.

"What's that mean for us?" Daniel said. "We gonna have work in January?"

"It ain't that bad yet," the site-boss said, and set his elbows on the desk. "Nobody's gonna be let go or nothin' like that. But work gets harder to come by this time of year. Some fellas'll lose hours for a while."

"All the ones who got their trucks out there in the lot?" Daniel said.

The boss started to say something and stopped. He leaned back in the chair. Then he nodded.

Daniel couldn't look at the man anymore so he stared out of the crossbarred office window. Acre upon acre of frozen ground with great muddied swaths in the white and cavernous pits dug out and waiting for foundations to be set within them. Miles of metal stacked in pieces or assembled already into half-built things. Ten-ton diggers and backhoes and bulldozers without their drivers. If you didn't know how that work was done or how many were offering to do it you would think it would last forever.

"Don't worry," the boss said. "It's only temporary. We get to the other side of winter and see what the spring has for us."

Daniel studied the site-boss in his chair. Brick of a man once, gone soft at the belly. Ill-fitting workshirt and a wedding band sunk permanent into his gnarled finger.

"I better get to it," Daniel said.

The site-boss waved and went back to his paperwork. Daniel left the office and shut the door behind him and went slow down the steps. When he got to his truck he opened the door and stood with one hand on the window frame and the other on the ridge of the truckbed. He felt the torn boltholes in the siding and squeezed until the metals broke the pad of his middle finger and his palmheel and then he squeezed a little harder and let go.

At the end of his shift Daniel was back in the lot taking off his gear and stowing it in the truck. He'd lost a metal fragment down his sleeve during a weld and it had burned a narrow ditch into his forearm before he could shake it loose. He examined the arm. The hair singed in a wandering line from wrist to elbow. It still stunk and so did his workshirt.

As he was searching the cab for antiseptic ointment, a huge welder called LeBlanc came out of the site-office and let the door swing. He had an envelope that he stuffed into the pocket of his coveralls. He walked past Daniel's truck on the way to his own. The man seemed to be talking to himself. LeBlanc, like Daniel, had been born and raised in the area, though he'd gone to the French high school and was a few years younger. Daniel applied the salve but he had nothing to cover the site of the burn. He rolled up his shirtsleeves to the elbow. LeBlanc got into his truck and it shifted under his weight and then shifted again when he got back out.

"They fuck you too?" LeBlanc said.

"Yeah," Daniel said.

LeBlanc shook his head.

"You want to go for a beer?" he said.

Daniel thought on it. He looked at his wrist by instinct but he'd not worn a watch in some years. He stared stupid for another second and then dropped the arm.

"I'll follow you," Daniel said.

They'd taken stools at the bar and nobody would sit close to them on either side. LeBlanc was nearly a full head taller than Daniel. He had the kind of hands you might see on a horror movie monster. Massive digits that had been broken and healed wrong and broken again. All of his fingernails were bitten down so that they were just calcified bumps. LeBlanc had cashed a paycheque through the bar and he seemed to be trying to drink his way through a fair chunk of it. Above the backbar there was a TV showing some kind of down-hill skiing championships. LeBlanc took a peanut up from a near bowl and flicked it whole at the TV screen.

"You ain't a skier?" Daniel asked.

"Has there ever been a sport more perfectly designed for assholes?" LeBlanc said.

Daniel laughed. Said there probably wasn't. They drank and made some more small talk about work, their wives, their kids. LeBlanc had four girls and a boy. The first before he might have even considered himself grown. LeBlanc stopped talking mid-sentence and went quiet for a minute.

"You still hooked up with the bikers and those Indians?" LeBlanc said soft.

"Pardon?"

"Under the table kind of stuff," LeBlanc said. "You know what I mean."

Daniel didn't even try to bullshit the man. He'd a belly full with beer and he gone tired right through as the evening limped by. He told LeBlanc that he didn't do that work anymore.

"Come on," LeBlanc said.

"I'm telling you the truth, pal."

LeBlanc's face soured. He drank at his beer.

"We known each other for a long time," LeBlanc said. "And you know what kind of guy I am."

"I do," Daniel said. "But I still can't help you. It ain't like what you think."

"You don't know what I think."

LeBlanc would barely look at him.

"You should do anything but what I done," Daniel said. "I'm being straight, man. You shouldn't even be fuckin' asking about it."

LeBlanc said no more. Daniel got up from the stool and went across the room, down the corridor to the bathrooms. The men's had the door marked by a wooden cutout of a rooster. Daniel went in and took his place at the end of a metal trough. Nobody else in the room. As he pissed he read the wall in front of him. Someone had written "Life Sux" on the plaster at face-height.

The door opened as Daniel shook and zipped his fly. LeBlanc took a step into the room but no further. He pulled his shirt off over his head and tossed it to the bank of sinks against the one wall. The man carried some extra meat around the midsection but he was heavy with muscle underneath, through his shoulders and chest and arms. Determined look of a drunkard in his eyes.

"What the fuck is this?" Daniel said.

LeBlanc just put his fists up high.

"I'll prove it," he said.

"Prove what?" said Daniel.

But the big man was already coming at him. The bathroom was maybe twenty feet in length and with the stalls and the sinks Daniel had nowhere to go. LeBlanc swarmed him and swung wild. Daniel covered up and he was calm enough to ask LeBlanc to quit. Got hold of LeBlanc by his neck and put his head under LeBlanc's chin and shoved him back. LeBlanc would not stop and he was long-limbed and on the way back he slammed a left hook upside Daniel's forehead and sent him teetering into the stalls. Daniel got back to his feet and he was moving funny at first. His right foot sluggish as he stepped the tile. When LeBlanc came back Daniel snapped a push kick into the huge man's stomach with his lead leg and that backed LeBlanc up a step. Then Daniel had his legs back and he whipped a hard right low kick to the meat of LeBlanc's thigh.

LeBlanc blurted something odd and started falling as he came forward on the stung leg. Still, he was moving too fast and had enough reach that he grabbed Daniel up and they both went over together. The bigger man falling onto Daniel and pinning him there to the filthy bathroom floor under his weight. Daniel couldn't see and he couldn't move LeBlanc. Acrid, damp smell that he couldn't help but inhale deep. Someone came into the room and could be heard swearing and then they went back out in a hurry. Hard footfalls in the corridor.

And there, buried under the giant, Daniel felt something he'd not felt in years during a fight, not since his early days as a green amateur. True panic. He tried to shuck loose as LeBlanc kept the weight on and near smothered him. Short punches landed to the side of Daniel's head and shook him, so big were LeBlanc's lunchbox mitts. Daniel settled himself and when LeBlanc tried to posture up Daniel elbowed LeBlanc from the bottom and managed to work to a butterfly guard, his knees bent up and his shins under each of LeBlanc's thighs. LeBlanc didn't know what to do there and when he began to throw punches again he was off-balance and Daniel elevated the big man and pushed him to the side. Daniel got his knee to the tile and pulled LeBlanc's support hand off of the ground and rolled him. Drove LeBlanc all the way down to his back and held him there.

LeBlanc tried to shift Daniel but the big man had nothing from his back and he was sucking air. Daniel had his arms around LeBlanc's neck and shoulder and he let go long enough to push LeBlanc's arm up against his massive head. Then Daniel got his grip again with his left bicep and forearm squeezing LeBlanc's neck, Daniel's head and shoulder pinning the big man's own left arm and putting pressure on that side. The choke was tight already but Daniel cleared his legs and swung them over LeBlanc's knees so that he was belly-down on the floor beside LeBlanc, completing the hold. LeBlanc tried to buck and hit Daniel in the back of the head with his free hand. Seconds like that and his fist drummed Daniel's back clumsily and fell away and then LeBlanc went limp.

Daniel let go of the choke and got to his knees. LeBlanc's arm was twitching a little on the floor. Daniel patted the big man on the chest and got up. He went to the mirrors by the sink. Welt at his forehead where LeBlanc caught him. Line of blood right down the middle of his chin from a cut lower lip. Scratches and scrapes on the one side of his face. Swaths of his shirt gone dark and damp with LeBlanc's sweat. He could not catch his breath. He felt weird right through and puked beer into the sink. Again and again until he was just dryheaving. When it stopped he drank water from the tap and rinsed the basin. Daniel washed his face and then let the tap run cold over his hands. Went back over to where LeBlanc lay. He knelt and put his hands to the man's face. Shook him a little. LeBlanc had already started to stir and come back. Daniel slapped the downed man across the cheek.

LeBlanc was still a little unsteady when they loaded him into the passenger seat of his truck. It took Daniel and another man on either side of LeBlanc and a waitress with armsleeve tattoos shoving LeBlanc in by his ass. The big man only lived a mile or so from that watering hole, and Daniel drove LeBlanc's truck while the waitress followed in Daniel's truck. Her shift was up and he'd agreed give her a lift home after, on the way out of town.

When they got to LeBlanc's place, all the windows were dark and there were no other vehicles in the drive. LeBlanc had recovered enough to speak and to walk but he didn't say anything. He was still hammered-drunk on top of his having been actually separated from his senses. When they got out Daniel and LeBlanc met around the front of the truck and the big man apologized and shook Daniel's hand. Daniel walked LeBlanc up the pathway to his own front door and LeBlanc fumbled with the keys until he found the right one. Daniel tried the key in the deadbolt but the door hadn't been locked. LeBlanc went in.

Daniel came back down the drive to his own truck and the tattooed waitress shuffled over on the seat. She had black hair and a lip ring. He didn't know of her or her family name.

"His old lady is probably going to knock him out as well," the waitress said.

Daniel looked up at the house. No lights yet by the windows.

"I don't believe anybody else has been living there for some time," he said.

ELEVEN

Daniel came home from work with hours of the day to spare. He sat on the step of his house in his workgear as if they might call him back in a minute. When he went into the house he opened the fridge and stood there. He got a beer and glanced at the clock and then put the bottle back.

He sat on the basement steps and wrapped his hands. Fifteen feet of cloth to better hold bone and ligament together. He had his near worn-out sixteen-ounce gloves with Velcro straps and he pulled the gloves on and fastened them tight. Daniel threw jabs and his straight right until the bag and his mitts shucked the dust clear. He moved on the balls of his feet. Shifted weight to either foot and shook his wearied limbs. He stretched his hamstrings and his arms and his neck and then he threw the jab over and over. He tried to throw hooks and nothing felt right. He went back to his jab and once in a while he threw the heavy right hand. The ball of his right foot grabbed concrete and then shifted power through his calf and his ass and his core. Torque of his wrecking-ball shoulder. The bags shook in its chains and the crossbeams rattled. When he landed the right-hand clean the bag bowed and bucked and swung a wide orbit. If anyone were upstairs it might have sounded as if he were taking a sledgehammer to the washing machine.

An hour later Daniel stood with his hands behind his head. Hauled as much air as he could. Finally he let his arms drop and he bit at the strap of one of his gloves and pulled it loose. He took the gloves off and set them down on the stairs and then he sat down beside them. Daniel unwound the sodden wraps and balled them up and tossed them at the washing machine. He got up and went over to the laundry sink and turned the tap on. He leaned in and drank water from the tap until his insides stung from the cold. He stood up and took great, heavy breaths and then drank again. Then he turned the tap off and went to the steps and picked up his gloves. Walked those stairs with his mouth open.

He had the truck idling in the roadside gravel, parked so that he could see clear across a small patch of stony field to where the house stood. Modest two-storey building in one of the town's older neighbourhoods. He observed changes made to the structure, an extension to the garage. A boat on a trailer out front, in its covers. They'd lately built an above ground pool and it took up most of the back yard. There'd been a pond there that they must have had filled.

That had been his father's house for forty-seven years and then it was Daniel's for just five more before he had to sell it so that he didn't lose it outright. They'd gone bankrupt not long after Daniel had to quit fighting and they only had the house because it had been left to them. Two years of piss-poor welding jobs that came and went and paid almost nothing had them remortgaging the place and another worse year had them on a second mortgage from the bank. When they sold the house they had credit cards and a line of credit and they were upside down on the mortgage and couldn't cover it all. They'd paid the bank but were still paying the other creditors, month by month. Daniel had even borrowed from Clayton the once but swore he'd never again, long as it took for him to work that through that debt with his hands before he could start to earn.

He waited awhile longer until he couldn't stand to look at the place. As he was putting the truck into gear somebody came out onto the back deck and looked toward him. Shielded their eyes with the flat of their hand. Daniel wound the window down and stuck his fist out, gave them the middle finger. The man on the deck kept looking. Then he waved. Daniel pulled out from the fringe and drove off.

Yellow buses came and went over snow and sludge. Daniel sat in his truck trying to remember if he'd ever rode in one but he couldn't. Kids ran with their bags dangling and some were dressed well, brand-name running shoes and backpacks and clothes bought new for they alone. The cuffs of their pants soiled gradual by grit and salt as they walked the pathways and parking lot. Other kids wore ill-fitting hand-me-downs and had home-cut hair and others yet were bedraggled with busted packs and sneakers. They were children that ranged in age from five to thirteen years old, and he saw faces of men he knew in some that passed, of girls he had known in his youth that would be in their thirties now. Still, there they went, some tiny and high-voiced. Some of the older ones had outgrown their age and Daniel guessed at their troubles or the troubles they'd cause.

Daniel got out of the truck and shut the door, stood waiting. Faint trace of his breath in the air. He wore a light jacket but the cold bothered him little. He saw parents in other cars, parents at the school doors talking to teachers and each other. He stayed by the truck. The girl didn't show and she didn't show. Nervousness deep in his chest that he couldn't control nor explain away. He waited there until almost all of the kids had cleared and then he pocketed his keys and started for the school.

He'd not been long in the truck, driving the roads around the school, when he saw her by the perimeter fence. Daniel knew her by her walk even with some hundred yards between them. The girl was trailing three boys and they were trailing another. Daniel about blew a stop sign and closed on them quick.

By the time he got level they'd begun the scrap right in the sidewalk, the three of them after the other kid. Quick mess of fists and they had the kid down in the snowbank where they battered him. Two of them were tall and thin and they'd pinned the smaller boy. The thicker of the three was punching the downed kid in the back and dropping knees to his flank. He threw mean and the punches had some weight to them. The kid on the ground had not been in good shape even before they started beating on him. They could barely hold the scruffy kid down and he was whining and growling and cursing them out. Daniel cranked the wheel and pulled up hard to the curb and the tire clipped it and rocked the truck. As he thumped the door open he saw they'd dragged the boy into the snow itself to smother him in it, stuffing mittfuls into his jacket and down the back of his pants. Daniel's boots hit the fringe just as Madelyn got there.

She turned the wide one by his shoulder and drove a straight right to his maw and he sat down on the pavement. Then she took the nearest of the taller boys by the neck of his jacket and horsecollared him to a knee. He was taller than her by plenty but he'd not seen her coming. The other tall kid turned and quit with the kid on the ground long enough to take her measure. The thickset boy was up again fit to kill her but Daniel hollered so loud the boy froze up and almost lost his footing again. Dribble of blood from his nostril. They cleared out but Madelyn had got tangled up with the tallest boy and she kept feeding him little shots to the guts and he wrestled her off her feet into the snow. Daniel walked through the other two and got hold of the tallest by his coatback and his belt and lifted him high, like he were a bundle of long kindling. The girl came up with the tall boy and they let each other go. Daniel just took the boy a few feet away and dropped him.

As soon as the scruffy kid lowered his arms and saw daylight he sprung up and swung on the nearest kid, the second tallest one who'd been last to get his licks in and was still upright. That kid took a haymaker to the ear and went back toward the road and banged up against an old utility box in the snowed-over fringe. He held the side of his head and had his eyes shut tight. The scruffy kid had filthy teartracks ran down his cheeks. His eyes were crazy. Daniel caught him and tied him up before he could take another crack. The kid tried to thrash clear but within seconds he slowed and all the air seemed to go out of him and he sat down heavy in the snow-bank again. His damp hair stuck out from his head and he'd snow in his earholes. His coat hung open, the zip-per busted. The tall kid who took a shot to the ear was already jogging away down the street and the heavyset boy was pulling his other friend off the ground.

"You fucking assholes," he said. "We're gonna come after you. And all your wagonburner buddies."

Daniel walked at him and the boys tried to scram-ble. They weren't quick enough and Daniel got a boot to the heavy kid's rear end as he started to run and the kid stumbled and took a header to the pavement. The tallest was up and running then. The mouthy one quick on his heels and he ran with a limp.

"I know your old man, son," Daniel called. "You can tell him who done it and ask him if he wants to talk about it."

The kid stopped long enough to flip Daniel the bird.

"If I was a worse person I'd tell you why he ain't gonna do a goddamn thing," Daniel said.

The kid spat into the road and then he kept running. Daniel stared after them for a little while and then he turned around to check on the kid they'd beat. Only Madelyn there with her face red and her ponytail pulled ragged. The other boy was gone.

"He took off," she said, and pointed.

Daniel looked around at the nearby pathways and the gaps between houses but he couldn't see the boy. There were bloodspots in the snow, a lone backpack that one of the bullies left when they fled. Madelyn had gone for her bookbag and came back brushing the snow from it. She got to the abandoned pack and picked it up by the handle and flung it wide. It clipped the top of the schoolyard fence and turned end over end, spilled its contents in the field. Daniel met her in the sidewalk and took her by the underside of her face in one hand. She stopped. Scrapes across her right cheek and on her forehead.

"You okay?" he said.

"Yeah," she said.

"Good," he said. "Now get in the goddamn truck."

Madelyn's window creaked and wound down in fits and starts until it was halfway open. She took the cold air over her face and put her hand outside the truck.

"Let me see that," Daniel said.

She brought the hand inside and he took it in his and looked at her knuckles. Redness but no more. He pressed each knuckle with his thumb and she didn't make a sound until he got to the joints of her index and forefinger.

"That hurt much?"

"A little bit."

He let go and she rubbed the hand, put it back outside. They said nothing for a long time.

"You pissed at me?" she said.

He shook his head, watched the road.

"I don't want you fighting."

"You fought," she said. "Hell, you even got in a fight the other week."

Daniel shook his head. He still wore some of the damage from his night on the town with LeBlanc.

"That shouldn't ever have happened," he said.

Madelyn was still breathing heavy from the scrap. Daniel reached over and squeezed her by the shoulder. The girl shook some. All that adrenaline run through her that had nowhere to go now.

"Maybe if you taught me..."

"That's enough," he said.

The girl went quiet. Daniel just watched the road. He seemed to shrink some in his seat. Madelyn let him be for a minute.

"Do you really know that kid's dad?" she said. "The one who swore at you."

"That's why I know what kind of ingredients are in the boy," Daniel said.

Madelyn set about fixing her ponytail, took the elastic out and retied it. Daniel surveyed the neighbourhoods as he drove. Houses of brick with naked oak trees and wooden fencing, custom-built awnings and decks. Subdivisions of wood and brick-facade with wide driveways and coloured siding. Houses of clapboard and tarpaper with rough, black shingling and brokedown garages, rockgardens and crabgrassed lawns covered in snow. They passed houses that Daniel knew and houses that he didn't.

"At least you threw that punch right," Daniel said. "Break a hand out there and you're done for."

He could see her smiling in the window reflection.

"Don't do it again though, hear me?" he said.

She said she'd not. Tried to stone-face him as she made the promise. Daniel looked at his daughter hard and knew that it was too late by years for her to keep it.

TWELVE

Early on a Thursday afternoon Daniel finished his half-shift and made for his truck. He sat in the cab and stared out at the site-office for a while. Bowed his head and breathed careful. He drove away from the site and followed the concession road out of town. When he was supposed to turn off for home he didn't. He kept on driving and saw the mouth of the road that he lived on from the highway overpass. Beside him on the seat he had an old duffel bag, stuffed full.

Half an hour later he turned into a pothole-ridden lot outside of an industrial plaza. A foot of snow on its flat roof. The truck tires ran through sludge and road salt. There were four units in the plaza and only one was occupied. The rest were barred and boarded shut and had notices pinned to the doors, offers of sale or rent or notices of dereliction. Daniel waited in the truck awhile. Three vehicles in the lot and he knew one of them. Eventually he shut the engine off and got out with his bag. He walked across the lot toward the lit front of the occupied unit. Light freezing rain fell about him. Icewater mist that blew at his hair and face as he went.

When Daniel got to the door he saw the front room empty, a computer left unattended on a desk. Worn-out office chairs on either side. Framed pictures were hung on the wall behind the desk and posters were tacked around the office and taped to the front window. Light at the end of a long, dim hall. He knew that the entrance door would be unlocked so he pulled it open and went inside. Smell of sweat and old leather, dampness, disinfectant. Then he heard a sound like gunfire. Bare feet shuffling. Someone unloading on pads in the distant, open room and the sound echoing against the bare cinderblock walls. Daniel smiled and took his shoes off where he saw other men's shoes. The front door had not closed full behind him and he pulled it shut and went down the hallway.

They stopped when they saw him. Just for a few moments. Then they went on. Two men were in the ring. One held the pads and the other wore gloves and shorts and nothing else. Another man skipped in the corner of the room atop green floormatting and he turned as Daniel came in and then went back to skipping and studying the men in the ring. A digital timeclock sat on a table by the corner of the ring and counted seconds. At five minutes a high tone rang out and the coach caught one last punch and then he lowered the focus-mitts. The fighter in the ring raised his arms and laced his hands behind his head. The coach spoke to him close and the fighter nodded and looked the coach in the eyes. The coach held the pads out and the fighter bumped them with his gloves and started walking back and forth. Wet canvas underfoot where he'd loosed sweat. Daniel waited ringside until the coach turned to him. Tan skin. Nose flat and the bone long gone. The coach leaned on the ropes. He squinted and then he smiled slight.

"What you doin' here?" he called out.

"Hey Jasper," Daniel said.

"Long time, man."

"I heard you opened up shop again."

Jasper stood full and gestured around at the gym, the new matting and ring covers and ropes. Freeweights on racks along one wall, the opposite wall lined with leather heavy bags and teardrop bags hung from the ceiling by chain. Lone, aged Muay Thai bag actually touching the floor where the sand settled and made the base alike to concrete pillaring.

"Beautiful, ain't it?" the coach said.

"It's somethin'," Daniel said.

"It's not like the old gym."

"No. But that's alright."

Jasper pointed to Daniel's duffel bag.

"You here to train?"

"That's the idea."

"You got all your necessaries."

"Yessir."

"Locker room's over on the left. You need tape or wraps or anything you just give me a shout."

Daniel nodded and picked up his bag. He walked the length of the gym toward the locker room door. The fighter in the ring was pacing back and forth and didn't seem to know anybody else was there. The other man training outside the ring had never stopped skipping. Now he eyeballed Daniel. His face gave up nothing. Dark skin laid tight over his crooked nose and patchwork brows.

Daniel arrived home by twilight. As he got out of the truck Sarah opened their front door. She looked him up and down as he climbed the steps with his duffel, then turned and went back inside. Daniel dropped his bag in the hallway and kicked it to the side. He hung his jacket and went into the kitchen to meet her but she was already coming out with their dinner.

"You didn't have to wait," he said.

"It's okay," Sarah said.

She set the plates down. Roast chicken and potatoes, salad in a bowl at the centre of the table. Two bottles of beer.

"Sit," she said.

"Where's the kid?" he said.

Sarah nodded toward the living room.

"I let her eat in front of the TV. She wouldn't sit still at the table. Then she was all over the kitchen. All I know is impatience isn't a trait she gets from me."

Daniel sat at the small dining table and waited there. Sarah was back in the kitchen turning the stove off and then she came out and sat. He cut some chicken loose and watched her past his chewing. They ate and said little. Sound came in from the living room and Daniel looked over his shoulder for Madelyn. He ate another bite and then did it again. Sarah stopped and rested her knife and fork against the table.

"Just go, you dummy," she said.

THIRTEEN

Near every day Daniel left the jobsite at noon. Drove his truck an hour out of town. With one hand he ate the lunch his wife had made him the night before. The door to the gym was open always. He would go inside where Jasper held pads for young fighters and sometimes the coach would be sitting on a chair outside of the ring while his assistants ran drills. On weekdays there were classes in the morning and young men would be in the changeroom when he got there, some of them quiet and some talking shit. None of them knew him. But they saw the curved mark under his left eye, the scar tissue through his brow, hands broke and rebroke with thick and hideous knucklejoints. Musculature of a man who had done a life's work in the ring and perhaps made part of his living on a farm or hauling a fire hose or shifting metal as Daniel did now. He would wait them out and when they left he went out to skip rope and shadowbox atop the new floormatting.

Often on those early afternoons there would be just a half-dozen men in the room. Some of those men knew Daniel by the picture of him that hung in the entryway or they knew of him by talk in the locker room or by rumours circulated in other gyms by other men. It was plain that Jasper paid Daniel some mind when he was working, studied him out of the corner of the eye while he trained other fighters. But Jasper would never lose track of the pads he held or the punches and kicks coming at him. If a fighter dropped his guard they'd take a pad upside the head or a shin half-thrown to the thigh and they would reset and forget about Daniel altogether.

For a week Daniel did no more than skip and shadowbox, worked the bags light. He stretched out ligament and tendon and rediscovered muscles that had long been ignored. He made sure to take deep breaths to his diaphragm as he worked. Exhaled hard through his mouthguard while he threw hands. Daniel dripped sweat until his bare feet slid on the matting. Then he'd change his sopping shirt and come back out onto the floor. Towel the mats down again and work until he had to start thinking about home.

In the last days of that month Daniel came into the gym and there was but one assistant coach and a young hundred-and-seventy-pounder at work. Jasper was not there. Daniel changed and stowed his things, went out to train. By then Jasper had come out from a makeshift bedroom in the rear of the gym and sat the edge of the ring and yawned. He saw Daniel and waved him over.

"You want to put all your gear on today? Get some real work in?" he said.

"Sure," Daniel said.

Jasper started to stretch his arms, pulled his elbow back behind his head and bowed a little to that side. The man had Thai and Filipino in him on his mother's side, Dutch-Canadian on the other. He'd lived most of his life in cities in central Ontario and had only been overseas at length to Thailand, to train and fight.

"Grab some shinguards from the back if you don't have none with you," the coach said. "Just warm up and give me a minute before you starting beating on me."

When Daniel was warm enough he strapped his shinguards on. Jasper was in the ring waiting for him. Daniel walked the short stairs behind the ringpost. He waited a beat before he stepped through the ropes, ducking his head as he went. Jasper likewise wore shin-pads on his short, treetrunk legs, worn shirt that caught at his stomach a little. More meat on him than Daniel had seen the coach carry before. Underneath it all his bones were yet like iron. Daniel felt the canvas by his footsoles, thin padding and wooden boards below. He studied patches of faded cloth where stains had been mopped and scrubbed.

"This ain't one of the aprons from the old ring? Is it?" Daniel said.

"It's pretty new," Jasper said.

"Yeah?"

"There ain't any of your blood in here. If that's what you're thinking."

"I'd hope and pray those old canvases were burned."

Jasper shrugged.

"All new," he said. Then he waved Daniel forward with his right mitt-hand.

Daniel walked over with his guard up, the thumb of his right glove pinned to the right side of his brow and the other held out slightly in front of his face to jab and parry. He moved back and forth, shifted weight from leg to leg. The coach let him settle and then he called for the jab, the right cross, double jabs and lead rights. He called for more head movement and if Daniel's hands dropped after a punch, Jasper whipped the focus mitts around and Daniel had to get his guard up before the pad slammed upside his head. Instead he took them on the glove, his shoulder, the crook of his elbow. The coach called for him to breathe and then he started calling for hooks at the end of Daniel's straight punches. Lead hooks, short hooks from in close, long left hooks at the end of a jab with his left foot pivoting hard and his foreknuckles drilling the pad.

Daniel started tense and wild and off-balance. He reset and fired until he got loose and gave up on throwing power and thought about his feet. He gradually settled lower in his stance, got more rotation with his hips and body. Shoulders, arms and hands to follow. The coach barked at him to crack hard and he stung the pads and his arms shuddered to the elbow. Gunfire again in the hollow of that concrete room. When the coach called time Daniel stepped back and put his hands up above his head and paced back and forth in the ring. The other two men working outside the ring had stopped what they were doing.

Daniel hauled air over his teeth for a short minute. The coach waved him back over.

Jasper had him set up right leg kicks with a one-two and let Daniel bury his shin into the meat of the coach's thigh. For a while Daniel was either too close to Jasper or too far. Had stepped too long when he threw his set-up punches, or he'd thrown his hands too light so that he'd be at distance to land clean. His hips weren't there yet and he couldn't get the torque he wanted out of them so he was never in the right spot. The coach repositioned him and called out for him to turn the kick over and finally he buried one deep into the coach's thigh and Jasper nodded.

"Better," he said. "More like that."

Daniel started getting the feel for it again and threw the kick hard. Jasper started turning his arm and putting the one pad down over his own leg. He told Daniel to switch up and had him stutter-step and throw a one-two and a left low kick. Daniel didn't have as much trouble with the switch, but his hips were still tight and his power wasn't there. He ran the drills and tried to mind his footwork, to stay light. He stepped and threw until he was struggling, his sweat-soaked shirt hung low from his neck. His arms got heavier and heavier but held up lest Jasper slam the mitts against his part-cauliflowered ears. The coach told Daniel to break and again he paced, his arms up high and his eyes on the steel rafters at the gym ceiling. Then the coach called him back.

"One-two. Low right swing," Jasper said. "Go."

Daniel bowed the pads with his hands and threw the kick behind and this time Jasper checked it, lifted his left leg wide with the knee bent so that his shin caught Daniel's shin as it came. Fire inside the meat of the leg, to the bone. Sensation of warmth after that spread through his calf and down to his foot before he settled back down into his stance. It didn't last for more than a few seconds. He'd not felt that sting for years. Daniel threw again and felt something like it, less and less. The coach worked him for a few more minutes. Made him alternate kicks and checked them each and all. Daniel took his time with the technique and turned his hips better now and when he connected his shinbones shook right through, but he suffered quiet. Jasper called time. He held one Thai pad out and Daniel touched it with his glove and then stepped back and shook his legs out.

"How'd that feel?" the coach said.

Daniel kept on moving, rubbed at the right shin. Picked up the foot and pulled it to his ass to stretch.

"Okay," Daniel said.

He loosed the foot and pointed with his glove.

"Somethin's wrong with those legs," he said. "I near forgot."

Jasper grinned.

"These legs?" he said. "I had them all my life."

"Somethin' that awful don't come like that to begin with," Daniel said.

Jasper unfastened the straps on his Thai pads and let them drop on the canvas. Started to work out cramps in his hands. He kept smiling at Daniel but he didn't say anything. Daniel took his gloves off and went over to the ring corner where he'd set his water. Jasper had gotten out through the ropes already and came over.

"You coming back tomorrow?" he said.

Daniel said that he would. Jasper reached up and pulled the ringrope down. Daniel took up his gloves and stepped through and then hopped down to the flooring and made his way across the room. The pads of his feet were raw and they spoke to him about it on the walk.

He came home in his workclothes just before six o'clock and when he got out of the truck his legs were already fucked. He stood for a few seconds and stamped his feet on the tarmac as if it would do something. Eventually he reached over and got his lunchpail and he was about to grab the duffel bag but he didn't. He shut the door and made his way gingerly up the driveway grade. By the time he got to the front steps he could just about cope.

In the bedroom he shed his workclothes and stopped before he could loose his belt. Thought he heard a car. He stood quiet for a time. Nothing. Sarah had worked the early shift until three and then she'd have gone for the girl and groceries before leaving town. He tried to place her on the road but he gave up and took his pants down and stared down at his reddened legs. They would bruise blue but there had been no true damage done. Still, he already felt bonesore and his muscles were spent and run through with lactic acid. He sat on the bed and examined the soles of his feet, each in turn. Then he set them back down on the floor and looked at himself in the mirror. Tried to remember what he looked like when he fought. Daniel got up and grimaced as he made his way into the bathroom, turned the shower as hot as he could take it.

Two days later Sarah and Daniel sat on the couch together. Madelyn slept in her room where whalesong could be heard playing on her small bedside stereo. That sound drifting ghostly down the hall.

"We're gonna hear that sad shit until the end of time," Sarah said. "You know that?"

"All I did was give her five dollars in the supermarket."

Sarah slumped in the cushions. They watched the news on TV. Nothing good was happening.

"You want a beer?" he said. "Or is it time to call it a night?"

She turned to him slow, like she'd not heard him. She closed one eye and opened it again.

"I could do one more," she said.

Daniel got up and walked the cold, warped hardwood in his bare feet. Moved through the kitchen. He set two empties in a case beside the back door and paused where he'd hunched over. Wind whipped against the wood and howled low in the frame-seams. Behind that the mewling and caterwauling of some animal. It wailed the once more and then stopped and he didn't hear it again. He stood up and opened the door. Nothing but the chill and the rear steps by pale lampglow, darkness beyond where wildgrass shook in silhouette. A small pine branch went past, needles bowed like a ship's sail.

Daniel came back into the living room. He too sunk in the couch and set the two bottles on the table and leaned in to open them. That was when Sarah reached down and lifted his pantleg up by the cuff. Daniel just sat there with his two hands holding either end of the beer bottle. Sarah studied the leg for a long time and then she let the cuff drop and checked the other. She let that pantleg go nearly right away and withdrew to her spot, pulled her hair back and tied it.

"So, when were you gonna tell me you were on half-days at work?" she said.

Daniel drank his bottle near empty.

"I don't know. Soon," he said.

She just looked at him.

"I didn't know how long it would be for," he said.

"How long's it been?"

He thought on it.

"About two weeks. Give or take a day."

She nodded.

"I figured that much," she said.

"How's that?"

"'Cause I'm the one that buys the bread and beer. I know exactly what amount of pennies we've got to spare."

Daniel put his arm around her and she let him.

"I also figured it takes time to get your shins beat to shit like that," Sarah said. "Time in a day that you wouldn't have otherwise had."

"You remember Jasper?" he said.

"Of course I remember him."

"He opened up a gym not too far down the road."

"Yeah?"

"I been going there afternoons. Just to see."

Sarah reached up and scratched at her cheekbone, let her palm fall to his knee.

"What did you find out?" she said.

Daniel drank at his beer again. The TV screen flickered and Daniel cleared her from his shoulder and got up and turned it off. He came back and planted his ass at the edge of the couch cushions with his elbows on his knees. They sat there together listening to the blue, nautical lament from their daughter's room. The drafts that likewise whistled in the dim coldness of their little kitchen.

FOURTEEN

They were more than a mile down the trail off the county highway when they stopped. Pretty clearing with wildflowers dotted around the place. Wallace sat the hood of the car near to Clayton's ledger. At one end of the clearing stood the hanging tree with long, heavy branches that bent in all directions and some bent back upon themselves. Clayton's nephew had strung a man to it in just his skivvies. Length of wire around his neck that worked back through a lasso and had gone taut enough to cut the skin. The man's hands were tied and the balls of his feet were pushing at a milk crate set at the base of the tree. Tarbell had split him by the eyebrow and ear and then Clayton told him stop and he'd gone to work on the man's body. The man was still cussing at them. He said he didn't owe.

Clayton went over to the car and Wallace handed him the ledger. He carried it over to the man and opened it to the right page, cloth band to earmark it.

"That's your name, isn't it?"

The man didn't say.

"That's your name. And that number here is what you owe," Clayton said, finger dug into the one page. "This number to the right. What you paid. It's not the same number."

"I got fuckin' time still," the man said.

Clayton shook his head. He pointed to the crate. Tarbell came over and the man tried to kick at him as he neared, almost caught him about the head but Tarbell slipped by and booted the crate clear. The man dropped and the wire stretched him out. He'd got his tongue caught this time and bit into it deep. Wallace came over and moved Tarbell aside and took the weight of the hanging man, his shoulder to the man's waist. He called for the stool. Clayton had gone back to the car to watch.

"You pass me that fuckin' thing right now," he said to Clayton's nephew.

Tarbell took his time coming back with it. Dropped it sideways on the ground. Wallace told him to fuck off and righted the crate and lowered the man again. There was blood all over his lips and his chin. Wallace reached high and managed to loose the wire enough so the man could talk.

"Last chance," Wallace said.

The man wheezed and moved his head all about like he might shuck loose. He'd plenty of fight left. He started his cussing again but none of it intelligible. Wallace cuffed him across the side of the head with an open hand. The sound of it carried through the place. Something skittered through the weeds near the treeline. He'd nearly turned the man sideways and the man was blinking hard and trying to move his jaw. Wide eyes on Wallace.

"I'm doin' you a favour," Wallace said close.

The man whispered to him. With his bit tongue it took a few tries for Wallace to hear him plain. Wallace backed up and looked deep into the man. Then he got hold of him again and hefted him all the way up. Anchored the man against the tree trunk as he reached up as he had before and made enough slack in the line to get it over the man's head. The man dropped heavy over Wallace's back and bled on his shirt. Wallace let the line swing. He hoofed the milk crate hard enough that it took air and went end over end into the near brush. He carried the man over to the car. Clayton had already got in and fired the ignition and popped the trunk. Plastics fixed there to cover the all of it. Wallace laid the man down in the hole and made sure he wasn't dead or dying. Then he closed him in.

When he came around to the front, Tarbell was sitting in the passenger seat. Wallace stopped short and spat to the clay. He opened the back door and got in behind the blonde. Knees high and drove into the seatback.

"Move the seat forward," Wallace said. "Right Fuckin' now."

Tarbell eventually found the switch.

"He's got the rest at his squat in the boonies," Wallace said.

Clayton put the car into reverse and swung it around to face the trail. He drove the road reckless and the man in the trunk could be heard yowling and bashing against the liner.

FIFTEEN

In weeks to come Daniel went to the gym every afternoon and each time he went he found his rhythm a little bit more. The near-crippling soreness that came in early days was gone and now he felt but a steady ache, telltale signs of muscle broke-down and rebuilding. His hands throbbed when the weather changed, when humid air hung fog through the fields and forest hollows. The skin of his knuckles had dried and split. He'd dents up and down his shins. He started to spar light with Jasper's assistants and some of their prospects. If there were things he couldn't do he still had a knack for teaching them to the younger fighters. He went to work at the jobsite with his cheeks purpled, slight swelling under his eyes, his forehead scraped up and gone red. Daniel worked hard and every day at noon he drove off the site-lot while men stood around in hardhats smoking and talking to each other, watching the rear of his truck with their faces gaunt and haggard.

Jasper had an assistant coach called Jung Woo that Daniel worked with plenty. Jung Woo had been a boxing prodigy in South Korea but his trainers put him in a tournament too young and in the semi-finals his nose was flattened by a punch and the surgeons that put it back together had called colleagues into the operating room one after another to shake their heads at it. They told Jung Woo that he wouldn't be able to box for a very long time but he still had fight in him and had to find somewhere to put it. He found Jiu-Jitsu classes in his town and then he went to Japan and learned to grapple and wrestle and when his nose healed he trained Muay Thai and took fights throughout Thailand, Australia, the Philippines. He'd scraps in Burma that he didn't like to talk about. He fought and studied chemistry at the university in Kyoto. He met a girl there and when he graduated he married her and fought three more times before he had his nose shattered again and had to retire. He won a scholarship to work on a graduate degree at the University of British Columbia and he moved there with his wife. Jung Woo found a gym in Vancouver that Jasper's cousin ran and he worked there while he studied. He spent more and more time at the gym and then he took another fight and tore a man's arm out of the socket with a Kimura lock. He didn't spend much time at home and within a year his wife left him for another man and moved to Seattle. Jung Woo took a job at the gym and he quit school and that was where Jasper had found him, penniless and smiling while he turned men inside out as they rolled on the mat. Where he plastered men to the ringropes with body shots and afterward explained how he had done it in timid half-English while they kneeled on the canvas, wheezing and nodding at him.

Daniel stood maybe four inches taller than Jung Woo and outweighed him by thirty pounds. But Jung

Woo's head was built right into his shoulders and he had thick legs and powerful hips. The two men worked hard and landed heavy shots but they were precise and their hands and shoulders and elbows were always there to muffle or parry punches. They were also both ex-fighters who saw men nearly half their age come into the gym and train. So they threw hands with speed and ill-intent but they didn't go in for the kill and they didn't brawl nor let the sparring devolve into the brutal practice rounds that an active fighter might use to get ready for his next bout. They spoke in the breaks and gave each other pointers and when Jasper called time one man always held the ring-rope for the other as both men went back down to the gym-room floor.

Jung Woo taught Jiu-Jitsu to young fighters and in the quiet afternoons he would roll with Daniel. At first those sessions were maulings where Daniel tried to power out of holds and chokes and poor positioning, Jung Woo clinging fast to him and shifting position with ease, always moving and making near imperceptible adjustments. If Daniel fought off a submission he would already be fighting another and in the end he would be caught and tap and he would sit there hauling air, his shirt turned wet rag. Jung Woo would be across from him, giving instruction, breathing gentle and often wearing only Daniel's sweat on his rashguard. Daniel had a decent ground game when he'd fought, but his Jiu-Jitsu was mainly defensive, used to prevent submissions and to get back to a dominant position where he could thump a downed man with punches and elbows or get back to his feet and box. Jung Woo could win fights with submissions or with strikes, but he didn't have Daniel's power and he was a bleeder. He cut too easy and his ruined nose had broke in all his later fights and he'd had trouble breathing and seeing clear.

During those weeks of training Daniel started to get his timing back and he became calm and fluid again in the ring. He took shots well and never staggered and his heavy hands were feared in sparring, even half-thrown. Jung Woo would call out to Jasper between rounds to watch them spar as if he were not already studying it. He would call out and he would talk very seriously to Jasper afterward while Daniel stretched on the gym floor.

During a bleak late-winter afternoon the two men warmed up and then wrapped their hands for sparring. Jung Woo had been waiting for Daniel and when Daniel came out into the gym in his gear Jung Woo was already shadowboxing and dancing the mats on the balls of his feet.

"What?" Daniel said. "You win the lottery or somethin'?"

Jung Woo smiled. Kept throwing light punches. He did that for a while and then he let his arms drop and shook them out at his sides.

"Today real sparring," he said. "Hard sparring."

Daniel had wrapped his hands. Started stretching his arms.

"Yeah?" he said.

"Okay?" Jung Woo said.

Daniel looked at him awhile and then he nodded.

"Sure," he said.

"Just hands."

"Okay."

Daniel sucked wind in the third round. He kept his hands up but his arms were heavy and his punches had lost some of their snap. The canvas was spotted with blood from Jung Woo's nose and the Korean had plugged his nostrils with tissue, since turned maroon. Even with the headgear on he couldn't hold his mud. Jung Woo moved as well as he had in the beginning, stepping light and strafing Daniel with jabs and combinations as he moved out of range. Daniel kept his hands high. Jung Woo went to the body. Daniel ate short hooks to the stomach and ribs and he took them well but knew they would slow him and sap his energy. He took chances and came over the top as Jung Woo went low but those punches came late or were blocked and then Jung Woo would be gone. By the last half of the round Daniel looked to ringside for the clock and Jung Woo stood him up with a jab and he didn't look for the clock again. Daniel could hear his heartbeat in his ears and little else. He breathed and he breathed and now he backed up and bounced on the balls of his feet and tried to get his legs to work again. He stalked Jung Woo and paid for it with a right hook to the cheek and then he tied Jung Woo up against the ringropes for a second and heard the one-minute warning from the timeclock.

Bedlam in that final minute. Daniel shoved Jung Woo clear and bombed him with punches. Jung Woo came off the ropes swinging and Daniel ate a left hook as he ripped Jung Woo to the body. Jung Woo grunted and stepped back, threw a right hand as he went that clipped Daniel on the forehead but had no power behind it. In the dying seconds of the round Daniel walked Jung Woo down and threw wild. He took shot after shot from the quicker man and still he chased. Eventually Jung Woo planted his feet and attacked. The two men stood in the pocket and traded. Blood and sweat sprayed the canvas and their feet atop it. Daniel landed heavier shots but Jung Woo landed more and his hands were faster and Daniel had to cover up. Jung Woo pushed forward but Daniel would not give and then he came untethered and drilled the Korean with hooks and an off-angle uppercut that sent the man sideways with his legs stiff and his glove drawing in the air as it came up late to block. They each ate the other man's right hand as the buzzer rang to call the round.

Daniel stopped and stood full while Jung Woo let himself go against the ringropes. Rocked back and grinned through his mouthguard. Blinked hard while thin lines of blood ran through the pluggings in his flat and boneless nose.

Jung Woo reached up and spat his mouthguard into his glove. Daniel put his hands up over his head, one wrist held in the opposite mitt. His jaw hung open and he blew hard over the black, fitted mouthpiece that covered his upper teeth. He took his hands off of his head and pulled at the strap under his chin and then wrested the headgear off and let it fall to the canvas. His hair stood up crazy, sweat-drenched and matted into clumps. Jung Woo had his gloves off when he came over and they were pinned under his armpit while he took his own headgear off with his free hand.

Bloodspots on his shirt by his chest and left shoulder. They bumped fists through their wraps and kept trying to get their wind back.

Daniel stood under the hot water in the gym shower for a long time. He could tell that the shower wouldn't take so he turned the water cold and let it chill him through. His head felt three sizes too big. The skin of his face and neck and arms was warm to the touch. He knew what kind of soreness would come that night, the next morning. He turned the cold tap wide-open.

When Daniel came back out of the changeroom Jung Woo and Jasper were sitting on the edge of the ring, legs dangling. Jung Woo had lately been skipping and the rope lay on the ground below him, his hand-wraps in a pile beside the rope. He spoke to Jasper and articulated by throwing different punches and combinations in the air. Jasper listened. Daniel walked over to the men with his duffel bag slung at his side, wet spots on his clean T-shirt. Jung Woo got up and shook Daniel's hand and sat back down again.

"This guy," Jung Woo said. "Real fighter. Good body. Punches like nuclear bombs. Getting very good on the ground."

"Real fighter?" Jasper said.

"Real fighter," Jung Woo said. "Still."

He drove home slow and when he got there Sarah was waiting for him. She sat on the steps by twilight and blew smoke. The wind carried it on. Daniel saw her before she saw him and when she did see him coming she tried to drop and bury the joint with her foot in the dirtied snow beside the steps. Daniel turned into the driveway. The rear wheels of the truck spun some as he pulled up to the house. Sarah didn't get up. Just sat there brushing her hair clear when the breeze laid it across her face.

Daniel got out of the truck with the duffel bag in hand. He shut the door.

"Your head is all red. It looks like someone plugged you in," she said.

"It's alright," he said.

Sarah stood and came over to him. She reached up and took his head in her hands, felt his forehead, his cheeks, the underside of his jaw.

"I don't know," she said. "Could be permanent by the looks of it."

Daniel took her hands away.

"You got a phone call this afternoon," she said. "I heard the message on the machine."

"What's the story?" he said.

She took her hands back and put them in the pockets of her coat.

"They want you to go back on full-time at the jobsite. They got some big contract they didn't think they'd get."

"No shit?" Daniel said.

"You'll have to give it a listen yourself. But it sounds like they weren't jerking you around after all."

Daniel nodded.

"See," he said. "I knew it'd work out."

Sarah hugged him around the waist. He dropped the bag so he could get both arms around her. When they broke he told her he'd be in shortly. She ran her hand down his hand and reached for the duffel bag, carried it on into the house. Daniel turned the handle on the garage door and pulled. He had to force it up and around the rails to get it all the way open. He went inside and came back with a bag of road salt and set about scattering it on the driveway. At the base of the drive he stopped long enough to take a chill. Dirt road there that ran past their house and led to lakewater and marshland. The country-run plough had built a massive snowbank where the road ended, humped some ten feet high and full with grit and gravel.

Later that night they lay together in their bed and Sarah held his hands in hers. She ran the pads of her fingertips over his knuckles and over bonespurs that sat thick in the middle of his hands.

"I guess you're gonna lose those afternoons in that gym now?" she said.

Daniel lay there at his side of the bed, nearest the window. A full moon showed part of him, shone narrow between the bedroom curtains.

"I guess so," he said.

"Well, it isn't that far. I'm sure you could still make it there sometimes if you wanted."

"I figured you'd be happy I couldn't go to the gym anymore," he said.

Sarah examined his hands for a little while longer and then she stopped and rolled over to face him.

"I just don't want you to get hurt," she said.

Daniel shrugged.

"You could see the difference. Just from you training again. There's a calmness that you get."

"Think so?"

"You know what I mean," she said.

"Yeah," Daniel said.

Sarah put a hand to his cheekbone.

"Did your eyes give you any trouble when you were sparring?" she said soft.

"They didn't."

"Did you feel like you could get hurt again?"

"No," he said.

They were quiet awhile. Daniel stirred and reached back to shift the pillow behind his head. He kept his arm there and stared up at the ceiling.

"I might go evenings after all," he said. "If I can muster it."

She didn't say anything. She was asleep. Her one hand rested on the bed near his face and the other had been pinned down under her head and her pillows. Her legs were bent at the knees like she might run.

Daniel took up her wrist and let go. It fell back down to his side where she'd left it. She woke for but a second and slept again. He let her be.

SIXTEEN

The van drew up against the curb and settled there, exhaust rattling. Wallace King in the driver's seat with two men in the windowless rear of the van. Clothed and hooded in black. Gloves on their hands and only their eyes plain through balaclava holes. Under their coverings they were Mike Moreau and Troy Armstrong, hired on again but without their scatterguns. Nobody sat in the passenger seat. Wallace got out of the van. Ash and elm trees lined the one-way street, bare branches reaching and some long enough to touch some twenty feet above the vehicle. The trees grew from the short lawns of hundred-and-fifty-year-old Victorian brownstones that were owned by the rich or had been converted into stores for the rich. Wallace shook his head. He snuffled hard and spat into the middle of the street. Starless sky above. Spotlights flickering there from the downtown core just beyond. The streetlamps were shaded by the thin tree-cover and once in a while some would blink out while others lit in turn.

Another like van had been parked down the street. That vehicle showed no running lights or exhaust from the tailpipe. Wallace got back into his van and almost right away a white face was there at the passenger-side window. The two men in the back jumped and Moreau stood up and cracked his head on the ceiling and sat down again. Wallace looked at that startled goon and took a deep breath. Moreau was still rubbing at the back of his head through the knitwork when Tarbell opened the door and got in.

"Nerves of steel on these," he said.

Wallace didn't acknowledge it. The blonde settled into the seat and waited.

"I seen two cruisers up and down these last few blocks alone," Wallace said. "You see any the way you came?"

"I saw one."

"Better get this over with. You know what you're doin'?"

"No," Tarbell said.

Wallace narrowed his eyes on the man.

"Pardon?" he said.

"I know what to do," Tarbell said. "But I don't know why I'm out here to do this petty shit."

Wallace turned back to the road.

"So what?" he said. "I could build a fuckin' mountain from the amount of shit you don't know."

Tarbell stared at Wallace King for a long time.

"Get out," Wallace said.

The pale-eyed man opened the door and got out and slammed it shut. Went to the other vehicle. Pulled a hood over his hair. Wallace put his van into gear and pulled out from the curb. When he passed the other van, Tarbell had the forefinger of his left hand pointed at Wallace and his cocked thumb as the trip-hammer. It took all that Wallace had not to swerve and put his fender through the driver door.

The gallery front was no more than triple-sheet-glass in the arched window frames of one of the

Victorians. Faint light in the upstairs windows, some in the main floor. A tiny red beacon winked at the sill. Wallace couldn't see the cameras but he knew where they were.

"Do not fuckin' look up. Except to see what you got your hands on."

The men nodded.

"Get everything I told you. You fuck it up, I'll kill you both."

They nodded slower that time.

"Okay," Wallace said. He pulled his hood up and tightened it by the drawstrings. Then he got out of the van. He looked up and down the empty street. Maybe a hundred yards afield there were people passing on the avenue. Drunken students and club-goers and finely dressed men and women. He paid them no mind. He walked around the van and pulled the sliding door. Moreau carried an eight-pound sledge as he set his feet to the asphalt and Armstrong held a prybar in each hand.

They hustled quick over a three-foot high wrought-steel fence and across the front lawn. Then Armstrong slowed up with the prybars. Moreau took long strides and raised the sledge up over his head and pulled it back like a warhammer at the ready. He broke into a short run and then planted his feet and let fly. The sledge went end over end through the air and blew the window in without slowing and slammed into the far wall of the gallery room. Glass pelted the hardwood and showcases. Alarms wailed. They took a prybar each and cleared the jagged leavings from one side of the window frame and then leapt the ledge.

Wallace took cover inside the van. He watched the sidewalks and parked cars and the neighbouring houses. In his rearview mirror he saw the busy avenue small in the distance. Life went on. By the busted shop window he could see the men levering the paintings from their wallmoorings. Moreau put his boot to an installation in the floor and bashed the display case apart while it lay prone. Four-inch fastener bolts stuck out of the bottom. Long splinters of hardwood clung to the bolt-ruts. Wallace studied the street again. When he turned back to the gallery both of the thieves were already coming out. Wallace got out of the van again and went around to meet them. They'd left the tools and now Armstrong had two paintings pressed together under his armpit and Moreau held a weathered wooden case to his chest. Moreau slid the chest into the back of the van and climbed into the hold and then took the paintings from the other man. Armstrong leapt onto the vehicle and he had barely cleared the lip when Wallace whipped the door shut.

The alarm-siren howled on but no other windows had lit anywhere on the street. Wallace made it to the driver door and reached for the handle. There he stopped. A stranger stood agog in the road, feet stepping uneasy on the pavement. Wallace turned his face away and opened the door to shield it. He was about to cuss the man out when he heard whistling behind a loud bang. Chunks of bark blew clear from an elm trunk not five feet from where the stranger stood in the lane. The young man blurted nonsense and got to the ground in fits and starts. Nothing in him seemed to be working right. He crawled the road strange and two more shots rang. Even Wallace cowed behind the vehicle door. From there he saw the kid scramble up and lurch out crazily toward the opposite sidewalk where he bowled through wooden fencework and somehow kept moving on all fours until he was lost to the gap between two houses.

Wallace got into the van and gunned the engine. The door carried shut as he drove. Soon enough he came upon the other van, Tarbell standing outside with a pistol in hand. Wallace put the passenger window down as he came close. He reached under his seat and brought up a pistol of his own. Aimed it at the blonde.

"Give that to me," he said.

Tarbell yet held the pistol, looked at Wallace blankly. Then he slowly let the clip out of his gun and held the clip and pistol together in his hand. He did not take his eyes off of Wallace. He stepped closer so that his hands were inside the van and then he ran the slide and loosed the round in the chamber. It all dropped to the empty passenger seat. He waited.

"You got any other shit that'll get you locked up?" Wallace said.

Tarbell shook his head.

"Motherfucker," Wallace said.

He took off and Tarbell barely got clear in time. Stood in the road and watched the van's taillights. Then he turned to the busted gallery. Perhaps two hundred feet between that building and the second, identical van in his charge. He sat on the rear bumper of the vehicle and crossed one leg over the other and waited. Soon he saw cherries turning the dark as the first cruiser pulled up to the scene. When the second cruiser arrived Tarbell stood and walked to the driver door of the van and got in. Turned the key and fired the engine. He had the handbrake cranked and his left foot heavy to the clutch. He shifted into gear and hammered the gas, spun rubber until he could see smoke in the sideview mirror. He dropped the brake and popped the clutch and peeled out loud. The van bucked hard over low speed bumps as he sped off down that suddenly electric side street.

The two cruisers caught the van before it got to the highway on-ramp, one unit trailing and belting threats from a loudspeaker, the other running the lane over until it got a car's length ahead. There the cruiser skidded to a stop on a diagonal and pinned the van up against the curb. The cops came out with their pistols drawn, hollering for the driver to keep his hands on the fucking wheel. One hulking cop came up to the door, eyes wide and white against near blue-black skin. He had his sidearm pointed at Tarbell's cheekbone. The other cop stood on the other side of the van, ginger-haired and taller than the black cop if not as wide. Yet another cop came up on the van from the rear, the smallest of the men.

"Is there anyone else in the vehicle?" the black cop said.

Tarbell said no. To have a look if they felt like it.

The cop stared at him and the ginger had made his way to the front of the vehicle where he could see into the van on an angle through the passenger window.

"I don't see anybody," he called over.

The black cop kept weighing up the driver.

"Anybody else comes outta there I'll fuckin' shoot you," he said. "You take your hands off the wheel, I'll fuckin' shoot."

Tarbell nodded. The cop reached over and yanked the door open. Tarbell sat low and calm, fingers loose on the wheel. He blinked a few times.

"What do you want?" he said.

The cop glowered at him and told him to get out of the van and put his hands behind his head. Then he walked Tarbell around to the front and had him lay his palms on the hood. Cuffed him and frisked him. The other cops had the van doors open and called it out as clear. The ginger cop came around to the front of the vehicle and sent word through his shoulder-clipped radio that they had stopped the van and had the driver in bracelets. The third cop was searching the back of it.

"You stay put," the black cop said. "Don't you move…"

"Or you'll fuckin' shoot. Yeah. I got it."

The cop snorted and backed up. He holstered his pistol but kept the clasp loose. He brought Tarbell to the side of the road and sat him down on the curb. Then he went over to the ginger cop. The smaller officer had left the van and sat in the cruiser behind and worked at a dash-mounted laptop, talking into his radio all the while.

"There's nothing in the van," the ginger said.

The black cop shook his head.

"Something's wrong with him," he said.

The ginger cop eyeballed Tarbell for a minute. Rubbed at his mouth. The third cop got out of the cruiser and came over.

"That van is clean," he said. "Plates and all."

"Fuck off," the black cop said.

"I don't believe it either," the smaller cop said. "But he didn't dump anything and he didn't change those plates. All we can do is haul the van and hold him until we get a better look at it."

The cops all turned to where Tarbell sat at the curb. Still as could be. The black cop looked away, out across four lanes of city thoroughfare. Dark storefronts with their pavements swept. Travellers leaving the city or coming back behind halogen headlamps.

"Have you seen him before?" the ginger cop said.

The black cop shook his head. He drummed his holstered pistol with the pads of his fingers. He looked at their prisoner again. Tarbell sat up straight on the curb. He'd not taken his eyes off of the black cop. They stared at each other for a very long time.

"There's something wrong with him," the cop said.

By mid-morning Clayton dozed in the driver's seat of his Cadillac. Sun through the windshield and creeping the interior. The windows were down. Wallace sat red-eyed in the passenger seat. He wore fresh clothes and he'd a baseball cap over his clippered head. They were parked inside a wrecker's yard between mountains of gnarled metal. Sound of gravel shifting somewhere else in the lot. Wallace shook Clayton and Clayton opened one eye.

"I was having a good dream," he said.

"You weren't even asleep," Wallace said.

"Didn't matter."

Clayton sat up straight and looked at the rearview mirror. The van rumbled into the yard with its tires spewing sand and rockpebble. It banked to the left and came up beside the Cadillac and stopped. The driver-door of the vehicle opened and stayed open as Tarbell set his feet down and came around the front of the van. His clothes were wrinkled from a night spent on a prison bench. Otherwise he looked no different. Had he slept or not nobody could have told.

He walked up to Clayton's window and stood there. Wallace spat to the ground and swatted a wasp against the side of the car. Clayton looked over at Wallace for a moment and then to his nephew.

"You gonna get in?" Clayton said.

Tarbell put his hands on the window frame and bent low to better see Wallace in the passenger seat.

"You got my gun?"

Wallace put a hand to his brow and kneaded his forehead. He said nothing.

"Seems like a lot of trouble for a bit of canvas and bullshit," the blonde said.

Clayton nodded.

"It does to you," he said.

Tarbell cleared his hands and went to the rear door on the driver side and got into the backseat. Clayton turned the key and peeled out of the lot. Left the van behind. They passed through the exit gate and Wallace waved at somebody in a makeshift office there and that man waved back.

They sped north along the two-lane highway, thumping over baked and battered macadam. Wallace's eyelids hung low and heavy. In the backseat, Tarbell watched the forest at the highway fringe. As soon as Wallace sagged in his seat Tarbell spoke.

"Who do you think's got more reason for hate?" he said. "An Indian or a nigger?"

Clayton glanced at the mirror but once, and brief. He found the stereo knob and turned the volume up.

SEVENTEEN

Daniel worked long days and came home tired. Those afternoons welding bracket and pipe and girder wore on him different than his hours in the gym. His mind would not leave him be while he loosed lighting from his torch, built metals upon metals. He thought about things he didn't want to think about and then he thought about them again. The men Daniel worked with kept their distance and he didn't take it personal. He often ate his lunch alone at the tailgate of his truck and once in a while he sat with a few of the other welders and carpenters and talked about the weather and weekends and the work waiting for them when the hour was up. If they talked about work they'd done in the past and places they'd lived and women they'd known he would smile and nod but he never gave back. If they did ask him something like that they didn't ask very hard. Those among the men who'd grown up in that town at the same time as Daniel asked him nothing at all.

If Sarah worked the mid-shift at the home, Daniel would stop at Murray and Ella's house to fetch his daughter. The house sat on the corner of their long, country lane and the wider concession road that led to greater roadways. Town to the north. City to the south. That house was nearly one hundred and forty years old. Home to farmers and their families before the land they farmed had true names or boundary lines. Murray had been born on the island reserve and moved west as a younger man to make enough money to buy a house in town. He met Ella at a hotel bar in northern Saskatchewan while she was travelling with her cousins and he was on shutdown from his worksite in the Northwest Territories. She was part Plains Cree, the first he'd ever met. He took years coming back east. When he did return to Simcoe County she came with him and they were barely grown and worked as farmhands for a dwindling Dutch family and then managed the farm when the elders of that family died and their children left to find other lives. When the farm closed down, Murray and Ella moved into town. Five years later they bought the property at auction and took up their implements again. They tended small fields of corn and soy and ran a meagre tree nursery and otherwise they let the fields run wild. They grew older and kneeled in gardens and sat on porches. Kept whiskies and cold beer at the ready.

Daniel drove up to the farmhouse in the early evening. He got out of the truck and stared up at the high-peaked roof where he'd helped set new shingles the year previous. There were two main floors and a triangular attic above. One lonely window had been lit on the second floor. Lamplight showed the front-decking and the cold soil and pale, flattened long-grass between the driveway and the house proper. The snow lay spare over the grounds. In a malformed bank where it had been shovelled off the frozen surface of a deep fish-pond. Daniel took his filthy workcoat off and left it in the cab of the truck. He went up the steps to the front door. The finish had been stripped years ago and the bare oak wore pockmarks and scars of storms long past. He drummed the wood with his knuckles. When nobody came he knocked one more time and went in.

"Hello," he called out.

"Who's that?"

Daniel went into the living room and there he saw Murray sitting in his armchair with a book in one hand and a beer in the other. Madelyn sat in the floor not two feet from the TV. She hammered on a video game controller with her nose wrinkled and her front teeth clamped to her bottom lip.

"Where's your better half?" Daniel said.

"In the kitchen. Makin' supper."

Daniel leaned out of the room some. Kitchen at the end of the corridor with the door pegged open, steam rising from a pot on the stove. He didn't see Ella there. He came back.

"That what you call being looked after?" he said to Murray. "You see the kind of face that kid is makin'?"

Murray set the book down on the tablestand beside him. He leaned over the chair arm and looked long at the girl.

"Looks like she's having a religious experience," he said.

Daniel shook his head.

"I hear this one got into a scrap," the old man said.

Madelyn turned so quick her hair flew. Murray paid her no mind.

"She tell you all that?" Daniel said.

"Some."

Daniel smiled at him funny but he didn't say anything. He heard shuffling at the end of the hallway and stepped back to see. Sound of cupboards opened and shut. A tall woman stood with her back facing the kitchen entry, long and grey-streaked hair. Once quite black. She stirred the great pot on the stove and set a wooden spoon on the countertop near the sink. She wiped her hands on her apron and then stopped and turned around.

"Daniel," Ella called. "Stop talking at him and come over here."

He went down the hallway to meet her. When he got there she hugged him hard and kissed him on the cheek. She stood only a few inches shorter than he. She let him go and studied his face and his clothes, the all of him. He still wore a bruise on his cheek from sparring and she thumbed at it rough.

"I heard you were back into those gyms again," she said.

"Just tryin' to get back into shape," he said. "That's all."

"You sure she knows that?" Ella said.

Daniel took a breath. Sat to the edge of the counter.

"She's smart as you can get," Ella said. "She knows more than she should already about what you do."

He glanced down the hall. Murray and the girl could likewise be heard talking but they were still in the living room.

"I always thought it'd be easier than with a boy," he said.

"You can never know what traits they'll take on," Ella said. "Doesn't matter that she's a girl."

"I know it."

The woman pulled the oven door partway down. Let it shut. She spoke to him in a hush. Hardness in her voice.

"Between the fights and that other work, you are lucky you're still in one piece."

"Yeah?" he said.

"I know life's not been easy, son. But I will be damned if I stand by quiet while you put that little girl at risk."

"I hear you, Ella," Daniel said. "But you don't know what you're talking about."

The woman drew herself up tall. Stood him off awhile and then settled.

"I just don't want her to lose her daddy for no good reason," she said. "To see her turn mean."

Daniel crossed his arms and looked off. Ella frowned at him. At a glance she often seemed no older than he, but she was at least fifteen years his senior. Up close her greyed hair gave it away, skin she'd spent under the sun, the yearlines around her eyes and mouth.

"You know that I'm done workin' with Clayton?" he said.

She nodded.

"I just hope you got out in time before anything took root."

"She'll be alright," Daniel said.

"I'm not just talking about her."

Daniel took her arm gentle and kissed her by the cheek. He said thanks for their watching the girl and started to leave but Ella had him at the elbow.

"You gonna stay and eat supper with us?" Ella said.

Daniel stopped by the door. Thought on it some.

"We put you out enough already," he said.

"Don't be sore," she said. "We got plenty, and I've seen what you feed her."

"It's alright," Daniel said.

Ella squeezed at his bicep. Let go and went to the stove. She took up the spoon and stirred.

"Call her in," she said. "See if those two don't make a run for the dinner table."

He stood there a minute longer and then he called.

Daniel and Madelyn ate and stayed on another two hours. Daniel drank beer with Murray and talked to the man and Madelyn helped Ella clean up. Daniel tried to help out but Ella told him to sit and then the girl told him again. He sat down.

"You should get off your ass once in a while," he said to the old man.

"It's not like I'm against it," Murray said. "But anythin' I do she does again. So I just let her be."

"Alright."

Later they said goodbye from the porch. Madelyn said her thank yous and Murray put his fists up to her. She punched him in the shoulder. He'd gotten sort of drunk but wore it well enough. Hugged the girl to him. A low wind whistled past through their part-open doorway.

"When it gets warmer we should all take a trip up north," Murray said. "Ella got that cabin from her aunt who passed."

"Yeah?" Daniel said.

"Yes," Ella said. "It's lovely there in the summer."

She leant down a little to talk to Madelyn.

"I used to go there when I was just a girl. Younger than you are now."

Ella winked. Madelyn looked up at her father.

"We'll have to see what your mother says," he said. "Neither of us get much in the way of holidays."

Ella nodded. She stood full but kept looking at the girl. Murray took a sip of his beer and set it down on the railing.

"They got poisonous snakes up there. Fish big enough to bite a paddle in half. Frogs as big as your head."

Madelyn blew out hard over her lips, made a fart sound.

"I'm not scared of any of that shit," she said.

Murray said he didn't buy it. They stared each other down until she smiled.

"We better get goin'," Daniel said.

"Tell Sarah hey," Ella said.

"Sure thing."

Then he took his daughter by her shoulders and trailed her down from the deck. Halfway she shook loose and hopped the last two steps to the ground.

"Try not to drop anymore punks," Murray called to her. "Unless they deserve it."

Ella backhanded him to the chest. She looked to the girl and shook her head no. The girl waved. She climbed into the truck and pulled the door shut. Wound the window down so she could better see them. Daniel dropped his own window as he pulled out, raised the one hand. The old man and woman stood there. The great house like an island in the snow and meltwater. Daniel took his hand back and turned the truck out toward the road. Madelyn leant out and waved until the top half of the house had been taken by the dark, and so the grounds beyond and before it. Until the old man and woman were but shapes.

EIGHTEEN

Daniel pulled into the gym mid-evening now, with the skies gone dark. There were sometimes a dozen cars in the lot and many more if a group was taught while he was there. Jasper and Jung Woo taught those classes, or they worked in the ring with up-and-coming fighters. Daniel beat the bags in the back of the gym and sometimes he came in to help green fighters get their mechanics down, their footwork, the timing of the fight as it played by round. He rolled with Jung Woo once in a while. But mainly he worked alone. He saw young men come and go with their lean muscle and quick feet and the confidence that came from their believing they had many years yet owed to them. Daniel drove out to the gym two or three nights a week at most. The gym built and more fighters came to train. Men who had scraps booked and needed other full-time fighters to get them ready.

Daniel put in lonely work on those late evenings and often he was half-spent when he warmed up and stretched on the mats. Rarely did he shadowbox in front of the huge wallbound mirrors in the rear of the building. Not nearly as much as he should have. Instead he ripped the heavy bags with brutal, rudimentary hooks. His kicks were methodically set up and thrown heavy. His hips and shoulders turning over full before a slow reset. If he felt short of breath or weak-limbed, he would grunt and power through until he could barely keep the gloves up. Some of the fighters watched him work but he seemed not to notice. He rarely spoke to anyone. Jasper and Jung Woo tried to train him when they could, but he didn't know when he'd be there or for how long and they had obligations in the ring with the active fighters. Daniel's work was uneven and sometimes outright chaotic. But he felt the good in doing it. In hours and hours of stilted work he had his moments. Ring of sweat circling the heavy bag where he stepped light and battered the thing out of shape, dug valleys into the leather. Light sparring drills where he slipped punches like he'd been told what was coming. Grappling contests where his raw power kept his arms intact and his neck free and gave him top position over an exasperated man. Nobody would hold the Thai pads for him except for the coaches. Afterward Daniel drove home through dark country where the snow had cleared and seed-filled soil lay black and damp. Nightbirds cried out and circled above. And at the end of the road his wife and daughter sleeping. Cold beer in the kitchen. The space where he would set his head down and hope for dreamless sleep.

NINETEEN

Sarah corralled her daughter into the entranceway of the bank and let the door close behind them. They'd taken a week of unusual warm weather through the county and there were people in the line who'd sweat partway through their shirts and dabbed at their brows. Madelyn sat down in a chair in the waiting area and Sarah told the girl to stay put. Madelyn saluted her. Sarah muttered as she made for the teller.

"What can I do for you today?" the teller said.

"I have an appointment."

Sarah told her the name. The teller stopped and tilted her head a little. Narrowed her eyes.

"You're Daniel's wife," she said.

Sarah just looked at her.

"I went to high school with Dan," the teller said. "He used to hang out with my brother. I knew him pretty good."

"Oh yeah?" Sarah said.

"How's he doin' these days?" the teller said.

Sarah took in the woman's round face and dimpled cheeks. Blonde hair to the shoulder. The teller was maybe a few years younger than Daniel and a few years older than Sarah. She still had all of her curves and wore an engagement ring with a pink diamond.

"He's good," Sarah said.

"Tell him I said hey, would you?"

Sarah left for the waiting area before the teller quit talking. The teller took a minute to figure out what happened and then she called over the next person in line and her smile came on crooked.

She'd been sat and waiting in the banker's office for half an hour. Madelyn still occupied the chair outside and Sarah could see the girl's back through the glass. She was very still. Sarah watched her all the while. The loan officer came back and shut the door behind him. He set her papers down on his desk.

"You didn't have to come all the way down here," he said. "When we spoke on the phone I thought we covered everything."

Sarah took the forms from the desk and put them in an envelope that the banker offered her.

"I just wanted to let you have a chance to explain it in person. Seemed like the kind of thing a human being might do."

The man was trying that trick of looking at her forehead and pretending to look her in the eye.

"It's just that, with your history, we're not in a position to take on the risk."

"All we're trying to do is pay you instead of all of these other places," Sarah said. "After what you made on the house, I figured it's the least you could do."

The banker frowned.

"I've been through this before with your husband," he said.

"Daniel."

"Pardon?"

"You know him."

"Maybe Dan has been working there a little longer, and we see some stability there, you could try again. I can't see the answer being no."

"A couple of months is a long time for some people," she said.

The banker started to say something but she reached out her hand and he stopped. He shook and then leaned back in his chair while Sarah put the envelope in her purse.

"She's growing up fast" he said, gesturing at Madelyn.

Madelyn had company now outside the office. A boy had sat in a chair beside hers, tall and tow-headed. The girl seemed to know him well enough by how she'd turned to him. They were talking but it was muffled by the glass. Sarah stood and straightened her shirt. Took up her things. She left the banker there without another word.

They drove into the supermarket plaza and parked on the far end of the lot. When they got out of the truck they had to cross a laneway and then walk the length of the plaza past the bordering shopfronts. Sarah asked Madelyn about her friend at the bank, and she was told that he was just some boy from school. They said little to each other after that. Sarah put the keys into her purse and turned over the contents. She found a pack of gum and went to give some to Madelyn but the girl was not there. Sarah spun and saw the girl near to a storefront window they'd passed. On the other side of the window young pups shuffled by sleepily and others pawed the glass as if they might dig through to daylight. They yapped at Madelyn and she made faces and spoke to them.

"These dogs shouldn't be cooped up like that," Madelyn said.

The girl had her hands pressed to the glass where one pup squashed its face ugly.

"You think we'll ever get a dog?" she said.

"Who'd look after it?" Sarah said.

"I can take care of a dog," the girl said.

"Not until we can figure out how to pay to feed it. Whenever that'll be."

Sarah could see Madelyn frowning in the plateglass.

"Dad said he'd think about it, when I asked," Madelyn said.

"You can ask me about it right now," Sarah said.

The girl did not seem to hear her.

"You wouldn't ask me though, would you?"

Madelyn put her hands in her pockets, turned to look at her mother.

"Anything you ask him for he'll try to give you," Sarah said. "Even if he can't. He'll try to give until he's broke and starving. You understand?"

The girl nodded. Sarah took a deep breath, brushed her hair back behind her ears.

"We got no money now 'cause he's not working nights. Right?" Madelyn said.

Sarah didn't answer.

"I know about him. I'm not stupid," Madelyn said.

Sarah walked a few steps and sat on a bench opposite the storefront. Dropped her purse down to the wooden slats.

"I know how smart you are," Sarah said. "But, honey, I promise you that there's still plenty you couldn't know even if I told you or showed it to you plain."

"Dad never talks about his fights. I had to read about them on my own."

Sarah shrugged.

"Things didn't turn out the way he wanted to, Maddy. They don't always."

"Do you think he can still fight?"

Sarah almost laughed. Caught herself. She had tired eyes and rubbed at them with her thumb and forefinger.

"Yes," she said.

"Will he fight again? Like, a real one?"

Sarah chewed at her gum. She dug her keys back out of the purse, held that hand out in the air. It had begun to rain. Madelyn kept waiting on the reply.

"If he's so good at it I don't get why he won't do it," said the girl.

Sarah stood and gestured for Madelyn to come away from the window. The girl was slow to move but Sarah unmoored her with a look. They walked back to the truck together. Madelyn pointed to the stores in the supermarket plaza.

"Don't we need anything here?" she said.

"We'll make do," Sarah said.

The girl waited by the truck quiet and Sarah set about wrenching her busted door wide enough that she could get into the cab.

TWENTY

The cruiser came toward the house at a creep. Dust trailing in the dry, spring air. Daniel sat in a wooden chair on the lawn with three cans of beer bound by the plastic tether, the other three rings empty. He sat in cargo shorts and a T-shirt and he wore no shoes. The sun had been out and lately left and now heavy black cloud rode across the northeastern sky. Warm winds across the fields. Daniel waited. The cruiser slowed and went on again. He made out the cop's face from far away while the cop was still squinting out at him over the steering wheel. The cruiser sidled up to the road's edge on the far side of the driveway. The constable got out and walked the length of the gravel drive while Daniel worked another can out of the plastics.

"Dan," the cop said.

"Constable Smith," Daniel said.

Daniel pitched the beer at him underhand. The cop caught it and looked at it. Still walking. He smirked and pitched the can back. Daniel caught it in his left hand and cracked it and drank before the foam spilled over the lip.

The constable stopped at the edge of the lawn and put his hands on his hips. The man stood about six-foot-three and he'd an athlete's build just beginning to go to seed under his blues. Square jaw that he'd not shaven in a few days by the look of it. The cop had played semi-pro hockey as a young man but he'd been a cop longer than any of that now. He looked up at the sky. Both skies.

"Was a nice day, wasn't it?"

"It was," Daniel said.

The cop looked at Daniel. At the house.

"Sarah home? Your girl?"

"Just me," Daniel said. "Am I in trouble or somethin'?"

"If you have anything you'd like to confess to, I'm all ears."

Daniel took a drink.

"No," he said. "Fuck. I don't have the time or the means to get in trouble no more."

The cop nodded.

"You find out what assholes stole my rig?" Daniel said.

"Not yet," Smith said.

"Well, I won't hold my breath on that."

Daniel set the can on his knee and studied the constable. He leaned heavy on the chair arm.

"Alright. Why in the fuck d'you come all the way out here?"

"I need you to come look at something," Smith said.

"What?"

"Not entirely sure. That's why I need you to look at it."

Daniel peered out across the fields. He took another drink.

"Do I have to?" he said.

The cop shook his head. Took a moment to reset.

"Listen," the constable said. "The both of us know what kind of work you've done around here. And I know that you've been straight a little while."

"Actually, I've never took a charge in my life. You can look it up."

The constable's radio crackled on at his chest and he listened a second and pressed a button to quiet it.

"Whatever you were into before, that's not what I care about," Smith said. "If you quit the work maybe you at least had the sense to know which way it was going when you left."

"How's that?"

"This is a county that used to have bikers growing weed and robbing each other. Now we're into war atrocities. Shit that'd even give you nightmares, Dan. That you'd not want your daughter to even know was possible."

Daniel sat there awhile. He rolled his shoulders and drank the rest of the beer. Dropped the can to the grass and stood.

"You gonna pinch me for drivin' now?"

The cop looked around.

"You don't even have a vehicle here," he said.

"Yeah. I need a lift to the end of the road there so I can borrow one."

"What?"

"I can't be seen in that fuckin' cruiser."

When they walked into the station house there were two cops sitting at desks in the back of the reception office. Heavyset man with a buzzcut and a young woman with her hair pulled back in a ponytail. Another tall cop standing at the front counter, stamping papers. All of them armed and uniformed. The man at the counter stopped what he was doing. Eventually the heavyset cop turned and saw who had just come through the front door. He coughed and the female cop looked up. She half-waved at Daniel.

"Hey, Mike," said the tall cop at the counter. "How's it going?"

"It's goin'," said Smith.

The constable waited at the door until he heard the buzzer go. Click of the lock as it unlatched.

"Come on," he said.

Smith shoved the door open and went in. Daniel followed him, looking down at the back of the cop's head as they crossed the threshold and the door shut behind them. Sharp crack as it set flush in the metal doorframe. Daniel felt strange. A chill right through him. He followed the cop down the corridor until they came upon the room that held the man's desk. Seven more in that humble space and nobody attending them.

Daniel was already sitting when Constable Smith came around to the other side of the desk and settled in to his seat. He'd not been there two seconds and he stood back up. He reached down and undid his belt and took it off. Laid it heavy on the table. Baton, cuffs, pepper spray, pistol and all. Then he sat down again. The constable leaned back with his hands on the chair arms.

"That bother you sittin' there?" the constable said.

"No," Daniel said.

"I'd always been told you don't like guns. That right?"

"They can make an awful mess."

The cop smiled. He'd laced his hands and now he popped the knuckles on his left hand, on his right. Then he leaned forward and took up a case file from atop his desk. He opened it up and turned it around and dropped it back on the desk in front of Daniel. Daniel just sat there.

"Please," the constable said.

Daniel waited a few more seconds and then he shifted in the chair. In the open folder he saw the first of a series of crime-scene photographs. He picked them up and went through them. Wide shots and close-ups. Greyed skin darkened by layers of bruising. Small black holes here and there. Blind eyes, clouded white. The insides of finger-joints like rings on a tree trunk. Daniel let his eyes wander to the corresponding paperwork left in the file. Constable Smith reached over and shut the folder and took it back. He shook his head. Daniel went through the pictures again. Muttered something. He set them down in the middle of the desk. He'd begun to breathe heavy. Couldn't hide it.

The cop waited.

"What?" Daniel said. And too loud.

"You know that poor fucker in there?"

"His name is Lucas O'Hare," Daniel said.

"He a friend of yours?"

"I wouldn't say that."

"But if there were violence, you'd not be on opposite sides."

"I liked the kid."

The constable nodded and then he took the pictures and went through them himself. By his face he'd likely done so many times before. He took a deep breath of his own and then laid them back down.

"You saw that they cut off his fingers? Pulled out his teeth? Set fire to parts of him?" Smith said.

"I saw."

"Well. It doesn't make a whole lot of sense to process a man like that. Not considering we knew who he was on sight."

"It makes sense if you know who did it."

"Yeah. Who?"

Daniel shook his head no.

"You don't know or you won't say?" Smith said.

"Pick one."

"What?"

"There's a lot of evil assholes out there I can think of that might have done it. One that I'd put at the top of that list," Daniel said. "But I don't know for sure. If I did I might even be stupid enough to tell you."

"And he's working for Clayton. Ain't he?"

"I assume you knew the answer to that before you asked it."

The constable nodded. He leaned in and put his index finger to the top picture.

"This is bullshit," Smith said. "We can't have it."

Daniel just looked at him.

"You don't have anything else to say about it?" Smith said.

"I'll say that you're in trouble if you don't lock him up quick."

The constable leaned back in the chair. Crossed his arms. He let his chin hang down near his chest for a moment.

"This has to disturb you, Dan. Being so close to home," Smith said.

"It disturbs me plenty. That was just a boy they killed. And not a bad one either."

"Yeah?"

"Yeah. Some of those guys are just tryin' to make a living. Whatever you think."

Constable Smith took the photos back and put them in the folder and closed it over. He loosed his shirt at the collar and rubbed at the back of his neck with one hand. Eyes of a man who'd not slept. Little bruise outside his brow that Daniel hadn't noticed earlier.

"I have trouble believing you are clear of that work. Entirely. That you don't have something else you could tell us."

"Well you should believe it."

"Why?"

"'Cause you will never see pictures of me like the ones in that folder. Not ever."

The constable studied him awhile.

"I appreciate that, Dan," the constable said. "But if you hear anything…"

"I make sure I don't hear nothin' anymore. You know everything I know."

"Okay."

Daniel started to get up.

"And what if you do end up back at work alongside these fellas?" the constable said. "If you gotta be in the same room as the man who's doing this heinous shit?"

Daniel made a funny sound. He patted his pockets for his keys as he stood.

"That ever happens and you'll get all kinds of help from me," he said. "You won't have to worry about that motherfucker ever again."

TWENTY-ONE

The man went up his porch steps two at a time. Long, long legs under his jeans. His hair would have reached his waist were it not pulled back and tied. He opened the screen door and let it slam behind him. Then he got his keys and opened the front door of the house. Out in the bordering wood he heard branches crack. He stopped and turned. Stared out into the dense treeline to the north. The sun shone full on the grass. Loons called from the lakewater to the rear of the house. The Mohawk man turned around and pushed the door open gentle. He had to duck under the lip of the doorway as he went in.

He crossed the length of the living room in four strides and reached for the top of the eight-foot bureau that stood against the wall. His great fingers touched only wood. The Mohawk held the rim of the bureau-top in his hand. He could hear the other man breathing somewhere in the space behind him. He did not know how close the man was until the floorboard between the living room and kitchen entryway gave off a groan. He turned around.

Tarbell stood on the hardwood in his stockinged feet. He held the sawn-off shotgun in both hands, aimed from the hip. The Mohawk's rifle lay on the couch near Tarbell with the bolt and magazine removed. The two men were but ten feet apart.

"You heard the board?" Tarbell said.

"I heard you breathin'."

The blonde smiled.

"Why didn't you go for that buckknife in your belt?" he said.

"'Cause you had the rifle, idiot."

Tarbell quit smiling. He snorted.

"That was a bitch to get down from there," he said.

"I bet," the Mohawk said.

Tarbell kept the gun steady. The Mohawk man straightened up. His shoulders were as wide as the bureau. He had a huge head and a wide face with pock-marks on his cheeks. Dark eyes. He had no man-made scars on his face.

"Where's Wallace and Clayton?" he said.

"They're not here," said Clayton's nephew. "They thought you'd be somewhere else. I thought you'd be here."

"How's that?"

"They think you're scared of Clayton."

The Mohawk said nothing. He seemed not to be moved by any of it.

"You're a big fucker. Aren't ya?" Tarbell said.

The Mohawk reached behind his back. He did it slow with the pale-eyed man watching him. The buck-knife came back with his hand and he stood there with his fingers settling their grip on the handle.

"Those things are a hell of a lot slower to fire when you ain't got the hammers cocked. You know that?" the Mohawk said.

Tarbell tilted his head to the side. Stared on and on.

The Mohawk gave no sign before he moved, step-ping hard to the right and then coming straight. He'd closed the gap to naught by the time Tarbell fired. Tarbell did not save either barrel and the shot blew from the muzzle in spitflame and hit the Mohawk's chest and stood him straight up. His shoetoes danced the floor and then he went backward and slammed to the hardwood like a tree felled to shieldrock. Somehow he was not dead. Blood bubbled at his lips and his eyes rolled but his chest still rose and fell and he still drew air by his flared nostrils. Tarbell had already broke the barrel and shucked loose the spent shells. He reloaded the weapon and held it fast, ready to slap the barrel straight. He stopped and stood with the short-stock stuffed into his right armpit and the broken shotgun draped over his arm like a waiter's cloth. The dark irises of the Haudenosaunee man were wound back to the top righthand corner of his eyesockets and his massive hand crept the floorboards and then reached out desperate. Nothing there. The buckknife lay out in the floor beyond the Mohawk's reach.

By the time Wallace came into the room Tarbell had the Mohawk sitting upright and was stood behind him with a fistful of hair. Edge of the buckknife dug into the Mohawk's forehead. Look of intense concentration on his face. Wallace was on top of them before Tarbell turned. Wallace got hold of the knife hand and tore it clear and then turned Tarbell's wrist until the blade dropped. Tarbell came clear as well and there the Mohawk fell back to the hardwood just a foot from his knife, a neat red line across the length of his brow. He didn't reach for the blade. He was dead.

Clayton came into the room where the dead man lay. He saw Wallace standing between the Mohawk and his nephew. Tarbell leaned against the wall, rubbing his right wrist with the opposite hand. Clayton had to survey the room again to be sure of what was in front of him.

"What is wrong with you?" he said.

Tarbell raised his head. He didn't seem to know that Clayton was speaking to him. Then he took a deep breath and stared down at the killed Haudenosaunee. Back up at Clayton with his cold eyes. He got up off the wall and walked out of the house. Looncries echoed in the outlying dusk. The pale-eyed man cried back.

PART THREE

The welding rig for the truck had been bought by Daniel on a five-month run out west. He went alone and left in late autumn, driving through that vast territory where roads ran in a wide, counter-clockwise arc from the southern tip of Georgian Bay to the western boundaries of Lake Superior. Rounding those waters to the north took him a day's worth of driving through smaller and smaller towns and through ragged wood with gaunt trees more severe than their like in the south. Massive rock faces on high cliffs and beside the rolling highway grounds. Ravens and eagles alighted and looked down from their perches. He saw hints of bear and deer. He saw one great moose that waited for him in the road under moonlight to stall or kill him.

He bought the welding rig from a Haligonian who'd just finished a five-year hitch welding pipeline on-site. The man went over the rig with Daniel and then they shook hands and they pulled the bolts and clamps from the Nova Scotian's truck and four men lifted the rig and set it down in the bed of Daniel's truck and bracketed it to the metal. Daniel paid less than he should have but the man wanted rid of the machine and he promised he wouldn't ever try to buy it back. The Nova Scotian wouldn't even have a drink with the men he'd been working with. The ex-welder went east and Daniel went north, so tooled, and travelled site to site. He slept in the truck until it started getting cold. Then he lived in motels and garages, bunkrooms, colonies of portable shanties where he drank smuggled whiskey and stood in his longjohns pissing into the frosted campside brush, snow to his bootcuffs. That was October. By December he stood pissing again at site's edge. Fire lit the sky atop great stone exhaust pillars, above gigantic kilns and metalwork framing. Burnt cloud smothered the sun and was there yet in blackest night, hulking over the world. Daniel didn't work that far north again.

He counted days until Christmas. Too many. At first Daniel wouldn't go into town with the men and then he would. He didn't fight. When he laid his hands on men and pulled them clear they knew something was wrong and stayed back. He drank beer and whiskey with the tradesmen from the east and the older men played guitar or banjo or mouth harp or washboard. They sung old songs and the younger men knew few words or none at all. Still they tried and many of them could hold a tune. One night three Newfoundlanders showed up with a jug of moonshine they'd bought from a group of Métis labourers near Peace River. That night in town a fight broke out between Daniel's men and a gang of lumberjacks back from interior British Columbia. Daniel hit the biggest of them with a straight right and he felt the man's jaw unhinge and then watched it list and spill two broken lower-front teeth before the lumberjack crumpled. He'd not *hit anybody in three years. Someone broke a full beer bottle over Daniel's head and he did not feel it and inside of a minute there were six men down and all but one were bleeding from the mouth or nose or eyes. All but one, who lay facedown over an upturned table, his shoulderjoint twisted out of the socket so that the whole arm hung stretched and simian at his side. That same arm had lately held a beer bottle like a bludgeon. If Daniel were able to remember the brawl he might have remembered that he studied the wreckage for a very long time and then said aloud that he thought the man might lose the arm altogether.*

He flew east for four days at Christmas and then he flew back. Nobody had known his name at the brawl. They told the police again and again that they had nothing to tell. Daniel moved about freely from site to site and job to job. He tried not to drink but he did drink. He got quieter and quieter. He drank alone and paid out of pocket to avoid campsites and colonies. Once in a while he went to a shithole pub or inn to watch the fights on TV. He talked to people sitting at the bar, only about the fights. Few pegged him as an ex-fighter. When they did he lied and had a few more drinks and then he left. He bought off-license beer and drank it in his truck and sometimes he woke there in brilliant morning with the battery dead and his bones frozen.

In late March he set out for home. All he had in the truck was a duffel bag of clothes on the passenger seat. The welding rig stood ugly in the back window of the cab and looked in at him. At the tail end of the bed were truck-mounted boxes that held his tools and some that were his father's. A storm had been predicted from the Northwest Territories and it was supposed to last for a week. Daniel left early to beat it. The weight of the truck kept him slow and he ran through gas quick and took pills to stay awake. He crossed the Saskatchewan border, tired through and ripe in his clothes. Daniel didn't see the boundary sign in the white. He couldn't see five feet of road ahead of him and when the wipers stammered and froze he had to open the window and lean out. Frost clung to his eyebrows and his hair and his eyes watered and he wiped them clear. He drove on and on and then at once the road was there and the sky was bright above where the clouds thinned. A weird fog trailed at his spinning truck tires for a mile or so and he drove faster and kept looking out at it and then it was gone.

TWENTY-TWO

Spring did not last long. Summer came in late May and settled hot through the county. It almost never rained. Streams dried to tepid runnels and last year's watermarks were written on the rock more than a foot above the small waves that passed in the bay. The crops came in too early and the young tree leaves went brown and curled like paper beside coalfire. There were ribbons of smoke rising from the west and then they were gone and later they would come back. At the end of one beach-headed concession road there stood a sign with a coloured semicircle and a wooden needle that the township moved to show the level of danger from forest fire and to show when a fire ban was on. Later in the month some kids from town got to the sign and a few passersby saw the sign itself on fire. That sign came down.

They left for the cabin at mid-morning, driving with the windows up until they got to paved road. There they wound the windows down and kept them so through gust and gale. Daniel drove and Sarah kept turning around to see if Madelyn was okay. The girl was still and quiet while her hair whipped around her head and showed her eyes and nose and ears in strobe. They drove north and skirted the town and went on. Single-lane highway with asphalt gone pale and fissured throughout. Concrete bridge-work that took them high over marsh and swamp-muck, weeded shallows, open waters lit by midday sun. Boats drifted by with their sails tucked, carried on by motor or current or just bobbing free in their windless channels.

Fifteen minutes later they came upon turn-offs to smaller towns and villages. Daniel took the truck to the far-right lane and they spiralled down to a roadway that coasted the water's edge. A detour they'd half-planned that morning. Other roads branched off of the main lakeside pass and some were shrouded in heavy tree cover and some were barely roads at all.

"Why is granpa all the way out here?" Madelyn called out.

"It's where he was born," Daniel said.

He looked at the girl quick over his shoulder. She'd put a baseball cap on but her hair still blew. Old, tattered lid that he'd forgot that he'd given to her.

"Do you want to go, Madelyn?" he said. "We don't have to go."

"Yes, we do," Sarah said.

She had her sunglasses on her head to hold her hair back and wore a tank top and shorts that showed a lot of leg. Her sandals were tucked under the seat and her bare feet rested one over the other, heels to the floor mat. Tiny beads of sweat at the nape of her neck.

"I want to go," Madelyn said.

Daniel nodded.

"We won't be in there long," Daniel said, and faced the road. They rode fast with trees close on either side. Sarah's window was open and its frame caught the tip of a long branch. A leaf fell to her lap in pieces. She bit at her nails.

The marker stood in the shadow of an oak tree. Thick-hewn stone, greying year after year in the rain and sun and frost. All that had been cut into the marker was his name and the years that he lived and a small Celtic cross at the centre apex where the rock had been rounded. The church had resisted his being buried there but Sarah wore them down until they allowed it. The man did not truck with religion much in his later years but he'd worn a silver cross alike to the one on the stone. He wore it because Daniel's mother gave it to him before Daniel was born. She'd bought it in Wales and had it blessed there and later she hung it around his heavy neck while he lay slumped over, sleeping the sleep of the drunk in a deep-set armchair. Now Daniel wore the silver and he'd worn it to births and battle and it had only come off when he'd stepped into a ring or cage and his cornermen took it from him and held it in the shirt pocket atop their heart.

They were alone in the cemetery. The three of them stood at the stone and Madelyn went up and laid her hand on it and then she kneeled in the grass and laced her hands in her lap and started whispering to the stone. All the blood went out of Daniel's face. Sarah started to go get her and Daniel took his wife's shoulder and she turned. She came back. Soon enough Madelyn got up and said goodbye and she left the gravesite. She stood beside her father. He didn't know what to make of the girl so leant down and kissed her on the head. Sarah started a prayer to the stone and it was short.

"Can I walk around?" Madelyn said.

They both said she could. She left them there.

Daniel stared down at the marker for a long time. He said nothing. Often he would look for his daughter and find her afar in the rows and then he'd look back at the grave. Sarah put her hand on his neck and held him tight for a moment and then she let go. He rested his fists on his hips by the knuckles and hung his head. He wiped his brow with the back of his sleevecuff. He looked up.

"Let's go," he said.

Daniel stepped out of the row and didn't wait for her to follow. He crossed the cemetery to where Madelyn had gone. Row upon row of markers that he passed. None too large. They were the graves of country folk and immigrants from England and Ireland and Scotland, Dutch and German, French names on the Métis markers and on the stones of the Quebecois who travelled the St. Lawrence River to live and die there. There were stones straight as carpenters' nails hammered through planking. Others had been put askew by wild animals, time, tree-roots that wandered subterranean. There were graves in that cemetery that were planted long before those great oaks and cedars were seed or sapling. Some older yet, by ages. And all of it penned in by dense and lightless forest that bowed under snow and wind and brokedown in part and fell to earth and grew again.

The girl had lately found a patch of grass with three markers planted flat in the ground. The names nearly wiped clear.

"They're all in here," she said. "This whole family."

Daniel leant in enough to see the names. He nodded once.

"Where's granma buried?" she said.

He kept reading the plaques.

"I don't know," he said.

The girl was waiting on him to tell her about it. He didn't.

Eventually he stood and turned and saw Sarah in the distance. She was at his old man's gravesite yet and seemed to be knelt or crouching there.

"You go on to the truck," he said. "I'll get her."

He walked back to the grave and came up close. Sarah did not hear him. She'd gone to the actual stone and when Daniel came upon her she was kneeling in the grass as their daughter had. Her head was not an inch from the marker and she could be heard speaking to it in a whisper. She took very deep breaths. Daniel watched her for a long time and he didn't say anything to her. She looked up but once. Out past the stonetop across the grounds, at the weather-worn rock and burnt shortgrass. He couldn't see her face. She lowered her head and said a few more words and then she turned around all at once and when she did her eyes were red. She seemed surprised to see him there. She put her palm to the ground and got to one knee and then drew herself up, kissed the pads of two fingers and pressed them on the stonetop. She came out from the plot and took Daniel's hand in hers and led him out of there.

TWENTY-THREE

The cabin sat in a clearing perhaps a hundred feet from the lake. It had been built of log and brick and mortar and looked down a gentle decline of rough soil and wildgrass. That land ran to rock just a few feet from the water. A granite overhang crept out past the bank. Four deck chairs were set on the stone in a wide semicircle and there was plenty of room to spare. Two lines of tall firs stood at either side of the lot and out in the waters there were no markers or boats or swimmers. Across the bay waves rolled up against the rock-lined bank of a narrow peninsula. That lonely building could only be guessed at from the road, smoke rising from the wood where its chimney might be.

In the cabin, Sarah unpacked her case. Madelyn had her bed in a near bunkhouse and she'd been putting her clothes away and evicting spiders with an old tin can left in the room. Daniel hadn't been indoors yet. He stood on the stone overhang and looked up at the cabin, windows at the side of the house facing the lake, drapes pinned back. The shapes of women moving about from room to room. Madelyn left the bunkhouse and went to the main cabin. Daniel surveyed the grounds aside the place. There was nothing else in the clearing but a woodshed and chopping block set back near the forest's edge. Firepit some thirty feet from the front of the cabin, walled in by hand with loose brick. Daniel saw the opening in the wood where they had come out into the clearing and at the other end of the property he saw another break in the trees where another road took up and led to deeper country. He spat in the dirt and then looked at the lake again. Beside the ledge he could see clear to bedrock, to black mud where reeds grew and sashayed back and forth with the undercurrent.

In the morning none were awake but the girl. She'd been down to the water near sunrise and washed there, went into the house to do her necessaries. Ella stirred next and went into the kitchen. Sarah made funny noises and then sat up all at once like a folding cot sprung from its fasteners. She shoved Daniel but he wouldn't shift. She pulled the covers off the bed and rambled overtop him, elbows sticking him in the stomach and chest. He smiled but didn't move so she gave up and left him there in the bed with his shorts on. In the other room Murray had been left alone from the get-go and he lay snoring with his bare, kegbarrel chest rising and falling. Battered hands clasped over his breadbasket.

At breakfast Madelyn stared the old man down from across the table. He'd come out of the bedroom wearing yesterday's jeans and his wrinkled and slept-in undershirt. He yawned and started in on his coffee. She was trying not to laugh at the state of him before the food made it to the table. Daniel and Sarah brought the toast and butter and set the plates in their places. They sat down and Ella laid down platters of bacon and eggs for them all. She fussed about the stove and the kitchen counter. The old man leaned back in his chair and stared back at the girl. She kept looking at him as if he were a bug in a jar.

"There's somethin' wrong with that kid," he said, pointing at her with his fork.

They hiked upcountry on a grown-out path, the two men and the girl. Murray led them on with the fishing rods over his shoulder, the handles to his palm. Daniel followed. Madelyn towed a metal cart with studded tires and their provisions inside. Cooler filled with beer and sandwiches at one end. Another for their catch. Bait and tackle aside it. Soon they came upon a wildgrass clearing and a width of river that ran quick to forest cover and to the lake beyond. They stopped near the riverbank and Madelyn pulled the cart into a thicket of tallgrass where it wouldn't roll. Sound of continuous thunder near to the clearing. Two-storey waterfall just upriver from them, rock steps that stuck out and split the cascade. The current broke on the rock and shot spray that caught sun and coloured the air. At the base of the falls whitewater roiled and ran south over polished stone.

"Come on," Murray called back. "The spot's just a'ways over."

Madelyn parked the cart on an earthen overhang maybe four feet above the surface of the river. Firs on the opposing bank caught most of the late afternoon sun and the grass brushed coolly against their ankles and shins as they set up. Murray took Madelyn's rod and cut the line and tied on a new hook and weights. He showed her how to cast the line sideways and it took only two or three tries for her to fling the hook far out into the river current. Daniel put a hand to her shoulder and she gave him a funny look and then reeled the line in crazily and cast again.

When the rod bent the first time, the girl jumped but she held fast. By the second dip she pulled the rod hard and started trying to reel the line in. Daniel put his hand on hers to stop her turning the handle. Then he got hold of the rod higher up and felt the pull on it.

"We gotta let the line run a bit," Daniel said. "Otherwise it'll snap."

Madelyn stared at the taut line and dug her heels. Daniel told her to flip the guide open and line shot off the reel by the foot. Madelyn watched it go.

"Now get hold of that handle again and, when I tell you to start turnin' it, start turnin' it."

He'd started reaching out to grab the rod from her if she lost it. She swatted his hand quick and got her own back to the rod.

"I can do it," she said.

"Alright."

Daniel turned. Murray was sat on the cooler and he was laughing. Can of beer in his hand. The girl had her tongue stuck out a little, bit between her teeth. The line ran awhile longer.

"Now," Daniel said. "Crank it."

Madelyn wound the handle and the guide came back and the line rose out of the water and went straight. The rod bowed and near doubled over but she held.

"Keep hold of that thing but let the fish pull it back the other way. Just don't let it run like before. Make it hard on him."

So she did. She held the handle-knob in her fist and let it windmill back toward her and come up the other side. Daniel had shuffled back some so that she had the space to work.

"You feel him startin' to quit?"

"I don't know," the girl said.

The line cut through the riverwater. Slacked some when the fish rose or came closer to the near bank and snapped tight again when the fish bolted. Madelyn held on and on and the torque on the rod lessened by the minute. The girl whiteknuckled the reel-handle now. She kept turning it slow. Sure-handed as could be.

The fish came up into the shallows like a phantom formed there. It thrashed in the last few feet of river and little waves carried out from the spot. Ripples on the surface that soon thinned and vanished. Madelyn kept winding and hollered when the fish came clear, twisting wild in the air, sunshine caught in its scalecoat. The fish had more weight out of the water and there Daniel did help Madelyn heft it but he didn't have to help much. Murray had set his beer down long enough to fetch the net. He handed it to Daniel and stepped back. Daniel went to the bank with the net in hand. Madelyn worked the reel. The girl had beads of sweat at the corners of her freckled brow. She brought the fish up as it bucked and spun on the line. When she had it a few feet out of the water, Murray came around to make sure the fish cleared the overhang while she kept the rod high and walked it back from the bank. Daniel stood at river's edge with the net and waited.

He netted the fish and brought it inland and set it down in the grass. Five-pound pike hooked through the gill, and yet it beat the ground hard, drummed its tailfin to the turf. Sucked air. Daniel kneeled down and reached into the net and got hold of the thing.

"Yeah," he said.

Madelyn came close in time to see the pike show its teeth. Daniel put the fish down and reached into his back pocket and pulled out a cutter-clamp and snipped the line. Then he laid the tool in the grass.

"He's done for," Murray said.

Daniel nodded.

Madelyn knelt down. She touched the pike but once with her fingertip.

"What can we do with him?" she asked.

"Even if we wanted to put him back we can't," Daniel said.

"Will we eat him?" she said.

"It's your catch. You'd have to clean it."

Madelyn thought on it.

"Can you show me how?" she said.

"Okay," Daniel said. "Now, go over and grab me that cooler."

The girl nodded and got up quick. Daniel watched her take three steps before he dropped the underside of his fist onto the pike's head and left it flat and lifeless. He pushed the barb through and took up the cutter-clamp again and pulled the hook clear, five inches of slime-sodden line that trailed it.

The sun hung low to the treeline as they left the woodland trail and came out into the clearing. Daniel and Murray led with the rods while Madelyn pulled the cart, the bait cans rattling on the metals as it rumbled over rock and soilclod. There were fishguts smeared on the top of the one cooler. Haul of three fish inside, two smallmouth bass and Madelyn's pike. One bass yet lived and when the girl stopped to switch her grip it could be heard sloshing in the riverwater they'd filled the cooler with. She'd tried to wash by the shore after she sunk the innards of the two fish but her hands had dried filthy.

Sarah and Ella sat in chairs near the bank, side by side. They had drinks at their chair arms, shirts sleeveless to the shoulder, bare feet heeling the dirt as they spoke to each other. The conversation stopped and Sarah sat up straight and turned. Madelyn called out and Sarah waved. Sarah turned back to Ella and spoke in a hush. Then she stood up and pulled at her wrinkled shorts. She lent a hand and helped Ella to her feet. The old lady went ahead to meet the cart. Stood in front of the girl.

"So missy, how did you do?"

"We did good," Madelyn said. "We got three fish."

"You catch 'em all yourself?"

"Murray got two. I got the big one. Dad helped."

"It was all her," Daniel said. "I didn't catch nothin'."

Ella took the rods from Murray and Daniel. She squeezed the meat of his right hand as he gave his up and asked Madelyn to show her the catch. She lifted the lid and pointed and turned over her hands to show Ella what she'd done. Murray came over to rib the girl. Daniel watched them a minute and then he walked the clearing and sat in the chair beside his wife. She looked at him just brief and drank deep. Tried again.

"What is it?" he said.

"Work called," she said.

Everyone sat outside while Daniel dialed out from the yellowed, wall-mounted phone in the kitchen. Murray had tried to talk Madelyn into helping gather up soilbound horseshoes in a nearby pit that had not seen action in a long while. The kid would not go. She sat in a chair near the old man and listened close. Daniel started speaking to someone and then it was long time before they heard him speak again.

"Sure," he said. "Yep."

Quiet again. Sound of a chair shifting on the hardwood.

"I bet you will," he said, and then a few seconds later the receiver clacked into the cradle.

He did not come out to the decking so Sarah stood and went inside. He sat there at the kitchen table and watched her cross the room. Weary eyes and weary soul beneath. He sat very still and eventually he crossed his arms and exhaled hard. Sarah stood beside him and her fingertips circled the fine hair of his neck.

"What happened?" she said.

"They got no work for me anymore," he said.

"Just like that? They do you that way?" she said.

He didn't answer.

Sarah reached back and pulled another chair close to his. Then she sat and leaned in. He looked up at her the once and then stared blind at the wall. She took hold of his forearms with both hands.

"It's okay," she said.

He nodded.

"I mean it."

When he didn't answer she got up and shoved the chair back and sat sidesaddle in his lap, her arms over his shoulders. He had his eyes closed. She put her forehead to his and leaned back. He looked at her.

"This is bullshit," she said. "It won't beat us."

He shook his head.

"We never quit."

"No."

"Say it."

"I won't quit."

She hugged him close but he held her weak so she reset and pulled him in rough. There he got his arms around her and nearly squeezed the life out of her and stood up with her like she weighed nought and set her down on the floor. He let go and his right hand lingered at her waist for a moment and then he went past her and out through the kitchen door. He stood there long enough for Murray to hand him a beer and then he trod heavy down the porch stairs and found his daughter out on the grass. She'd been walking it in circles and he put his arm around her and spoke to her as serious as he ever had before. The way he might speak to any of the others. Her heart beat near his shortrib. Daniel loosed her and trod toward the river alone. Downed the beer as he walked. When he got close enough he pitched the bottle sidelong into the bay where it spun and skipped and then dug the surface and stopped. The bottle bobbed once and then took water over the lip. Sunk its neck under and went down into the deep.

Daniel could feel the truck tires clipping seams in the bridge lanes. The window rumbled against the back of his head and he tried to wedge a sweater in there but he gave it up to keep the cool glass to his scalp. He started to drift but snapped to all at once, his hands slapping upholstery and doormolding. His nose was clogged and his jaw hung. Sarah kept an eye on him in the rearview mirror. Madelyn rode in the passenger seat and every few minutes she'd turn around in the seat.

"What's going on up there?" he said.

Sarah and the girl each looked at the other.

"Did you just take a sharp left and a right or is that just me?"

"I might've swerved for a porcupine," Sarah said.

"Bridge-porcupine?"

Sarah nodded.

Daniel pushed himself more upright. Far as he could manage. His arms lay limp at his sides for a moment and then he collected them over his stomach. He blinked hard.

"What's wrong with dad?" Madelyn said.

Sarah wrinkled her nose up, switched lanes.

"Lots," she said.

Madelyn studied her father close.

"Are you okay?" she said.

He gave her a thumbs-up. Then he peered out of the window at the mess of woods and waters and road-ways, the commotion of it all, not any of it enough to distract from the goings on in his skull.

Sarah kept taking measure of him in the rearview mirror.

"What's the damage?" she said.

"You're looking at it," he said. "It ain't good."

Monday morning came and he got up to walk the girl to the end of the road where the school bus stopped. She asked him what he'd do. If he'd train. He said that he'd have to beat the pavement for another job. The girl kicked roadgravel as they neared the stop.

"If you go back to the fight gym, can I come sometimes?" she said.

He kept walking.

"You used to explain it all to me, the techniques and everything. Then you just stopped."

Daniel raised his fists to her so she could look close to the knuckles. To the scar tissue and mutated joints and bonespurs. None of it bothered her. When the bus coasted up the rise in the roadway he dropped his mitts and hugged the girl. Let her go.

"We can talk about this later," he said.

The girl accepted that. The bus rolled to a halt and the door opened. Madelyn climbed the steps and Daniel nearly came forward to put his arm around her and carry her off the bus, take her back home with him. He shoved his hands in his pockets and watched the door unfold and pin shut. Dust whirled at his feet as the bus drove off. Grit in his nostrils. He spat into the tarmac and stared after the thing.

TWENTY-FOUR

There were four bodies laid out in the trailer. Three of them were brothers and the fourth their cousin. The last of a small band of hillbilly thugs and cooks who'd run afoul of Clayton's new play for the area. They'd all been shot save for the biggest of them. He'd been cut through the neck with Tarbell's stolen buckknife and his head turned a horrific angle when they piled him in the trailer. The men were killed outside in the hollow so as not to rupture the works in the trailer and blow them all to shit. Wallace had picked up all the loose casings from the property and pocketed them. He came back to the trailer and went in. Tarbell was near to the bodies, pissing on the upholstery. For a moment Wallace thought he was fixed to piss on the dead men and that would've been all that he could bear. Tarbell and Wallace were both covered in the blood of the biggest hillbilly. The blade had severed the artery and it seemed like all he had in him exited the body through that cut.

It took Wallace a long time to cool by the edge of the site. An old hut beyond that they'd used to meet the hillfolk for years even when they were thinned to just a few and these some of the last in that part of the country. Ages ago there was bushwhiskey brewed up there and that was all. The old hut still carried some of the jars and boiler parts, long wasted and filled with rust or rot. Wallace's phone shook his jeans pocket. He tried to wipe his hands before he fished it out but there was not a clean strip of fabric on the man. He pulled the phone and bloodied up the buttons.

"How'd it go off?" Clayton said through the speaker.

"Like a fuckin' plane crash," said Wallace.

"What?"

"I've about had it with this shithead."

Clayton just asked him if everyone was accounted for. Told Wallace to get a hold of himself. That it would get worse before it would get better, but, when all was said and done, they were set to change the way things were run up there forever. He asked if he could still count on the big man.

"I would lay down in traffic, you asked me to," Wallace said. "But this motherfucker ain't you."

Clayton said okay and Wallace hung up the phone.

When they blew the trailer it was about as sophisticated as the way they'd dropped the bodies. Wallace had a rag jammed into a bottle of solvent and he lit the cloth and hurled it from across the hollow. It flew a high arc and blew apart on the corner of the trailer where the near side met the roof. Carpeted half of the thing in flame. Had he overthrown just a touch more it might have skipped off and into the woods.

They were already running before the fire spread to the insides of the trailer. On and on until they were sucking air on the trail. They were a quarter-mile clear and the detonation sounded like a meteor touched down. Shook the ground underfoot and put heat to the air behind them. At the car, they could see a column of black smoke going skyward fast and linear. Wallace watched it for a few seconds and then he started taking his clothes off.

"Hey," he said.

Tarbell turned. Looked at him incredulous. At the wingspan of the big man, black ink on brown skin over his chest and stomach and great patches inked solid at his shoulders and upper arms.

"Strip," Wallace said.

"What?"

Wallace had his clothes and shoes in a garbage bag already and wore just his gitch and his socks. He tossed the bag over the car and it hit the dirt near to Tarbell.

"Put your bloody fuckin' rags in there," Wallace said. "Unless you wanna drive through town lookin' like a goddamn nightmare."

Tarbell stepped out of his shoes and dropped his pants. He took his holsters and pistols and put them on the hood of the car where Wallace had dropped his own. The buckknife and sheath atop them. He buttoned his shirt and loosed it. Wallace saw enough to turn him while the man stuck his shirt in the bag.

TWENTY-FIVE

He would take Sarah to work and then drive through town in the truck. Houses rebuilt and others gone to rot. New roads and subdivisions at the high side of town. River valley where the body of a local girl had been found. A debris-strewn promontory near the docks where a grain elevator used to be. Malls and superstores on the westerly edge of town atop forest where he'd rode and ran. Entire universes that he'd invented as a boy paved over, places now for plazas to squat and shit. He passed by with the truck seat half-buried in resumes, filled-out application forms, a tie that his wife had knotted though she knew he'd never wear it. Daniel pulled into near-empty lots in front of factories and jobsites and went to their offices to hand them papers. Secretaries and foremen took them like rubbish offered up by a child. He shook a hand where he could. If they would even take the thing. Some reacted to it like it was electrified. Everyone saw the scars on his face. Daily he'd drive the curving road by the southern lakefront until he got to factories that had windows blacked or boarded, shredded flags whipping at their poles. There he'd pull off the road and mount the curb and park at the base of a brokedown concrete pier. Daniel would walk out and sit at the pier-edge with his legs dangling and he'd watch the grey-blue baywater break and roll.

One Thursday morning Daniel woke up hungover and haggered and tried to prop himself up with coffee as he took Sarah to her shift. They said little on the drive and Daniel guessed she was annoyed by his condition. Just outside town she turned the radio quiet.

"Yesterday I heard your underwear drawer rattling," she said.

"What?"

"I was putting the laundry away and found a phone in there. Guess who was calling?"

Daniel yawned into the crook of his elbow. He looked at her.

"You check it and see how I never answered the thing since I forgot it was in there?"

Sarah nodded.

"That's the only reason you're still breathing, honey," she said. "Also, I got rid of the thing."

Daniel slowed for a red light and when the car stopped he turned to her.

"I ain't never going back," he said.

Sarah narrowed her eyes on him. When she'd seen enough she leaned in and kissed him hard. He put his forehead to hers and held her there, fiddled with her ear with his thumb and forefinger. They sat like that until they heard the horn from the car behind them.

He came to the gym with sparring gear, legs already warm from running on hard dirt road and fieldtrail. Jung Woo would skip with him on the floormatting, sweat ringing his shirt neck, black hair matted down with rogue greys throughout. They rolled on the mats and Daniel controlled position from within Jung Woo's guard, his heavy legs on either side, hips forever shifting while Jung Woo held Daniel's wrists and looked to sweep or submit him. Daniel rolled with four-ounce gloves and he would bomb down and try to shuck loose and move out of Jung Woo's guard to side-control, to mount. He made mistakes. He got caught in armbars, Jung Woo's legs across his face and chest as he pulled Daniel's arm back to his own chest against the natural bend of the elbow. If Daniel threw punches and didn't get both arms clear he'd end up in a triangle choke with his head pinned by the crook of the Korean's bent knee while Jung Woo hooked that leg's foot under the other kneejoint, one arm and shoulder trapped there, and pulled Daniel's head down until it went blue. Daniel had to tap, but once he didn't and the world went dim and quiet and just before he went out Jung Woo let go of the hold. Daniel kneeled on the mat and wheezed. A vein had risen in the skin of his forehead. Jung Woo sat up in front of him and pointed.

"Next time you tap. You tap or you go out."

Daniel looked up at him. He'd not seen the man angry before. Daniel croaked out something like an okay and then nodded the affirmative, head hung level to his shoulders as he held onto his own knees and hauled air.

In sparring he battered Jung Woo all over the ring. His footwork had come back to him day by day and he walked Jung Woo down and cut him off and beat him to the punch. If Daniel ate leather he didn't seem to feel it. He kept his hands high and his chin down and threw with power. He found punches he didn't think he'd ever had in the first place. Jung Woo threw kicks and Daniel checked them low and fired back, whipped his lower-shin against Jung Woo's glove and forearm. Jung Woo reeled back and grinned black mouthguard. They worked from the clinch against the ringposts and Daniel handfought to get the Thai Plum, one hand clasped over the other behind the other man's neck, and there he pinched his elbows together and ragdolled Jung Woo, stepped wide and flung him across the canvas, pulled him back to where knees could be landed if they'd been thrown. Daniel sprawled and stuffed takedown attempts, underhooked Jung Woo's armpits, stood the man up and shoved him clear to throw hands at him again. After weeks of this, Jung Woo started to rotate out and send other men in on Daniel. No rest between rounds and fresh young fighters diving for his legs and ripping sly punches at the ex-fighter. He held his own.

Active fighters came into the gym to train with Jasper and Jung Woo, to spar on those the late afternoons. When they came in now they saw an ex-fighter beating the hell out of their training part-ners and teammates, their actual trainers. Some of the fighters knew Daniel and they knew his past and they would sidle up at ringside and watch him work. More than a few hollered at him to soldier on. Some had already started coming earlier to spar with the man and test themselves. They wore the minutes in blue-black bruise and knotted shins. Daniel calmed under the worst abuse. He never took a step backward unless he wanted to. The fighters skipped near to the ring and kept their hungry eyes on the man. They nodded when they saw something slick and cursed at the matting where their feet danced.

During an afternoon training session, a half-dozen fighters were watching Daniel hammer their like when another fighter came up. Six-foot-four with shoulders like an oxcart yoke. Flat-nosed and cat-eyed with a fade upside his huge head. He had little more than spider-webs of scarring under his eyes. He had wrestled as a youth and moved north and boxed in Montreal and he went from gym to gym sopping up fight knowledge and technique, honing his weapons. Jasper liked him as a fighter. Jung Woo did not like him at all. But he rolled with the man anyway and wore a pumpknot at the back of his head for it.

The big man stood ringside while Daniel took two glancing shots and answered and sat his sparring partner down in the middle of the ring, the ropes and ringposts shuddering when ass hit canvas. Daniel backed out with his hands high and let the other fighter up. The man shook his head and came forward. He was sitting again within seconds. The big fighter at ringside had only ever put that man down once in sparring. He rapped his knuckle against the shoulder of the fighter in front of him.

"Hey," the big man said.

The ringside fighter turned and scowled but when he saw who stood behind him he quit his mean-mugging all at once.

"Johnson. What's up man?"

The big fighter just cocked his chin toward the ring.

"Who in the fuck is that?" Johnson said.

TWENTY-SIX

He could see her silhouette flickering in the candlelit kitchen window. If she had heard the truck pull in she didn't show it. She raised her hand to her mouth, a smoke there. She inhaled deep and let out. Her head bowed some. Daniel went quick up the front steps. The front door was open and when he tried the screen door it was unlocked. He walked in and let his bag down to the entryway carpet and went through to the kitchen with his shoes on. Sarah didn't turn when he came into the room. She didn't quit smoking either. Daniel moved opposite her at the table and sat. Her eyes were red. She had teartracks long dried on her lovely cheeks and they showed faint.

"What happened?" he said.

She didn't answer. Just stared at him across the table. She seemed to be inventorying the new damage on his face, scrapes and swelling around his eyes and chin.

There was an open bottle of red wine on the table with maybe a flute worth left in the thick glassbottom. Daniel reached over for her half-full glass and took a swig. Taste of her lipgloss, the caustic taste of weed smoke in the claret. He slid the glass back over to her and she looked at it, stared at him tired. Daniel leaned back in the chair to where he almost toppled and got hold of the fridge door and pulled it open. He reached in and came back knuckling three beers. He shut the door and leaned forward to clatter the chair legs down again.

"How much of that shit you had?" he said.

She smiled for maybe a half-second. Passed him the joint. He took a haul and handed it back. Coughed hard into the crook of his elbow.

They sat there in silence. They drank. She smoked for a time and then got up and put it out in the sink and came back. She brought her hair back with both hands and tied it there. Then she bent down and fished through her purse on the floor. When she sat up again she had a torn-open envelope in her hand. She wiped her eyes and slid the letter across the table to Daniel and then she looked up at the ceiling.

He set his beer down and took up the envelope. He pulled the letter and unfolded it carefully as he could. He read. When he was done he put the pages back in the envelope and held it in his hand for a while. Finally he slid it back over to Sarah. She just let it lie on the tabletop in front of her.

"You are gonna go to that school, Sarah," he said.

She shook her head and ran a knuckle under her eye again.

"Did you see what it costs?"

"There's government loans they give for that."

"I can't be off work that long. If something goes wrong we're done for."

Daniel got up with the chair in hand and set it down beside her. He sat and put an arm around her. She was rigid but he kept on.

"Is that what you want to do or isn't it?" he said.

"I wanted other things I didn't get. It won't be the last one."

Daniel cupped her chin in the valley between his thumb and forefinger.

"Trust me when I tell you that eventually you can come to a last one. You can come to it all of a sudden."

Sarah took his hand in hers and put it to her cheek. She let go and sat up straight and poured more wine. Took a swig from the glass.

"I'll get work," he said. "Don't matter what it is."

She levelled her eyes on him.

"Yes," she said. "It does."

He tried to smile for her. She drank again. Took a few breaths. Emptied the glass. Then she pulled his arm up by the wrist, wrapped it around her. They watched the candles melt down and spill. Their like in the black windowglass behind.

"You are going to that school," Daniel said.

Her head nodded slight at his shoulderjoint.

"I'll find a way to get you there."

"Okay," she said.

TWENTY-SEVEN

He went to factories and foundries in neighbouring towns, those off the highway along service routes and industrial laneways. He did this for days and days. On the last day he could see the southernmost suburbs of the city by the time he stopped and turned back. He had to pull over at a rest stop because he couldn't see the road anymore. Daniel skidded to a stop on the part-paved laneway. Gravel flew and skittered away from the truck tires. Sunshine on his shoulders as he stepped over a roadside barricade and went out into a rivertrench beyond. He sat in the blanched highgrass with his knees pointing out from the grade and his fists curled in his lap and he was there for hours.

Dusk fell on the warehouse plaza and on Daniel's truck in the lot. He waved to the young lady at the front desk and went through the gym to the change-room. When he came out he had his hands wrapped and he skipped for twenty minutes. All the while he watched the action in the ring. The fighter named Johnson, with his long, cordmuscle arms. Unshod feet. Fists distending his gloves. He stalked another man on the canvas. Jasper and Jung Woo leaned on opposite ringposts and called out instructions to the fighters. The big man did not seem to need them and his sparring partner couldn't hear them. The hurt fighter staggered back against the ropes with his forearms up and there he took a stiff jab and an inside leg kick and then a right hook to the body that folded him and he balled up with his knees and forearms and forehead flat to the canvas.

Jasper climbed through the ropes and knelt beside the downed man and finally got him to stand. That man went clumsily out of the ring and walked slow across the gym floor to the corner of the room. There he leaned heavy on the wall and then finally slid down and sat huffing, his eyes swollen and lower lip split and bloodied. Jung Woo had come down from the ring and followed the beaten fighter and knelt beside him. Jung Woo spoke to him at length and the man nodded solemn but he wouldn't look up.

Johnson took water in his corner and glanced over at the man he'd beat. He drank again and spat it out of the ring to the matting below. When he came back to the centre of the ring for the next sparring partner he saw Daniel and looked right through him. Daniel skipped on. Johnson thrashed two more men, peppered them with jabs and low kicks at range and then mauled them against the ropes and ragdolled them to the ground and walked away. He didn't seem to want to be there. He listened to Jasper sometimes and other times he fought wild and reckless and got away with it. The old coach stared into the ring steely-eyed.

Jung Woo had come up to Daniel as he wound down his warm-up. Daniel doubled the rope over and tied it into a loose knot.

"You know this fuck?" Jung Woo said.

Daniel shook his head.

"He box for a while in Montreal. Undefeated. Now he fight Muay Thai and fought seven times in MMA. Good wrestler. Never lost yet."

"He's got somethin'," Daniel said.

"He's an asshole."

Daniel nodded.

"Natural athlete. Big. Strong. Quick. But a fucking asshole."

"He's runnin' out of people to beat on."

"Shouldn't be here. Jasper train him for next fight and then get him out of here. This kind of guy bad for the gym."

They watched Johnson do away with another up and comer. He had the kid hurt and the kid looped a right hand and the big fighter slipped it. The kid's right cheek lay naked for a counter and Johnson didn't let up. He came over the top with a long left hook and caught the kid clean on the chin. The kid dropped jawjacked to the canvas and tried to get up but he couldn't.

Daniel was already up at the ring apron and he hung his forearms on the ropes. He eyeballed Johnson hard while Jasper attended the downed fighter. The big man looked at Daniel from above as if he were a stray dog at his doorstep. Jasper came out of the ring with the hurt young fighter and then Daniel said something to the kid as he went by and the kid smiled brokenly and walked on. Jasper came back and stood next to Daniel.

"You need another body?" Daniel said.

"No," Jasper said, and started up the short steps.

Daniel caught him by the elbow. Jasper turned.

"Let me in there," Daniel said.

Jasper looked him over. Gave nothing away by his eyes. He turned to Jung Woo for just a moment. Turned back to the ring.

"Warm up," he said.

"I'm warm enough," said Daniel.

He came out and took the centre of the ring. Johnson threw at him right away and Daniel parried or blocked all but one long right hand but he walked through it. He'd already started cutting off the ring but Johnson was stone-faced and pumped a jab at him over and over from range. The bigger fighter moved light on his toes and he raised his left leg and stepped it up and down. He leapt in and dug his feet into the canvas and there he bombed Daniel with a powerful straight right and a series of hooks to follow. Daniel covered up and drove ahead and shoved the big man back against the ringposts, bowed him backward over the ropes as Johnson tried to step out to the side.

They were tied up there for a second and then Johnson managed to force Daniel out to arm's length and there he threw a knee that caught Daniel high in the gut. Daniel had braced for it but the weight behind the blow kept him at distance and the big man turned hard into a round kick and his right shinbone found deep thighmeat on Daniel's left leg. Daniel's left hand dropped a little and Johnson snapped Daniel's head back with a lead right. The big man thought he had Daniel hurt but when he tried to throw the right leg again, Daniel reared his left leg and checked the kick. The taller man's leg came back stung and Daniel had already stepped in to throw a straight right and left hook. Both landed and Johnson staggered.

Fighters were hollering in the naked stone hanger. Daniel faked another right hand and the man tried to slip it and fire back over the top with a looping left hand, but Daniel's punch had not come. Johnson had his hook blocked by Daniel's pinned up elbow and forearm as Daniel turned hard to his right and buried a short left hook into the big man's nose and upper teeth. Johnson sat down hard on the bottom ringrope and fell to his side. His lip had split against his mouthpiece and his eyes were very white and very wide.

Daniel went back to his corner and by the time he'd got there Johnson was already up to one knee. Jasper had gone in the ring to talk to the man but Johnson just took out his mouthpiece and gobbed blood and spit onto the apron and then stood up. Every other man in the gym stood ringside at a hush. Jung Woo behind Daniel in his corner with his knuckles paling where he held the top rope.

"Look out now," he said. "Hands up. Always up."

Daniel didn't turn around and he didn't speak.

In the ring Jasper followed Johnson to his corner and gave him shit. He did not want them to go so hard. He did not want them to kick in the early rounds. The fighter nodded over and over and Jasper said everything again and then came away shaking his head. He backed up into the middle of the ring.

"You heard what I said, Dan. Say yes."

"Yes," Daniel said.

Daniel took the centre of the ring again and he'd not moved more than a step into range when Johnson pivoted on the ball of his left foot and whipped his right shin at Daniel's head. The big man threw the kick with all he had, his hip turning over hard and his arms and torso pulled taut like horse-muscle. He threw it to kill. But he had telegraphed it in his footwork and his posture and the tensing of his thighs and groin. Daniel saw it coming and by the time shin would have cracked jawbone he had come forward into the pocket, stepping in so that his hips and flank stifled the kick at the big fighter's knee. Johnson could not get his hands back up to his face and Daniel's head dipped low under cover of his left arm and there in its place came an overhand right like the executioner's axe.

Johnson dropped atop a buckled left knee and Daniel reached down and pulled that ill-bent leg straight and then walked away. He paced the length of the ring and breathed but shallow. Jasper and Jung Woo were in the ring on either side of the downed fighter and then were calling for the other trainers. Mayhem around the ring. Fighters were walking circles with their hands atop their heads and others were pushed up against the ringropes. Trainers came with cold water, ice, gauze, adrenaline, smelling salts. One held a cellphone in his hand and waited for the word from Jasper about calling an ambulance. Jung Woo peeled off and let another trainer in with a bag of ice. He went over to Daniel. Grabbed him at arm to stop him pacing. He looked into Daniel's eyes and thumbed at his cheeks and jawbone and then he reached up his thumb and forefinger and pried the mouthguard from Daniel's upper teeth.

"You okay?" Jung Woo said.

Daniel nodded.

"How's it look over there?"

Jung Woo glanced back over his shoulder.

"Out cold. Gone."

"He'll be alright."

"Think so."

Jung Woo left Daniel and went back to Johnson. They were propping him up now and he sat bloodied and bewildered. Jung Woo clogged the man's crushed nose with gauze and it soaked red near instantly. Johnson got to his feet all at once and tried to walk to the stool but his legs would not work right. The men guided him to his corner where they sat him on the stool. He faced the ringpost with his forehead pressed up against the padded column. They tried to turn him to get to his nose but he couldn't be moved.

Jasper kneaded Johnson's cannonball shoulders and said a few more words to him and then left him in Jung Woo's care. Daniel had stepped out of the ring and Jasper went down and caught him on his way to the locker room. The coach had scissors in one hand and he put them up in his teeth and unlaced Daniel's gloves. Then he took the gloves off and got the scissors and carefully cut the tape from Daniel's hands.

"Can you get me a fight Jasper? A real one, outside the gym," he said.

Jasper kept working the tape loose.

"You don't fight no more. Remember."

"Can you get me one?"

"That shit ain't real enough for you?"

"Please," Daniel said.

Jasper looked into his eyes.

"What for?"

PART FOUR

The little girl got sick and after a few days she got sicker. Her forehead like a coalfire had been lit under it. Sarah woke her father-in-law and he stared at her through the shadow like he did not believe she was there. He shoved the covers down and swung his stockinged feet out of bed, thick grey hair crazed at one side of his head. He coughed to clear his throat and then he got up and followed her downstairs.

The old man drove through blinding white, the truck tires spinning wild on the buried road. Snowdrifts sent them skittering. He righted the truck and went on. Lightning flashed crazily in the southwestern sky. The old man tried to wind his window down but it had frozen shut so he thumped it with the underside of his fist and tried again. He drove with his head out of the truck and his eyelashes frosted and his beard thick with snow. They skidded through the sleeping town, through red lights and rusted stop signs with him peering out into the void for other travellers. None there.

At the head of the hospital road the truck climbed an unseen hillock of snow and stopped. The old man came around to Sarah's door and took the blanket-swaddled girl from her and hefted her up to his chest, pallid skin and damp hair and weak arms and all, cradled against his heavy flannel coat. He took off down the wood-shrouded pass, the little girl's legs hooked over his forearm at the knee, feet dancing in her coverings as the old man carried her through the mire.

The old man found Sarah on the handmade benchseat at the end of his long, narrow yard. She wept small but in keeping it quiet she shook and shivered. Fish circled gold and silver in the murky waters of the pond before her. The old man sat down on the bench, his knees crackling as he sunk. She only looked up at him for a second before she let her head hang and sobbed another lonely song.

The old man leaned forward to better see her. Alike to Daniel but not. Deep grooves of age in the rough skin, eyes very blue and very different. Salt and pepper hair curling out from the edge of his cap. He had a good build but he did not walk as well as he should have. Massive forearms stuck out of his shortsleeves, white-haired and scarred throughout from metal burns and wounds ill-tended.

"I need him back," she said.

He took hold of her by the shoulders.

"He's a stronger man than I ever could have made him. And by God don't you see that he's the weaker of you?"

She came back to the house to shower and change her clothes. Cold, cold night and black. Up the drive she went with her

eyes full with fatigue and fear. Those same eyes saw rectan-
gles of light in the garage door. Sarah pressed up to the sec-
tioned metal and saw the old man on his workshop phone,
bottle of rye whiskey on the countertop beside him. A glass
half-filled. A water jug. He spoke long with his huge, knotted
fingers strangling the receiver. He drank deep and filled the
glass again with whiskey and a little water. She could not
hear what he said.

Later she woke to him kneeling aside her, scent of whis-
key and a clean man's sweat. He'd shook her gentle until she
took hold of his bicep and stopped him. She'd being sleeping
upright and half-dressed in an armchair, her hair still wet
from the shower.

"What time is it?" she said.

"I got him," the old man told her.

"Where is he?"

"On the road back. Comin' now."

She smiled at the man and then she started to cry. He
let go of her and touched her light on the head and told her
he'd be downstairs. Waved at her from the bedroom doorway
before he eased the door shut. He did not tell her that he'd
been all night on the phone talking to men he knew in the
solitary northwest. That he'd sent a runner to a camp outside
of High Level where Daniel was known to be working but
could not be raised by phone or radio, though he likely had
both. The runner had been paid by proxy and left out from
Peace River in bleak early morning. And there at the end of
the world the he'd found the man in the camp canteen, wild-
bearded and terrifying, and the runner told him his daughter
had pneumonia that had nearly killed her and that it was
time to go home.

TWENTY-EIGHT

Sarah dressed and undressed and dressed again. She'd not been out on the town in a long while, but some of the girls at work had talked her into it. Thirtieth birthday for one of the receptionists. Sarah had her hair trussed up in a towel and the cast-off skirts and dresses on the bed. Eventually she just sat on the edge of the bathtub in her underwear and smoked a joint. She burned it halfway and then wet her thumb and forefinger and pinched it out. Sarah took up the first dress she'd tried and stepped into it. She loosed her hair and fired the hairdryer.

Someone knocked the door a few times and she didn't hear it. But she did hear a man's voice over the whine of the dryer and shut it off. He was saying hello. She waited there quiet until he spoke again and she knew it was Murray. Sarah brushed out some lengths of her hair and went out to meet him. The old man hadn't gone farther than the landing and he had his cap in his one hand. He was trying to get his own hair under control with the other.

"Everything okay?" Sarah said.

Murray stood up straighter when he saw her.

"Oh, yeah," he said. "The kid's fine. When are you headin' out?"

"Shortly," Sarah said.

"You look nice," he said.

"Well, sure," she said.

Sarah came over to where he stood and turned.

"Zip that," she said, and he did so with some difficulty. Sarah told him to sit and asked if Murray would have a beer. He said he would. She checked the clock in the kitchen and then pulled two bottles from the fridge. She uncapped them and came back.

They sat near to each other and drank. Murray tried to smile at her.

"You seen Daniel today?" he said.

Sarah shook her head no.

"Do you think that he's gone back to work for Clayton and those fellas?" Murray said plain.

Sarah didn't answer. She got up sudden and went down the hall into the bedroom. Murray stood. Then she came back with the rest of her joint and sat down. She lit it and took a pull.

"He tells me that he's not," Sarah said. "That he's at the gym."

"You believe it?" Murray said.

"If I don't then I don't know what to do," she said.

Murray sat forward heavy in his chair.

"Is he even fit to fight again?" he said.

"We won't know unless he actually fights," Sarah said. "But, whatever he thinks, I don't believe he's the kind of man to just take this back up as a hobby."

Murray nodded. Sarah took a drag and offered the joint to the old man. He looked at it a second and then he pinched it away and smoked. Again. Handed it back to her.

"I've lived in this county most of my life," Murray said. "And I seen the railways and the grain elevators go. And the farms. Most of the factories."

"I know," she said.

"Whatever reason a man has to outlaw, I understand," he said. "But it's gone to hell out there and you can't be living in a house with a man who's neck-deep in it. Not with a little girl."

Sarah slumped back into the couch cushions. She drank from her beer and let her dress wrinkle.

"I knew what he could do when I married him," she said. "I didn't even think most of it was wrong, to be honest. But we were young then."

She looked spent where she sat. Murray leaned in and put a hand to her knee. Rough palms that picked at her tights. She didn't care.

"I love Daniel, and I will do whatever I can to help the boy," he said. "But, if he takes up with Clayton again you need to have a plan to get clear of it."

Sarah nodded. She ran her hand hard across her brow. Put the rest of the beer away and set the empty bottle down. She stood and so did Murray. Sarah straightened the collar of the man's shirt.

"I'll not tolerate him if he's lied about all of that," Sarah said. "Believe me."

"I know it," Murray said.

"As far as fighting goes, we'll have to see."

Murray looked at her long. Smiled sincere this time.

"It'll be okay," he said.

Sarah didn't say anything. She stood there and watched him put his shoes on at the door. Forearm leant hard to the wall. Before he'd shod both feet, Sarah's ride pulled into the driveway and laid on the horn.

The streets were dark where she walked. Toward the brokedown tavern near the edge of town. The traffic lights were changing for nobody. When she got to the place there were two men smoking by the entryway arch. They shuffled out just enough to let her by. She went in through the heavy front door. Inside the barroom were tables of thick-hewn timber, the finish worn pale by the years under the shifting of glassbottoms and elbowbones. The heads of moose and deer hung high above the bar with their dead, glass eyes. All of it shown by the warm glow of lightbulbs burning in antique wall-lanterns and table lamps, prettier than it should have been.

Sarah walked up to the bar and sat. She didn't look at anyone direct. Only by the backbar mirror, and then just to make sure she saw nobody she knew. She wore jeans and a black tank top. The neck cut low and showed her collarbone. She wore very little makeup but she stood out all the more for it. She hailed the bartender with a raise of her eyebrows.

"Scotch, please."

"What kind?"

"A good one to start, and the very best of your cheapest after that."

The bartender smirked and went away. He stood tall with hair to his shoulders. Handsome face with a part-crooked nose, lean build under his collared shirt. He came back with a half-full glass of good scotch.

"We'll call that a single and the rest of it I spilt," he said.

"Okay," Sarah said.

"You got a tab here?"

"I need to talk to Clayton."

The man took his hands off the bar and looked to the side. He turned back to her.

"I know he's here," she said. "So you call him or call whoever is allowed to call him and tell him I'm out here. He won't be mad. We go back."

"Miss…"

She stopped him with a look.

"Trust me," she said.

The man shook his head and went to the end of the bar where a decades-old wall-mounted phone hung without dial or digits. He picked up the corded receiver and covered it when he spoke. After a while he hung it up and came over to her again. Sheepish look on his face.

"He says you can go back."

"Thanks," she said, and got up off the stool, drink in hand.

The bartender started to tell her the way to Clayton's office.

"I know where he's at," she said.

She went around the bar to a corridor to the rear rooms. The bartender watched her go, polishing the same glass over and over while those men sitting at the bar tried to call him.

Sarah knuckled the door twice. She'd not finished taking a sip of her drink before the door opened up. Wallace King filled the frame almost entire, his hand on the inside knob. Clayton sat in a chair across the room. He'd lately been watching TV but he shut it off and set the remote down on an end table to his side. The room smelled of cannabis and old leather.

"Sarah," Wallace said.

"You make a better door than a window, buddy," she said.

Wallace stepped back and waved her in. She went by. He shut the door behind her and she watched him turn a handle to a mechanism that bolted the door on either side. After that he walked by her and leaned against a naked brick column deep in the room. Sarah saddled up half-assed on the top of a nearby couch. She took another drink.

"You haven't seen him tonight, have you?"

"Who?" Clayton said.

She frowned at him.

"I've not seen your man. Not since he quit," Clayton said.

Sarah looked him up and down. She nodded. Finished her whiskey. Clayton turned to Wallace and pointed to the corner bar. Wallace got up off the pillar and took a bottle from the counter.

"Hey," Clayton said.

Wallace stopped and put that bottle down and picked up another one.

"Fuckin' choosy," he said, and went over to Sarah. She didn't lift her glass at first. Wallace shook the bottle at her.

"This is the good stuff," Wallace said.

Sarah stuck her glass out. Wallace filled it and went back to the bar.

"I heard he visited with the police," Clayton said. "That true?"

"You hear a lot for someone who's not keeping tabs on him," she said.

"Well."

"He wouldn't tell them a thing. You know better, Clayton."

He nodded.

"I know."

"You sure you don't know where he is?" she said.

"I heard that he's been working his way back to a fight."

"Yeah?"

"He might even get one, I hear."

Sarah took another swig. She ran a hand through her hair.

"Nobody ever gave him a decent job in his life," she said. "Can you believe it? A good man like that. It makes you wonder…"

Wallace chuckled. Sarah shifted so she was square with him.

"I didn't know you traded in fine art, Clayton," she said.

Clayton had his glass halfway up from his knee and it stopped right there. Over by the bar Wallace stood up tall. A series of paintings rested tarp-covered against the brick wall behind him. The oilcloth covered the all of them but she knew anyhow. Sarah raised her eyebrows at Wallace and then turned back to his boss.

"I'm a busy man," Clayton said. "But I've got hobbies. You wouldn't want to hear about a lot of them."

She nodded.

"I know a bit about paintings," she said.

"Sure you do."

"They still sell art private through private auction houses, in cash," she said. "As far as I know there ain't many other businesses in the world still run like that. Probably somebody could use a painting like a chit to move a shitload of clean money from one fella to another."

Clayton grinned at her. He drank slow and watched her all the while over the rim of his glass.

"How in the fuck d'you know any of that?" Wallace said.

"I read a lot when I work nights."

"Will you go out on a date with me?"

She looked him up and down.

"I don't date art buffs," she said.

The men laughed strange. The air in the room seemed to get thinner at once. Sarah downed her whiskey and raised the glass as a goodbye. She got up and went to the door. When she tried the handle to the lock it wouldn't turn. The muscles aside her spine went cold and then Wallace came over. He flipped a latch and wrenched the handle. Pulled the door open for her. It took everything she had to not flee. She turned around.

"You swear to me you've not seen Daniel?" Sarah said.

In the back of the room Clayton shook his head no. Sarah said okay and turned to leave. Wallace was still there.

"Will you walk me out?" she said to him.

Wallace turned to his boss and Clayton waved him out.

They walked out of the room and kept on and on and after an eon of hallway Sarah heard the office door clack shut. Wallace stopped by the exit door and waited.

"What?" he said.

"You got a family too," she said. "What happens to them if you're gone?"

Wallace leaned back against the wall.

"They'd be fine," he said.

"How can you say that?" she said. "With the fathers you and Dan had. How they ended up."

"Not the same."

"How?"

"They did it to themselves."

"But you know how that feels," she said.

"Sure, I found them both. Didn't I?"

Sarah took hold of Wallace by his shirtsleeve. He'd not look at her.

"His was purple when I found him," Wallace said. "Mine was yellow."

He cleared her hand off his arm. Went into his pocket and came back with a little metal canister. He gestured to her with it. Sarah just pushed the empty whiskey glass to his stomach. She shoved the door open and left Wallace there with the tumbler in his hand.

Then she was outside in the night, warm air on her shoulders. The moon shone full and far too close with shadow in its skullhole craters. She did not follow the road but rather went alleyward, her shoes barely visible under that orange flowermoon. She walked fast and her eyes kept trying to adjust. Sarah weaved through side streets to where she knew of a taxi stand. When she could make out the shape of highgrass in the bordering field she followed that line and made sure that no one else did.

She opened the door to silence. Small light from the kitchen. She couldn't see Daniel's shoes and then she saw them. Sarah wobbled on one leg and pried her own shoe off. When it fell she loosed the other one. Then she sat right down in the entryway and stared at Daniel's shoes. She'd thoughts of his never coming home again and of him buried shallow in the hills and even of her killing him. Let the worry and the fear wash over her, dread that couldn't be explained away. She let it take her under and turn her until it had run its course. When finally she stood she had to wipe her eyes and wait for her legs to work proper.

She trod soft on old carpet and groaning floorboard as she went to the bedroom. She flipped the light on and saw the bed he'd made that morning. Nearly as neat as she might make it but different. Sarah went back down the hallway to the girl's room. There he slept, sitting on the floor and leant against the foot of her bed. The girl in a ball on the mattress. Her arms hung off the bed to the elbow. Daniel wore his jeans yet and a T-shirt pulled askew as if he'd moved odd in sleep. The moon had followed Sarah home and it shone a column of pale grey over the sleeping man. She watched his chest swell and recede by that moon as if he were but another sea or body ran with tides.

Sarah could only see stars in the sky by her bedroom window, standing plainly drunk in her shortsocks and underthings. By and by she thought about a star and what it was and she didn't want to look at them anymore. She got onto the bed and lay back against the headboard and sipped at a bottle of beer from her sidetable. The bottom came to rest against the meat of her thigh, cool glass on her skin. She closed her eyes. When she opened them again Daniel was standing in the doorway. She closed her eyes again and soon she listed left with the mattress and all that side of the world got warm and smelled of him.

"Where did you go?" he said.

Sarah took another drink but she didn't open her eyes. The base of the bottle found her leg again.

"I went into town with some of the girls. Then I left."

"What for?"

"Stopped by Clayton's bar. Make sure he hadn't seen you."

"Jesus, Sarah."

"It was two days ago the last time we were both in this bed together. I guessed where you probably were or weren't but I needed to know for sure."

Daniel shifted heavy and faced her sidelong. He'd stripped down to his shorts and had the makings of a black eye along with scrapes and bruises frequent from his forehead to his toebones.

"I asked if they could get me a fight," he said.

"I was wondering when you were gonna say that," Sarah said.

She took a last pull from the beer bottle and slid it gentle across the night table. Folded her hands atop her stomach.

"What if I say no?" she said.

"Would you?"

"I fucking well should."

He reached out and held her far hip in his hand. Rough fingers pressing into her outside thigh, the back of her knee, her stockinged foot. A sock slid loose and flew. She shook her head.

"When did you get the kid home?" she said.

"Picked her up about ten. She fell asleep inside an hour, but Ella called to say she'd left her books at the house, so I went back," Daniel said. "I wasn't gone three minutes and that was three minutes too long."

Sarah opened her eyes.

"What d'you mean?"

Daniel told her how he'd come back down the road and saw the front door open. Half of their shoes on the steps and on the driveway. He nearly let the truck roll off by how quick he'd left it and ran through the house. The girl was not in her bed and she was not in any of the other rooms. He blew out of the place with a hammer in his right hand. Hollered the girl's name and searched the front and sideyards. No sign of her anywhere. He tore up damp, black soils as he made for the fields in back of the property. There she walked in her bare feet and shorts and her nightshirt. She didn't stop when he called and when he got to her she was talking and not to him. He didn't know if he should wake her but he did.

"She didn't flip out like they say," he said. "But the look of her coming back probably cost me some years."

Sarah reached over and corralled her husband, eased him down and put his head in her lap. She stroked his short hair and the sunburnt skin at the back of his neck.

"I never seen anythin' like that," he said. "Scared the living shit out of me."

"You did everything right," Sarah said.

"She ever done that before, when I wasn't home?"

"No," Sarah said. "But I heard you were the same, when you were a little boy."

Daniel tried to sit up but she held him and settled his head down into her lap again. She ran her hand up and down the middle of his back.

"At least that's what I was told."

After a minute Sarah moved him and swung her feet down from the bed. He tried to stand but she told him stay. She crossed the room and went out and closed the door gentle behind her.

TWENTY-NINE

He had his hands taped in the dressing room for visiting singers and visiting comedians. Mirrors ringed in lightbulbs and signed pictures of celebrities put out to pasture on the casino circuit. There were some eight hundred people in folding chairs in the banquet room where they staged the fights. Daniel could hear the chatter of them through the open door. He had Jasper and Jung Woo there and they both wore shirts with Jasper's gym insignia on the back. Face of a tiger wreathed in the woven rope of the Mongkhon. Thai script above. Daniel wore nothing but his shorts and shoes and the silver cross that stuck to his neck by the sweat from his warm-up. A few officials from the band that ran the casino were in the room to supervise. They weighed him up all the while.

Daniel made his walk and partway he thought about turning back around. He was glad for the nerves. If he didn't have them he'd have known that he was doomed. There was no cage built for the fight, just a standard boxing ring with ropes and four cornerposts. Mixed Martial Arts and Muay Thai fights were made legal in the province the year before and had been fought sparely on reserve land until then. In the states or out of province. The officials and his cornermen took Daniel to the staging area at the edge of the ring and the cutman assigned to him daubed Vaseline on his nose and eyebrows and rubbed it even through his cheeks. Another official checked his cup and the fingerless four-ounce gloves and the signature on the tape around them. They had him show his mouthguard and then waved him up the steps. He put his arms around Jasper and Jung Woo and the Korean told him to kill.

It was a heavyweight fight and the other man stood six-foot-three and weighed nearly two-hundred and forty pounds. Daniel weighed just shy of two-twenty and he gave up an inch or two in height. The other man had death's head tattoos on his arms and a grenade inked on the back of his right hand. Scars about his mouth and eyes. Not a shred of fat on him. They did not touch gloves and the other fighter belted himself about the cheeks and showed his black mouthguard.

Minutes in and the man had Daniel bullrushed to the ringpost, tried to can-opener him by pushing Daniel's head back, his massive forearm and one hand jammed under Daniel's chin. Daniel fought the hands and shucked his head loose and kneed up to the man's guts. The man took them well and threw knees of his own to Daniel's sides and quads. One that caught the cup and could be heard plain but the ref didn't see. Daniel fought for position and got an underhook on the man's one arm and drove his head under his opponent's chin. He stepped quick and turned the man. There he could tell that the other fighter lacked in his footwork and his rudiments. The man clawed at him and threw uppercuts up the middle, one that numbed Daniel's upper teeth and set his ear ringing. Daniel kept at the knees. One of them made the man put a hand down and Daniel worked both hands behind the man's head and put one over the other in a Thai plum. Pinched his elbows together and pulled down. The man couldn't defend quick enough and Daniel ragdolled him against the ropes and they bowed under the weight and made it harder for the bigger man to get his footing. Daniel threw brutal knees to the body from range, stutter-stepping to the mat and driving full with his ass and hips. The crowd groaned whole at the sound. Daniel blasted him again and when the other fighter's hands dropped to defend his body Daniel elevated and ripped a knee flush to the man's forehead and the man crumpled and nearly went out through the ropes.

Somehow he got back up on unsteady legs and swung hooks that whiffed as Daniel slipped and waited to time his attack. The big man's right eye was shut and his forehead above had already begun swelling monstrous. Daniel lit him up on the ropes, long punches to the bad eye and the contusion. He feinted and bombed power shots off-time. When the man next shelled up Daniel stepped wide on his right foot and turned on that toe and whipped a hard left round kick to the other fighter's liver-side. Impact like he'd took a baseball bat to the man. The man's body seized and quit and he dumped to the canvas. Daniel started to back off and raise his arms but the ref just looked at him so Daniel loped in and hammered the man upside the ear with another right hand.

He sat by the slots with two beers on the counter and his right hand in the ice bucket. Daniel still wore his fight shorts with their bloodstains, hoodie that he'd already sweat damp. He played quarter bets and pulled the lever. Jung Woo and Jasper were near the box office talking at the events manager and some of the pit bosses who'd seen the fight and were mimicking the clinch and the knees. The manager paid them out and shook hands with both men. He waved over to Daniel where he sat. Daniel raised a hand back. He put the last quarters in the machine and flushed them.

"You ready, champ?" Jasper said.

"Sure," Daniel said.

He downed his first beer. Took the other up as he stood and pulled on it as he left out across the casino floor with his trainers.

THIRTY

Daniel leaned back in the truck seat and waited. Chewed a toothpick and flicked it out the open window and got another. He watched the front of the tavern from over a hundred yards, his truck parked on a diagonal against the metered curb. Warm spring wind blew in at him, pushed a riderless, training-wheeled bicycle into the road where it toppled. A small boy came over to fetch it and started to wrestle it up onto the sidewalk. His young mother helped him right the bike and then she went around and got the front wheel between her pink legs. She turned the handlebar and straightened the wheel up, skirt dancing at her thighs. She gave the bike back to the boy and tried to rub the tire marks out of the skin at her knees. Soon she gave up. The little boy was already trundling past. The young woman stood up to call for him and there she saw Daniel in the truck. She waved at him. Red in her cheeks. He knew her but he couldn't remember her name. He waved and she turned and went on.

Daniel looked to the tavern again. A minute later the front door swung open. Tarbell walked out into the street with barely a glance in either direction. A passing car had to slow for him. He went on without gesture. Collared shirt and khakis and good shoes on the sand-strewn asphalt. He appeared to be talking to himself.

A behemoth cloud drifted high above the town, lesser clouds herded on before it. Midday sun simmering behind them. Tarbell got into a maroon sedan and drove away. Daniel watched the car pass by in his rearview mirror. Then he backed away from the curb enough to straighten up in the lane. He drove down the road to the building.

He went through the doors and the bartender saw him. The young man set his rag and dripping pint glass on the counter and his hands were under the bar.

"Easy on, buddy," Daniel said. "No reason for that."

The bartender just stood there.

"You new?" Daniel asked.

The bartender didn't say. Daniel stared at the man until he brought his hands back up to the counter. He didn't take the rag up again. Daniel heard the flat thud of a heavy steelbolt. Sound of a door broaching its frame. Shoe soles padding the hardwood. Wallace came out and looked at Daniel. He nodded. Then he looked at the bartender and laughed. The bartender gave Wallace the finger and set about cleaning the glasses again.

"Come on," Wallace said.

They went into the back office and Wallace closed the door behind Daniel.

"Clayton's in the john," he said.

"Okay."

Daniel took a seat in a worn-out leather chair like a giant catcher's mitt. He settled back. Wallace sat across from him.

"He ain't got you killed yet?" Daniel asked.

"Who?"

"That blonde motherfucker."

"Not yet. But he's tryin' awful hard," Wallace said. "You just missed him."

"I saw him cross the street," Daniel said. "You'd think there could be a drunk driver coming down that road. Somebody who spilt hot coffee in their lap. But no."

"Did you not wanna say hello?"

"I just didn't want the bartender to have to clean him off the ceiling."

Wallace grunted. Daniel sat forward in his chair.

"You believe the story Clayton is spinnin' about that dude?" he said.

Wallace looked to the bathroom door. No sound from within.

"He was adopted by Clayton's half-sister," said Wallace. "Real father was from Akwesasne. Supposedly the mother was long gone."

"Yeah?"

"That's about the fuckin' limit of what I cared to know. But it's true."

The bathroom door came open. Clayton shut the light off and walked into the room. He sat beside Wallace.

"You ladies are a gossipy bunch," he said.

"Well, I'm done talkin' about it," Daniel said.

"So, what do you want to talk about?"

"A bet."

Clayton leant forward to the edge of his seat. He pinched at his nose and sniffled.

"On what?"

"On a fight."

"What fight?"

"The next fight I'm in."

Clayton backhanded Wallace at the chest and then got up and went across the room to the corner bar. He held up a bottle of whiskey and looked back at the seated men. Wallace nodded.

"Dan?" Clayton said.

"Sure."

"What about your trainin'," Wallace said.

"Gonna let myself have a drink today. But just today."

Clayton was studying him from the other side of the room. He came over with the drinks, handed them over and sat heavy on the couch again.

"I know you've been crushing tomato cans," Clayton said. "But I also heard you nearly killed some guy in the gym. A fighter with a name."

"I didn't think that'd get around."

"It got around to me. But that's me."

"Good. They got me at a five-to-one dog in this next fight."

"It's been a while since you fought on a real card, Dan."

"I know it."

"What about your eye?"

"Doc said it's fine."

"That kind of thing heals?"

Daniel nodded.

"What kind of money you after?" Clayton said.

"Ten thousand."

Clayton frowned. He drank half the whiskey in his glass.

"You can't get ten grand if it goes wrong. We both know that."

"I'm gonna smash this guy."

"Why not go for a hundred then? If it's a done deal."

Daniel started to get up out of the chair. Clayton stepped forward with his hand out and settled him back down.

"You know how it works if I lay that down for you," Clayton said.

"I do."

"I don't think you should do it, Dan," Wallace said.

Clayton turned to him slow. Wallace shrugged. Clayton turned back to Daniel.

"You win I take the ten back and five for laying the bet. You lose…"

"Yeah," Daniel said. He downed the drink and stood up. Clayton met him in the middle of the room. Eye to eye. They shook hands.

"I'll call you to come get the ticket," Clayton said.

"Give it to Wallace. We'll meet up somewhere. I ain't comin' back here again."

THIRTY-ONE

Night came late to the farmhouse. Twilight over the field and before the decking where the old man and his wife waited for company. Murray sitting low in a Muskoka chair. Music played soft through the screen door and the living room windows. An old country ballad here. Fiddle music. Some Delta blues like a haunt over the farm. Murray tapped his foot and drank a short of rye. He heard the crackle of tires on gravel and stood in time to watch the truck through the thin trees at the edge of the property. He patted at the pockets of his shirt like he might have lost something. When the truck turned in to the long drive he took another drink.

"They're here," he called into the house. Then he set the glass on the arm of his chair and went quick down the steps.

They ate by candle and lamplight. Warm nightwind slipped in through the kitchen windows and screen door and circled about their legs and feet. Mosquitoes pestered them some and were swatted or stuck to a flystrip at the corner of the room. Daniel had already begun his weight cut for the fight and his cheeks were sunken. His neck and arms were nothing but muscle and vein, cord and bone. He ate skinless chicken and not enough of it. He ate uncooked vegetables and drank water. Every other plate had red meat and roast potatoes with gravy, buttered frybread. Daniel ate slow so that he wouldn't finish before them. The girl was talking Ella's ear off. Sarah and Murray fussed over Daniel but he ignored them until they gave up to eat. The old man wolfed his food down and sat back with his hands on his chest. He drank from a bottle of beer and got up for another.

"Will you take a beer?" he said to Daniel.

"I could have a glass of wine."

Murray nodded and came back with two bottles of beer. He uncapped the bottles and handed one to Sarah. Then he sat and took up a bottle of red and poured a glass for Daniel. They all touched glasses at the centre of the table, Madelyn reaching with a can of Coke and Murray leaning to meet her. Daniel drank careful and then he drank again. He let the glass rest on the table-cloth, the delicate stemware neck turning by the enormous pads of his thumb and forefinger. He had a little more and then he slid the glass away to his right, where Madelyn was seated. She didn't know what to do.

"Go on," Daniel said.

The girl looked to Sarah. She said okay. Madelyn took the glass up slow and sipped. No change in her face. She sipped again small and set it down. Quiet through the place now. Sound of crickets outside in the grasses, but even those calls seemed to thin. Daniel was bolt-straight in his seat with his head tilted back slight. Forearms resting heavy on the wooden arms of his chair. Nobody would look at him for long.

"Dad," Madelyn said.

"Yeah?" Daniel said.

"How long does the next fight last?"

"It could last one second. Or it could go for fifteen minutes."

The girl thought on it awhile.

"That isn't that long," she said.

"Let's hope not," Daniel said.

She picked up her glass to drink and then set it back down. Her cheeks had already took on some colour.

"Are you scared?"

He shook his head.

"Not the way you mean," he said.

Sarah got up and started carrying cleared plates to the sink. She gripped a handful of her husband's hair and then loosed it. Daniel reached up for the hand but it had gone. Murray rocked back on the hind legs of his chair and took stock of them all. He came forward and laid his gnarled elbows on the table.

"You know when those kids at school say their dad is tougher than everybody else's dad?"

Madelyn nodded.

"Well, you're the only one who's tellin' the truth when you say it."

She kept watching the old man as if she were waiting for him to wink or smile. To make a joke out of it. He did not.

Sarah led him into the house and left the place dark. She got hold of him and kissed him. The door swung into the stopper at the wall, blown back and back again by the humid night air. His shirt was up at the back of his neck and her fingers dug into his shoulder blades so hard that it hurt him. He stooped down to get his forearm under her legs and then he lifted her off the floor with her knees pinned to his left side by the crook of his elbow. She tugged him close, pressed into him so that he could feel her stomach tensing, filling with breath as a singer's might. He kicked the door shut and went through the house by memory alone.

Her sweaty head was warm at his neck. She talked to him in whispers and he whispered back. He felt the ridges of scar tissue at her shoulder and the fine hair at her upper arm. Her pelvic bone dug into the meat of his thigh, wet below. He worked out a cramp in the bridge of his left foot. There they lay for a very long time and he wouldn't think about what he looked like to her. He didn't weigh his luck and didn't need to. He knew he had too much of it. To be loved and to know it. He shifted like a man shaken out of sleep.

"I am scared," he said.

"Only fools aren't."

"I am."

"No, you're not," she said.

THIRTY-TWO

The sedan pulled into the motel lot at early evening. There were three other cars in the place. Two were parked in front of their lot-facing rooms. The other car sat on an angle with its hood well under a canopy that ran the length of the building. Front of the vehicle maybe two feet clear of the nearest room's door. Tarbell parked at the far end of the lot and came past to see the crooked car. He strolled between the stuccoed outer wall of the motel and the car's fender and went on down the walk to the motel office and let himself in.

He checked the time and calculated the hours he had to get his work done near that isolated village-town. The room was rented for the night and he'd made his calls to Clayton to say that he was where he was supposed to be. There'd been a local constable come to the bar to speak with Clayton, and the officer made no bones about his interest in their evolving operation. Talk of bodies and blown meth labs and special investigations. Tarbell was told to take care of one piece of business that day and another in the morning. He'd been told as hard as he could be. To take his time coming back and be wary as nobody had gone out there to back him. Tarbell had no intention of waiting until tomorrow for the second job. The fights from Montreal were on pay TV and he'd already scoped out a bar near to the motel that carried posters in its windows. He figured on how long it'd take him to get back to Marston.

He had his clothes laid out on the bed in small piles. Beside his clothes the sawed-off and his pistol. Three full clips and a box of double-aught. He sat in a chair wearing only a towel around his nethers. Pale musculature of his chest and abdomen. He had a mark alike to an appendectomy scar, but too long and too deep. Countless scarlines raised in his skin that crisscrossed his stomach and his upper arms. He wore a hole in the meat atop his heart, a gouge the size and depth of a half shotgun shell. The wound ran with pinks and purples. It would have been ugly anywhere on any man, but dug into his skin it seemed uglier yet.

The man got up and took his clothes from the bed. He dressed in a collared shirt and dark trousers, grey socks and custom leather shoes, leather straps over his shoulders for the holster. He sat back in the chair and watched the sun go down by the lot-facing window. Red skies to the west. When he could no longer make out the treeline he stood and took the pistol from the bed and holstered it. He put his jacket on and left the room with the butt of the sawed-off cupped in his palm, the gun upended and hidden by his arm. On the way out he passed a beautiful and bedraggled woman with a little girl tugging at her hand. The gun was plain to see for the girl but she didn't know what it was. The woman didn't see it at all. She'd her eyes on the man alone. He smiled as he passed and then walked across the dark lot. The woman turned when she got to her room but there was nobody out there.

THIRTY-THREE

Daniel rode in the backseat of the car. Jasper drove and Jung Woo sat shotgun. Daniel wore a sweatshirt with the hood pulled up over his head. He took long breaths and watched forests pass. Collapsed barns like dinosaur bones. Country chapels with gabled belltowers. They crossed a border. English moved from the top of the road signs to the bottom. Daniel saw a dirtied young boy at the side of the county road trying to put the chain back on his bike. The boy held up a grease-stained hand. Daniel took his hand out of his sweatshirt pocket and waved back.

They got to the hotel mid-evening. City lights shone in the valley below, in the water beyond the portlands. Jasper and Jung Woo shared a room and it was connected to Daniel's room by an adjoining door. The coaches went out and came back with Daniel's dinner. Eight ounces of grilled fish from an organic market down the road. He ate slow and drank water. He had about eight pounds to cut before the next day's weigh-in. When he closed his door to them at eleven o'clock he lay down in his bed and watched the television, found a hockey game in French and turned the volume low. He heard the door shut in the other room. Eventually he turned the television off and lay there with the windows open, a gentle breeze rustling the topsheet. He went to sleep hungry and had strange dreams that he couldn't remember.

Daniel slept late and Jung Woo finally came to get him at ten in the morning. The fighter ate a breakfast of fruit and egg whites. They weighed him at two hundred and fourteen pounds on a bathroom scale. He needed to weigh two hundred and six by four o'clock. He went down to the lobby to speak to the promoter and the press. Five reporters interviewed him. Many of the younger, would-be journalists didn't know his story or they didn't care. He shook hands with a few of the fighters and spoke to a journeyman from lower on the card who had fought nearly forty times though he was five years younger than Daniel. The man asked about Daniel's eye and Daniel told him it was fine but not to bring it up again. The man said he wouldn't. The journeyman had to cut sixteen pounds before his fight and Daniel shook his hand and wished him luck and then he went back up to his room to get ready.

He gnawed ice cubes through a handtowel while he waited for the coaches to help him get the plastics on. Long-sleeved shirt and pants made of airtight vinyl, taped at the wrists and ankles, tight at the neck and tucked in at the waist. He wore the suit into the sauna and took turns shadowboxing and riding a stationary bike. The weight came off. Sweat pooled at his lower back and spilled down into his shoes. His throat dried until it hurt but he didn't want to speak anyway. He suffered quiet for the better part of an hour and then he sat alone in the dim wood-lined room and suffered some more. When they came to get him he had the eyes of a wolf at the kill. They weighed him at two hundred and four pounds and he had half an hour to wait before they put him on the scales. He looked like he'd been carved out of wood.

The man he fought was a young contender from Boston, beaten twice in the early part of his career. Undefeated since. He stood a half-foot taller than Daniel and he had stopped sixteen men in a row. Daniel felt weak in the legs when he left the changeroom to make his walk. Every step closer to the cage he got them back. Felt his heart banging and rubbed his knuckles hard through the gloves. He came up the steps and ran a lap around the matting. He wanted that bell to ring so bad it near hurt him to wait through the announcer calling out their names. When they met for the staredown the younger man showed him nothing. They were told to protect themselves at all times. They touched gloves. Daniel kept his eyes on the other fighter. The announcer left the cage with his microphone and the attendants closed the door and bolted it shut. The other man glanced away for just a moment. Daniel opened and closed his fists.

When the bell rang Daniel took the centre of the mat quick and stung the taller fighter with an inside cut kick and an overhand right. The man buckled and recovered. He threw back. Daniel blocked the punches or ate them and walked the man back against the cage. The man tried to shoot for his legs but Daniel sprawled hard and stopped the takedown. He feinted and threw a long lead hook to the man's eye. The man came back strong but in the exchange he got caught with an upper-cut and knelt on the canvas. Trainers cried out from cageside for the younger man to clinch. He tried to hold Daniel as he stood but Daniel shucked loose and landed straight punches and hooks until the other man caromed off the cagefencing with his head in his hands. Daniel ripped a left hook to the taller man's body and when the man lowered his hands Daniel caught him with a right elbow and another left hook to the cheek. The man fell. Daniel followed him to the mat to take mount and there he blasted the downed fighter. The man kept his elbows tight and tried to roll out but he couldn't. Daniel's arms were stained red from glove to triceps. Finally the hurt fighter bucked and turned over to his side. The referee called down to the men but he didn't stop the fight. Then he did. He shoved Daniel clear with his shoulder and lay over the beaten fighter, one black-latexed hand waving back and forth.

Daniel circled the cage with his hands on his hips. He stared over at what he'd done. Officials came in through the door, doctors, cutmen. A suit-jacketed man stopped Daniel and asked him how he felt, took a good look into his eyes, lifted Daniel's hands and turned them over. He told Daniel it was a good fight and then he went on. The crowd were screaming and whistling. Daniel raised his hands and they saw it and got louder. He let his arms drop and went over to see the other fighter. His opponent's face was in ruin but he smiled at Daniel from where he sat on a short-stool. The fighters shook hands and the bloodied man patted Daniel's shoulder before the officials eased Daniel away so the doctors and cutmen could go back to work.

Jung Woo and Jasper hung over the top of the cage and Daniel went over to them. They each clasped his right hand in turn and told him it was a good fight but they were otherwise very solemn. Jasper glared over at the referee who stood at the other side of the cage and spoke to the judges through the fencewire. The promoter had come into the cage and had words with the referee and the athletic commission officials. He looked over at Daniel's corner just for a second. He turned away from the referee in mid-sentence and left the cage shaking his head.

The fighters were called to the centre of the mat with the referee between them, one of their wrists in each hand. The beaten man had his nose pinned back against his right cheek and a forehead like a boiled potato, scarred and swollen. His left eye was entirely closed.

"What the fuck, ref?" he said.

The referee didn't answer.

The call came from the announcer. Disqualification from strikes to the back of the head. Daniel tore his wrist clear and walked away. He came back and there were officials in the ring between him and the referee. The other fighter had his hand raised but he pulled clear as well and came over to Daniel. Raucous boos shook the place. Someone threw a lidded cup of beer at the cage and it broke apart at the bottom of the fencing and sprayed the canvas.

"It's bullshit, man," said the other fighter.

They shook hands and half-hugged. Daniel left the cage. The referee was nowhere to be seen but Daniel had already stopped thinking about him. He walked up the aisle where fans slapped at his arms and shoulders and hailed him as the winner between curses and calls for riot. He went into the tunnel and made for the exit.

Doctors and commission men tried to block him and make him take his post-fight medical. They told him he would never fight again if he didn't stop. They said they'd take his entire purse. He held up long enough to take their measure. He wouldn't go back. The promoter came over to him with a doctor in tow and had them examine him on the spot. He promised to pay Daniel the win bonus. Daniel let them cut his wraps and check his hands, his vision, his heartbeat. Minutes later he walked out through the exit doors and they swung hard against the outer wall of the arena. He beelined for the car, his bare feet turning black-heeled as they padded across cold tarmac.

THIRTY-FOUR

Murray took the receiver from the cradle and listened. He called Ella into the kitchen and when she came he handed her the phone and went into the living room. He came back with his mobile and started dialing. Ella had a pen in her hand and Murray laid a pad of paper down on the counter and she started writing. Murray listened to ringtone for a very long time. Someone answered.

"Sarah?" he said.

"It's me."

"Dan call you?"

"Yes."

"He's on the other line with Ella right now."

"Okay."

"Madelyn's upstairs sleepin'. She won't stir for awhile."

"I'll be back at seven."

"We'll be waitin'. Don't you worry now."

Murray said goodbye and he sat down at the kitchen table. A half-full bottle of whiskey stood on the topboards. He had three fingers of the stuff in a glass beside it. He stood and took the glass to the sink and dumped it. He was about to set it down but instead he took a few steps back toward the table and turned and pitched the tumbler at the sinkbasin. The metals rang and glass flew. Ella spooked and dropped the phone on the floor. She cussed at Murray and he picked the phone up for her and handed it over. Then he went back to the table and corked the bottle, sat there staring at it.

He hadn't been there for ten seconds when Ella waved at him. He got up and took the phone from her.

"Where the hell are yous all now?" Murray said.

"Just outside Cornwall. I'll be home in five an' a half hours."

"What do I tell the girl if she wakes up?"

"Tell her the truth," Daniel said. "I lost."

THIRTY-FIVE

There were two men barside. Blue halos of smoke rounded them. Tall cans of beer crowded the counter, overfilled shotglasses. They'd lately been watching the television mounted above the backbar. They cussed and argued. One man coughed hard and downed a mouthful. On his right hand he was missing a length of thumb from third-knuckle to fingernail. The bartender came over to take their empties. She knew them both by name. They shot their whiskies and ordered another round. Then they argued some more.

Tarbell sidled up to the bar and sat on a stool near the men. There were two commentators talking at each other on the TV and they looked to be setting up for the next fight. Tarbell called for a drink before the woman had even seen him. She turned and stared at him like he he'd kicked her cat. He stared back, still dapper in his shirt and jacket beside men in steel-toed boots and workshirts. Rank scent of sweat in their backcloth. The drink came to him slow. The local men returned to their conversation. The nearest one wore heavy fireproof coveralls and he filled the all of them, scratched at the hair under his ballcap as he swore at the man with the cropped thumb. The girl behind the bar eyeballed Tarbell. He drank in short sips and many. He heard something and turned on his stool.

"What did you just say?" he asked.

The men at the bar mumbled to a halt. Cigarettes ghosting trails of smoke from between their fingers. The man in coveralls glanced back and then angled away slightly. Tarbell whistled to them loud. Cropped-Thumb clasped his hands on the bar counter and shifted.

"What?" he said.

"You watched the fights?"

Cropped-Thumb said they did. That Tarbell had missed the most of them, including Daniel's scrap.

"Who won?" Tarbell said.

The workman raised his tallboy and chugged. He set it down and burped against a closed fist, plainly showed the club-digit.

"The local guy lost. DQ'd. Load of bullshit if you ask me…"

Tarbell downed his drink as he stood. He took a ten from his billfold and laid it on the bar. The local men were talking at him about the fight. Tarbell raised his palm to quiet them.

"Nobody cares, shut up," he said, and shoved the bill toward the bartender.

Coveralls sat up straight, took his dirty cap from his head.

"You're a real ignorant piece of shit. You know that?"

Tarbell stepped clear of his stool and walked to the door. He shoved out with his shoulder and paused long enough to look back at the workmen. The door shut behind him and wind whistled in the crooked jamb.

Partway across the lot he heard the door come open again and footsteps on the asphalt. He took a sharp turn to his right, toward a shuttered roadside filling station with one lonely bulb casting small light to the near ground.

They started calling out to him. Tarbell loped low and reached into his boot and then he turned. Both were far bigger than he. The man with the half-thumb led. Tarbell lunged and the workman blocked with his forearm and then backed up holding the arm. Arterial red pumped over his fingers. Tarbell came again and by the look in Cropped-Thumb's eyes the man knew the cost. The blonde held a two-inch bootknife between his first two knuckles and he snaked a punch over his foe's rising guard and put the triangular blade into the man's neck. He pulled the man close. His left hand braced the man's sweaty head as he stuck him again through the Adam's apple.

The bigger man in coveralls had come to help. He pulled Tarbell clear by the back of his jacket and the knife came out and painted a maroon line in the pavement. The man with the half-thumb sunk and keeled. When Coveralls saw all of the blood coming out of his friend he loosed his grip and stumbled back. Tarbell wheeled and swept the blade through the bridge of the stunned man's nose. Coveralls screamed tonguelessly and then he started running. He ran faster than he should have been able with his steel-toed boots and husky build, blood in his mouth. Only steps from the bar Tarbell caught him and stabbed him in the liver-side, hobbled him by dragging the knife through his hamstring. Tarbell hooked his arm around the wounded man's neck and pulled him gimpedly into the blackness behind the bar. There he opened the workman's throat and bled him white. He laid the man in a cut of wildgrass not ten feet from the rear of the building. The man gaped at starless sky and his eyes dimmed. Tarbell waited on his haunches until he saw the last plume of fog depart the workman's lips. Then he walked out of the brush and went across the half-lit lot with his shirt and suit jacket balled up in the crook of his elbow.

THIRTY-SIX

The black Cadillac rolled up the grade and waited in front
of the building. Sarah got up from the desk and looked
at it through the office window. Shifted her weight from
one foot to the other and then she came around to the
security doors. She turned her key in the lock and went
out, pocketed the keychain in her scrub apron. Clayton
got out of the car on the passenger side and came around
to meet her. She could see Wallace King behind the
wheel. She waved to him and he waved back.

"Let's sit," Clayton said.

"Okay," Sarah said.

They walked over to a wooden retaining wall and
there they sat on the topbeam. The timber was damp
and cold under their asses. Patches of newly-laid sod
behind them. Clayton pulled a joint from his shirt
pocket and offered it to her.

"I'm at work right now," she said.

"I won't tell," he said.

Clayton lit the joint. He dragged deep and blew
smoke.

"You won't hurt him, Clayton. Don't you dare."

"Who said I would?"

"There's a lot of stuff I know about you all and a lot
more I could guess at that'll turn out to be true if the
cops dig at it."

"Careful," he said. "That's a bad way to talk."

"What d'you think you could threaten me with if you already went after him?"

"There's still your daughter to worry about."

She turned slow. Stared a hole through him.

"I guess I could just kill you," she said.

Clayton took hold of her hand. She made a fist but let him have it.

"I don't plan to hurt him," Clayton said. "He isn't just anybody."

"What about the money?"

Clayton let go of her and put his palms on his knees. He studied the bordering pines.

"He'll have his purse to hand over. And I heard they paid him his win bonus anyway. That'll get us more than halfway."

"Then what?"

"Then I might have some work for him."

Sarah cleared her throat. She hung her head and put both hands over her face. Then she dropped them and sat up straight. She seemed like to puke but she'd not give in.

"He'll come home to you in one piece," Clayton said. "Both now and later. I won't work him like before. He's got some fights left. Probably I'll oversee them."

Sarah pinched the joint from his fingers. She took a drag and looked into his eyes. Clayton looked away first.

"You're gonna be his manager?" she said.

"Of sorts. People know what he did in these last fights. To real fighters. Bullshit calls be damned. There's money to be made before he truly does get old one night."

Sarah stubbed the joint out in the turf behind her. Flicked it into a nearby trashcan. She leaned back on her palms, saw the sky above.

"You are not doing any of that. I'll tell you right now," Sarah said. "But you will make sure all your fucking buddies know that Daniel is to be left alone."

She stood up. Clayton stood with her.

"I looked out for him before," he said. "Many times."

"There's just no way we all live through this if you don't leave him be."

Clayton raised a hand to Wallace. The car engine fired.

"We can talk about it later," he said. "But your man's safe. I've no intention of harming him, neither will anybody else."

"Promise me," she said and held her hand out.

Clayton looked her in the eyes and they shook on it. Then Sarah turned and walked the pavestone pathway to the security doors. She went inside without another word. Clayton climbed back into the car. The Cadillac circled the empty north end of the lot and came back past the office. She wasn't there.

Wallace drove through desolate town avenues. He took most street signs and stoplights as suggestions. They pulled up to a stop sign by the police station and Clayton scoped the building. Wallace wound his window down and spat. They drove on.

"How long until we meet my nephew?" Clayton said.

"About five hours."

Clayton looked to the clock in the dash.

"That's awhile yet," he said.

"Yep."

"You couldn't get him on the cell."

"That fuckin' lunatic ain't answerin'," Wallace said. "Could be he pitched it. Could be he's sleeping."

"You think?"

Wallace frowned.

"I wouldn't be surprised if he don't sleep at all," he said.

"He'll show on time," Clayton said. "Once he's done what he was told to up north."

"Okay."

They neared Clayton's bar just before daybreak. Wallace parked and shut the engine off.

"I'm going in the back to try and sleep awhile," Clayton said. "You keep trying to turn him up. Then get some sleep yourself."

Wallace nodded. He got out of the car and stretched as tall as he could, settled back on his heels. Clayton went in through the great saloon doors and let them swing shut behind him. Wallace sat on the hood of the car and glanced over at the doors. Like a huge passway golem, his feet flat to the ground and his knees bowed and his long arms crossed over his chest. He heard the squealing of bats as they pinwheeled home in the early morning pale. Wallace took his tiny metal cylinder from his inside jacket pocket and uncapped it and tipped some white into the cap. Snorted it through one nostril and put the container away. Felt the gunmetal slung against his chest. After a moment he moved his hand and took his phone out and dialed. He waited long before he hung up. Then he dialed again.

THIRTY-SEVEN

The girl woke to fingers sweeping the curls from her forehead. She'd barely gone under in the small hours but when she did sleep she slept full. It took some minutes to raise her but then one lid opened. The other followed. Sarah sat on the bed with one hand pinned to the mattress at Madelyn's side, the other running hair behind the girl's ear.

"Mom?" said the girl.

"Hey."

"Did you hear from dad?"

Sarah nodded. The girl started to shuffle out of the covers drowsily.

"No, honey," Sarah said. "You're gonna stay here a little while with Murray and Ella. I'll be down the road waiting for dad to come home. Then we're both coming back to get you."

"Okay," Madelyn said.

The girl's head started to list. But before her cheek touched pillow she shook herself awake again and tried to sit up. Sarah settled the girl back down. She'd not left the bed.

"What is it, Madelyn?"

"I knew he'd win."

Sarah put her chin to her shoulder and looked off into the shadowed corner of the room. She squeezed her daughter gentle at the wrist.

"Tell dad I knew," the girl said.

"I'll tell him. Now go back to sleep."

THIRTY-EIGHT

Dewfrost clung to the edges of the sideview mirror where the man's hand turned over its reflection. The sun had yet to clear the fir-tops and he could see the faintest trace of his breath in the car. He leaned back in the seat and stared at the rear tire in the mirror. The tread had sunk an inch in the untilled fieldsoil. Tarbell surveyed the southeasterly corner of the distant house, the county road that led there. He waited for risen dust, birds flown, low rumbling in the earth.

Tarbell opened his eyes to the steering wheel, dials in the console. He propped himself up in the car seat and cast about for his bearings. When he looked out at the house again he saw the truck in the driveway, the front-third hidden from view by the building. He got out of the car in his undershirt, damp cotton at his lower back that he pulled out to cover the butt of his belt-hung pistol. He left the door open. Cussed himself out for drifting. Tarbell started across the field and then stopped and came back. He went into the car again.

As he walked the worn-down croprow ruts a landed flock of sparrows pulled up from their pickings and flew. He carried on toward the house with his right arm dangling, the short-barrels of the shotgun passing his knee like a pendulum.

Sarah wrung her hair in the towel and then threw it over a high hook on the bathroom door. Lengths of her hair gone very dark. The ends wet the shoulders of her shirt. She went down the hallway barefoot and into the kitchen. Coffee dripped in the percolator and she poured a cup and drank, raised one foot from the cold tile and pressed it up against the cupboard door in the counter behind her. She turned and set the mug by and took a bottle down from a high shelf. She poured a slug of whiskey into her drink and stirred it with a spoon. Turned again to lean on the counter. She drank in near quietude and listened to the sound of her breath, the soft complaints of the old house around her.

She put the empty cup in the sink and looked out of the open window. A long shadow stretched out in the lawn below, shape-shifting all the while. Narrow stick-shade lengthening at the figure's side. Sarah stared at it for a second and then she dropped. She could hear feet walking the crabgrass. They stopped and Sarah clung to the low cupboards. The footsteps kept on and faded out. She waited.

A minute later they came back and passed the other way. She turned and looked over at the kitchen door. Slanted light shone through cracks in the wood slatting and lined the near tile. When she saw the thin beams break and vanish she got up and located the drawer in the opposite counter where the carving knives were kept. The doorknob started turning. Sarah went fast to the door and fitted the chainlock plug into its anchor and stepped back. When the door opened the chain rose taut and held. Sarah waited in the middle of the kitchen with her guts gone cold. The door eased back and the chain sagged. A man's hand came into the kitchen through the gap and reached for the lockplug.

The hand had just found the end of the chain when Sarah ran in and drove the door back with her shoulder. She hit hard and the edged timber crushed the arm against the framing. She heard the snap of bone and the man's forearm took a new angle from where the edge struck. Then the arm was gone and the door closed hard enough that Sarah stumbled forward and knelt against it. She was up again to turn the deadbolt and she could hear him screaming. She ran to the front door of the bungalow and bolted it and then came back through pushing the kitchen table.

Before she crossed the middle of the room the door blew inward as a wall of shot and torn wood and the thunderclap boomed through the house. Sarah had been lifted off the floor entire and now she lay in the kitchen entryway. Not long and Tarbell broke the top half of the door away with the stock and moved through the rag-ended lower half and into the house. Mud on the back of his pants and shirt, in his hair. He howled yet for his injured arm. He stopped when he saw her lying there. Then he sidestepped the wood-littered table and walked over to her.

Sarah's shirt blossomed in crimsons. She had one hand over her heart and the other held the squared column of the entryway framing. Tarbell set the shotgun on the kitchen counter and walked past her. Through the living room and down the hallway to the bedrooms.

Pistol drawn and cocked. Sarah lay alone and stared at the ceiling. She took a breath and let it go. She never took another.

PART FIVE

*S*he crossed the southern border to Montana on a Friday
*afternoon. Her sister had not seen the child yet and
hadn't seen Sarah in over two years. Sarah called
Daniel to say she'd arrived but she didn't call again. When
Daniel phoned her that Sunday evening she didn't answer.
He got in his truck and drove south on Highway 2 and eventually passed through the forty-ninth parallel.*

*The town where she'd been born had four traffic lights
and a gas station. A brokedown inn above a greasy spoon.
He got the address for her sister's place from the girl at the
diner's lunch counter. He went to the house, little more than a
trailer on blocks. Rotary clothesline turning in chinook wind.
Nobody was home. Daniel went back to the diner and found
out where their father lived.*

*Daniel drove down black nightroads until he saw the farm-
house sitting lonely in a barren field. When he pulled up to the
place a porchlight came on. As Daniel walked up to the house*

the door opened and a tall man with white hair came out onto the decking. He held an infantryman's rifle in his wiry arms and levelled it at Daniel. Hollering from the house that carried in the dark expanse around it. The old man turned and barked back into the room. Daniel didn't slow and when his foot hit the first step the old man put his finger to the trigger. Daniel went up the steps and felt the hard muzzlesteel against his chest before he swept the barrel wide with the outside of his hand and shoved the old man backward into his own kitchen. Sarah and her sister were in the room when he came in and Daniel gave the gun to the sister and put his arms around his wife. The old man still sat on the cracked linoleum, drunk and slow in his motions.

The old man eyeballed Daniel from across the table while Sarah got the baby. The sister stood by the kitchen counter with the rifle safetied at her side, the bolt removed. They'd found Sarah's passport and driver's license in a coffee tin in the cupboard. The old man drank bourbon by the glass and after a while he started to cry. When Sarah came out with the child she left the house without a word and Daniel got up to follow. The sister laid the rifle on the table in front of the old man and chucked the loose bolt into the sink before she walked out. Daniel stopped in the doorway and watched the old man wipe teartracks from his rough cheeks, tip the bottle again. After a long time the man turned.

"You had a gun pointed at you before?" he said.

"No," Daniel said.

The old man nodded, drank deep.

"You took it well, son."

"I ain't your son," Daniel said. "You're never gonna see her again."

"Okay."

"You cross north I'll bury you up there."

THIRTY-NINE

Murray heard the shot and went out to the back yard. He strained to better see the little house but a copse of trees blocked the most of it. So he looked to the fields and saw the car parked there. He tried to figure the make and model and then he went into the house and locked the door behind him.

He hurried the girl into the cellar with Ella trailing. Madelyn kept asking questions but Murray shushed her and the girl clammed up. He left her sour-faced, huddled on an old Chevy benchseat against the blockstone cellar wall. He squeezed Ella's hand and she wouldn't let it go at first but finally she did. Then Murray went back upstairs.

He went quick to his bedroom and the wardrobe against the west-facing wall. All he had for arms was a twenty-two rifle for groundhogs and vermin. A half-spent brick of rounds in a drawer. He turned the bolt-handle and ran the bolt back and forth, blew hard into the chamber. Then he put a round behind the breech and slid it forward. Ran the bolt again. He pocketed the rest of the bullets and went back downstairs.

They were only ten minutes in wait when muddied shoes passed by the small window above them. Murray saw them and corralled everyone into the corner of the room. He didn't see Tarbell stoop and stare in through the silted windowglass, move on. Soon they could hear knocking at the front door. No more than a pitter-patter at first. A series of loud, deliberate thuds following. Murray raised the rifle and thumbed the safety off. Fifteen minutes later he was still holding the weapon and there had not been another sound from the house, without or within.

"Maybe it was Daniel?" Ella said.

Murray shook his head.

"He would have called out to us," he said.

They waited and waited and then Murray got up.

"Just where the hell d'you think you're going?" Ella said.

"I'm just gonna take a looksee."

"I'm going with you," Madelyn said, and she stood.

"You are not," the old man said.

"Like shit," she said.

The man caught her by the bicep before she could make for the stairs. She got hold of his wrist in the one hand and his collar in the other. He all but lifted her off the ground to move her. Ella cussed them both and pulled them apart.

"You will goddamn well stay put," Murray said. "That's the end of it."

Ella had got between them and managed to keep the girl wrapped up. Madelyn looked like she might cry and that nearly set the old man off.

"Keep her here," he said to his wife.

"Be careful," she said.

Murray said he would and then he took the girl's hand gentle and held it. She didn't fight. She squeezed once and let go.

"Hold the fort down, kid," he said. "Can you do that for me?"

Madelyn nodded.

Murray let her go and kissed his wife and then he went up the cellar stairs. He bolted the door shut behind him.

Within half an hour the kitchen door opened and shut again. Heavy bootfalls above. The cellar door unlatched and Murray came down the steps with his face ashen. He saw them sitting there and closed his eyes, swallowed, stood the rifle up and squatted low to the cold cement floor. Then suddenly he was up again and coming to them. He lifted Madelyn to her feet, stared at her long. Turned to his wife.

"We have to go," he said.

They put Madelyn in the backseat of their car with a small suitcase of her clothes. Told her to buckle herself in. They'd lied through their teeth to even get her that far. When the old man closed the doors he flipped the child-locks but the girl didn't see it. Murray was coming into the house and met Ella on her way out. She dropped the bags she was carrying and put her arms around the old man. Murray held her fast to him and cupped the back of her head in his rough and calloused palm, stroked her hair.

"Dear God," the woman said.

"We have to get away from here," Murray said.

Ella nodded and let go of him. She rubbed at her eyes with her thumbknuckles and then picked up the bags. Murray started to pass her and go farther down the corridor when he heard the grumbling of a vehicle on approach. Murray and Ella looked at each other and then went out quick to the porch to see the car that drove the county road.

"Is that the one you saw in the field?" she said.

"No."

Ella raised a hand to her brow and squinted.

"It's Daniel," she said. "Daniel is driving that car."

Murray hustled down the steps and ran up the drive, hitch in his right step as he went. Soon enough he cleared the hedgebrush at the edge of the property and loped out into the road grimacing, waving madly at the vehicle. The old man stood tall in the lane until the car slowed and stopped. He put his hands to his knees for a second, rose up. Daniel got out of the car and came over to him. When he saw Murray's face he slowed and then stopped altogether.

"Where's my daughter?" Daniel said.

"She's fine. We got her in the car."

"Where's my wife?"

Murray stood and walked over to Daniel. The old man had tears in his eyes. He was making an odd noise through his teeth.

Daniel took a step back and looked out in the direction of his house through the treeline. He tried to turn but Murray got a mittful of his shirt. The old man raised a fist and shook Daniel hard. He unclenched his fist but then he cuffed Daniel at the cheek with the flat of his hand. Daniel didn't seem to feel it but he looked at the old man like he'd never seen him before in his life. He tore loose and shoved Murray backward and went to the car. He drove around the old man and fishtailed into the cross-running dirt road that led home. Murray stooped in the lane and held his knee-caps again. Dust and dirt in his hair. Taste of roadgrit in his mouth. He listened to the diminishing whine of the car and after a moment he stood up straight. Ella was talking to the girl down through the window of their car. Madelyn had figured out her situation and was hammering on the windows with her palms. Kicking at the front seats and at the doorhandle. Murray spat to the tarmac. Took a deep breath. Then he turned and started off down the road, laid his footprints one after another in the tire-tracked clay.

FORTY

Wallace King took the call on his burner. He wrote the particulars on his hand. The rural route address where the cruisers were going. He got out of his car and went into the tavern. Into the safe room and through to the back where Clayton now slept in an army cot. Wallace knelt down and shook his boss. Clayton opened his eyes but he didn't move. After a few moments he raised his watch up to see the hour. Wallace had his hand over his mouth.

"What is it?" Clayton said.

"Your fella at the precinct just called me."

"And?"

"Cops are talkin' about a body on the radio. Out at Dan's place."

Clayton rose, swung his legs off the cot and stood up.

"Give me your phone," he said.

Clayton made two phone calls. The first from his office and the second on the way through the main room of the tavern. Wallace went to the windows and looked out. He turned back and shook his head no. Clayton went behind the bar and poured a glass of whiskey as he spoke into the headset. Then he hung up and set the phone down on the bar counter. He had just raised his glass to drink when a car came off the street and pulled up against the building's front curb.

Tarbell came through the saloon double-doors in his wrinkled slacks and soiled undershirt. Filthy through his ass and back. He had tied the arms of his suit jacket together and hung it around his neck and shoulder as a sling for his broke left arm. Sleepless eyes fixed on Clayton, a look of cold craziness.

"What the fuck did you do?" Clayton said.

"I was looking for the fighter," Tarbell said. "He wasn't there."

Clayton's nephew did not get to explain more. Wallace stepped long and drilled a straight left into Tarbell's side-jaw. Tarbell crumpled and went facedown to the barroom carpet, the exposed soles of his shoes thick with mud and fieldclay. He did not go out completely and rolled away until he hit the base of a nearby table. His hand went sluggish to his waist and Wallace stood hard on the blonde's wrist. Drew his own pistol and aimed true.

Wallace King stood over Tarbell and looked to Clayton.

"Where do I kill this piece of shit?" he said.

"Call the doc," Clayton said.

Wallace stood harder to the man's arm.

"You gotta be fucking kidding me," he said.

Clayton didn't answer him. He just poured himself another whiskey and sat on the backbar until Wallace disarmed Tarbell proper and holstered his gun. Then Wallace took his mobile out of his pocket and sat down in a nearby booth. He made the call under Clayton's watch and then chucked his phone onto the table beside him.

FORTY-ONE

The constable stood in the sideyard of the house. Straight line of sight to the obliterated door and the blood-spackled framing just above the latch receiver. He did not look past to the kitchen where the detectives did their work. He had been through the house once and that was enough. All of the living room furniture was broken and thrown into one corner. The television stuck out of the lawnturf amidst a constellation of plateglass from the front window. The main hallway had been gutted of its drywall and there were blood prints on the pieces that yet hung. Out he went into the fields, eyes to the earth where the killer had driven. Constable Mike Smith came to the spot where the killer had parked in the early morning to watch the house. There the constable paced between the soil-pitted marks made by the killer's car tires. He stopped. In the distance he spied the old farmhouse that bordered the county road.

Constable Smith went window by window and not a room was lit. Everything had been locked down. There were plugs pulled from the wall sockets in the living room. He knocked loud on the front door. Nothing stirred. He walked the porch and looked into the living room a second time and there he saw the girl's backpack on the hardwood. Books and papers littered about the floor. He left and came back ten minutes later with a pickset in his back pocket. Constable Smith studied the lock and took his torque wrench and rake pick out. He went to work in the keyhole. Part of the lock gave. He moved on until he'd set all the pins and then he turned the bolt. Smith twisted the doorknob and went into the house.

There were no signs of struggle, nothing upended or damaged. Constable Smith took his boots off in the entryway hall and went room by room on the main floor of the old house and then he climbed the stairs to the second level. He found a spare bedroom that the young girl had made hers in the chaotic leavings of her days there. He saw an open closet with a long gap of naked clothes rail. Bureau with the drawers open and part-emptied. It was the same in the master bedroom. The constable went downstairs to the kitchen and looked through a clutch of bills and letters on the countertop. He read notes and lists written on a small whiteboard. Studied photographs and cards magnetted to the refrigerator door. There were no tickets or itineraries, no addresses listed. The constable felt eyes on his back. He looked over his shoulder but no one was there.

He found the cellar door and stepped down into the damp below. He felt a ripcord on his cheek and pulled it. By a dirtied hanging bulb he examined prints in the dust-layered cement. A man's shoes. A woman's slippered feet. Padprints of a teenager or adolescent. The constable pulled the cord again and saw the place by the narrow light of day from the tiny basement window. He walked over to the glass and found himself staring across turf and wildgrass at the patch of field where he'd been standing not twenty minutes before.

His radio crackled on and barked at him. Called out his name.

"I'll be right there," Smith said. "You find the truck yet?"

They said they hadn't.

"There's no vehicles here either," said Smith. "Tracks all over, but not a set of wheels to lay them down."

"Alright, come on back," they said.

"Will do," said Smith.

Before he left the house, the constable examined the kitchen again. He lingered on a photograph of Daniel and Sarah and the girl, centre-pinned to the fridge door. He shook his head.

"We gotta find him now or we ain't ever gonna find him," he said.

In the front hallway the constable put his boots back on. He let himself out and closed the door. Took out his picks again to shoot the bolt. It moved easy.

FORTY-TWO

The doctor came with his trove of painkillers and
antibiotics, needles and gauze, splints and wrappings.
He anaesthetized the injured man and reset the arm.
Stitched the bonebroke skin and bound the limb in
a soft-cast. All on the longtable where Wallace and
Clayton had drugged and dropped the patient. The doc
left three vials of pills for the pain and one to hold off
infection. He cleaned part of Tarbell's shoulder and
readied a tetanus shot that the man tried to bat away
drunkenly until Wallace pegged him to the hardwood.
The doc told them what to do with the pills and that
the arm would need to be cast better, and sooner rather
than later. Wallace dropped two thousand dollars into
the doc's bag, rolled bills bound by elastic. The doctor
left the men with the drugged patient dribbling to the
bar table.

"I don't fuckin' get it," Wallace said.

"What about it don't you get?"

"Why he ain't under ground."

"You think that'll help?" Clayton said. "It won't."

"We're fucked then."

"I don't think that's settled yet."

Wallace leaned up against the wall. He looked anywhere but at the man lying prone on the table in front
of him.

"Clayton," he said. "I wouldn't say I'm an emotional guy. But I hate that motherfucker like you wouldn't believe."

"I know. It was a mistake to bring him here. But now we'll need him."

"For what?"

"For the only thing he's good for."

"Look where that got us," Wallace said.

"Daniel will come for him and neither of them will walk away whole," Clayton said. "He isn't dead after then we correct the fucking error I made."

Wallace King slumped some against the panelling.

"The idea of him killin' Dan makes me sick."

"Me too," Clayton said. He went over to Wallace and reached up and grabbed him between his neck and shoulder. "I love that man. But I loath that he'll fucking kill me."

Wallace nodded.

"I want to be here tomorrow," Clayton said, shook Wallace once. "I don't love anybody enough to not take the right steps to be."

Tarbell left in the late afternoon when his meds wore off. He drove out in his car. Clean-shaven by his good hand. Showered and dressed in Clayton's suit. He had arms enough to storm a police barracks. He was to secure the safehouse where they would soon join him and hole up. Wait for what might be coming. Tarbell walked past two newly arrived men in body armour, grinned at them as he went. Moreau and Armstrong entered the tavern one after another. Armstrong stopped long enough to see Tarbell drive away through the tired streets of that town.

There were no men at the gate when Tarbell arrived. He had to get out of the car to work the keypad. The great steel barrier unlocked and began to move. When he passed through he stopped on the other side, made sure the gate slid shut and locked again before he drove on through the forest corridor. He parked in the frontlot and carried an army duffel onto the front deck, set it down heavy and went back for another. He brought the bag up the steps and unbolted the security door. Then he carried each duffel bag inside, one by one. When he came out again he surveyed the grounds. No other soul but he, bound by woods and fencewire and water to the south. The firs bowed gently in the wind.

He went through the house room by room, checked the locked metal doors and barred windows of the main floor. Then he took the bags upstairs. The man wore a military issue ballistic vest and he tightened it by the straps. He inventoried his arms and set them by on a huge spruce roundtable in the study. He checked a bank of monitors, each with a live feed from cameras set up throughout the grounds. Last, he fastened a leather sheath to his belt. Took his time with the one unslung hand. He picked up the buckknife that he'd stole from the murdered Mohawk and sheathed it, drew the blade and sheathed it again. Tarbell stared down at his injured and bound arm. Worked his fingers slow in the half-cast. He unfastened the sling and let it fall to the floor. His sawed-off lay on the table and he broke it to load the shells. Afterward he holstered his pistol and went back downstairs. There he sat on the bottom step and watched the door. The shotgun lay across his knees like an offering.

FORTY-THREE

Wallace King stood in front of the tavern at dusk. The lanterns came on and shone soft. He saw nothing out there that worried him. Inside the bar the two armoured men were sitting at a longtable, guns and water glasses on the tabletop in front of them. Wallace made a call from his cell but heard only dial tone. He pocketed the phone and went back into the building. Moreau and Armstrong turned to him expressionless, but Moreau's leg was dancing under the table, up and down. Wallace went past them and rapped his knuckles on the office door. Clayton came out.

"I can't get Dan," Wallace said.

"What about my fucking nephew?"

"He's all set up."

"Get ready to move," Clayton said.

Clayton came out from the office and went to the front windows of the bar. Moreau got up and Clayton shook his head at him. The man stayed standing. Clayton moved the drapes and stared out into the street. He came back toward the office and Wallace passed him going the other direction and stood near the entryway. He took his cell out again and turned to take another look through the window. The world darkened all at once. The phone dropped but quick from Wallace's hand and he dove to his left as the wall broke open and threw jagged timber and brick across the room. Sound like a train derailing into mountain woods.

There came the front-end of Daniel's truck fixed with a v-plow and it climbed the rubble and ran Moreau and Armstrong down where they sat at the bar table, plateglass in their armour. The truck rode over its front axle and scudded on toward the rear of the building. It stopped short of the back office and the metal frame of the vehicle rung like a church bell as it came to rest in a fog of brickdust and insulation fibres.

Wallace King lay on the ground with his right leg crushed and turned unnatural at the knee. He hollered for Clayton. Daniel started climbing out of the truck by the broken driver-side window. The man could barely fit through the mangled framework and he gouged his hips on stuck windowglass before clearing the gap. Handplanted on a slab of wood siding as he tumbled out. Daniel got up slow, his nose broke and cut through the bridge, blood in his mouth and beard. He had a raw spot on his forehead and his knuckles and elbows were part skinned. He spat filth to the bar floor and then turned to see Clayton scrambling toward the back office, red dribbling to the ground as he went. Daniel ducked low to study the men he'd run over but he couldn't make out what weapons they had through the mess of brick and cloth and meat. He shrieked into the wreckage and went after Clayton, caught him at the door and turned him around. There he grabbed the man's neck with both hands and throttled him. Clayton purpled and tried to claw loose before giving up one hand to reach for his belt. Daniel caught the hand as it came back up, wrenched it wide. Clayton fired twice into the ceiling plaster and Daniel put his forehead into Clayton's mouth and sat him down in the doorway.

Daniel stood over the man and hauled breath past his bloodied teeth. The pistol had gone behind the bar somewhere. He reached for Clayton again. Crack of gunfire as he bent down. Plaster rained down over his shoulders and the back of his neck. Daniel got hold of Clayton and rolled so that Clayton sat straddle-legged on the floor in front of him. Daniel put his right arm around Clayton's neck and held his own left shoulder with the palm of that hand, his left forearm behind Clayton's head. He shuffled backward into the office with Clayton in tow, the injured man sputtering and stomping at the floor.

"Wallace," Daniel hollered.

Another shot went high and wide and something fell from the wall in the barroom. Daniel dragged Clayton farther into the office and when he loosed the man he felt wet through his jeans and shirtcloth. He lifted his shirt, studied his stomach for damage. Shifted back onto his haunches and let Clayton loll to his side and hit the hardwood. A pool of red brimmed around the man. Daniel pulled Clayton's shirt up and saw part of a chair leg run through his liver-side, broken off crooked where it showed through his back. Clayton had a revolver hung there in the bloodwet leather of its holster and Daniel pulled the piece clear and tried to clean it with his shirtsleeve. He did not know if it would fire. No matter. He stood up and went back into the barroom with the gun drawn. Wallace shot again and hit the bar itself and on his next shot the hammer clacked and no bullet fired. Daniel came out from cover as Wallace pulled the slide back on his pistol to clear the jammed round. Daniel took aim with both hands around the revolver and fired on Wallace. Wood and plaster flew and the windowpanes shattered above Wallace's head. The second-to-last round tore a furrow through the top of Wallace's right shoulder and he dropped his pistol and cried out and clapped his left hand over the wound. Daniel kept trying to fire but the chamber spun with spent casings. He pitched the revolver at Wallace and then strode over and dragged the jammed pistol clear with his shoe and pocketed it. Got down low to see the destroyed leg and the shoulder shot through. He stared into Wallace's eyes and then stood up and round kicked him in the face. The big man's eyes rolled white and he doubled over to the carpet. Daniel left him there and walked to the back room over wreck and ruin.

Daniel lifted Clayton off of the hardwood and dropped him heavy in his leather armchair. The man groaned and looked up at Daniel with sickly eyes. He'd gone pale and sweat trickled from his hairline and rounded his sharp cheekbones.

"Did you know?" Daniel said.

Clayton shook his head.

"No," he said.

"Where is he?"

"Out at the lakehouse. Waiting for us. All the guns in the world."

Daniel just stared at him. After a minute he walked to the small back room of the office and flipped the lightswitch on. He threw the army cot and moved a small dresser to show the door of Clayton's safe, the steel built into the actual wall and bricked over. He came back into the main office.

"Open it," he said.

Clayton did nothing. Daniel lifted him out of the chair and dragged him into the little room. There he set the bleeding man on the floor beside the safe and waited. Clayton reached out shakily and turned the dial. When he was done he pulled a lever and the door cracked open. Daniel picked the man up again and brought him back to his chair. Clayton slumped into the leather upholstery and looked up at the ceiling. Into Daniel's eyes.

"That isn't all my money, you know that," Clayton said. "There's people beyond me and they will come for it."

"You had that fella steal my rig. To keep me workin'," Daniel said. "I suppose he's laid out somewhere. No ceremony and no marker."

"I took care of you all those years."

Daniel was not moved.

"I knew you since you were a boy. Knew your father. I wouldn't ever have hurt Sarah, or Madelyn," Clayton said. "Is the girl safe?"

Daniel's body nearly quit on him at the sound of their names. His hands were shaking and he grabbed one fist in the other and squeezed. He breathed and breathed. Lone whimper that slipped his teeth. Blood from his damaged nose. He had to sink to his haunches to keep his legs under him. He reached over to Clayton and took him by the shirt, pulled the man close and ground his forehead to Clayton's. Shook the man. Clayton half-tried to put a hand against Daniel's face. Daniel coughed hard and loosed Clayton. Took a pen from Clayton's shirt as the wounded man came free, red mark printed to his brow. There Daniel figured out a way to stand full again and he put the end of the pen high up in his nostril. Braced it with the ridge of his thumb and forced the bone straight. He bellowed but once and then he flung the pen away. Blinked and wiped at his face until he could see Clayton plain.

"He's your dog," Daniel said.

Clayton's eyes rolled some and then came back. Daniel took Wallace's pistol from his jeans pocket and pulled the slide back. A cartridge lay in the chamber and he took it out and blew into the breach, studied the machine for a time before he put the bullet back and let the slide snap shut. He put the gun to Clayton's head.

"See you later on," he said.

The man kept his eyes open. Daniel fired.

He was going through Wallace's pockets for the car keys when the big man stirred and tried to lift his head off of the hardwood. Daniel turned him over. Wallace howled and grabbed fistfuls of his own shirt. He went into his jacket insides and came back with a set of keys and his little steel container of cocaine. Daniel took the keys and watched Wallace open the vial and shove it into his nostril. Snort deep and cough blood back over his lips.

"Clayton?" Wallace said.

"He's fuckin' gone."

Wallace stared up at the ceiling.

"He suffer?"

"No."

"Will I?"

FORTY-FOUR

Daniel pulled over at the grass verge of the dirt road and got out. He saw dirty, roiling clouds perhaps a county over. But where he had parked birds still sang at the dying of the day, the evening sky clear and already lit spare with long gone stars. When night came in earnest, Daniel went to the trunk and dropped the side of his fist on it twice. He put the key into the lock and opened the door. Wallace lay there with his eyes closed, his knees to his chest, his broken leg purpled hideously under the makeshift splint. Daniel put his fingers on the big man's neck. He slapped him hard across the cheek.

Wallace's eyes showed sudden.

"Where are we?" he said.

"You fuckin' know where," Daniel said.

Wallace started trying to climb out of the trunk. Daniel pulled him clear and let the big man sit on the rear bumper. The vehicle sunk on its springs. Wallace went into his pockets for his coke and his pain pills. He took probably too much of each. Daniel didn't know how many he'd ate on the ride.

"If you take off on me you won't get far," Daniel said.

Wallace shook his head.

"I ain't your enemy," Wallace said.

"Fuck you."

"I'd have tore his fuckin' heart out before letting him do what he done," Wallace said. "You gotta know that."

The passway had gone very dark. Daniel came close and took hold of Wallace's ruined leg at the knee. The big man bawled and ground his teeth. Daniel let go. Wallace hunched some and came back winded. Daniel gave him a moment and then he got under Wallace's arm and hoisted the man up off the fender. Carried him over to the driver's side door and shoved him into the seat. Wallace took another bump from the canister and tried to catch his breath. Daniel closed the door on him, gauged his path through the blackness between the firs.

"You sure he's alone?" Daniel said.

"Very much so," Wallace said.

Tarbell stood pissing in the upstairs toilet with the door wide open. His shotgun lay on the sinkbasin. As he shook his dick he heard the low hum of a car engine. He went down the hall with his weapon and flattened himself against the wallpaper. He looked out long enough to see Clayton's black Cadillac rolling down the grade. Floodlights showed the grounds but Tarbell couldn't see clear through the vehicle's windshield. The car banked right and stopped, the driver side facing the house. The window slid down and there sat Wallace King. He was looking to the windows of the house one by one and when he saw Tarbell he stopped and gazed up at him. Wallace raised a hand and Tarbell nodded.

Tarbell lingered a minute and then walked back down the hall. He passed Clayton's office on his way downstairs. He went to each of the windows in the front room and moved the drapes an inch. Angled himself to see the entire porch part by part. Nobody was out there. He unlocked and unbolted the security door. Edged it open. He kept the outer cage locked and peered through the steel mesh. Wallace watching him cold across the lot. Tarbell beckoned with the shotgun but Wallace stayed perfectly still. Clayton was not with him. Tarbell panned the grounds and then he shut the door.

He'd got halfway up the stairs when something crashed loud into one of the caged front windows. Windchime tinkling of glass as it fell to the planking. Within seconds the acrid scent of woodsmoke filled the foyer. Tarbell watched dark grey plumes leaking pigtailed from the slatting of the wall, light dancing behind the window-dressing. He made for the weapons room. Heavy footfalls lower on the stairwell as Tarbell reached the landing. He started to raise the scattergun and turn.

Daniel was already on top of him with his fingers around the gunbarrel as he drove Tarbell back toward the wall aside the hallway bathroom. The shotgun hit the plaster and Tarbell couldn't hold it with one arm and he couldn't get his finger to the trigger and then the gun was loose. The blonde clawed at Daniel's eyes and tried to shove him off. Daniel took the smaller man's head in his left hand and rammed it back against the corner of the bathroom doorframe, let go and drove his left elbow into Tarbell's eyebrow. Something gave in his face and the man sunk to his haunches. A gash had been hewn into Tarbell's forehead and it spilled blood and his eyelid worked frantic to clear the pooling red. Daniel picked him up by neck and shirt-collar and carried him into the room. Swung him to the left and then pulled him back and drove Tarbell's head through the sinkbasin. A half-moon of porcelain broke loose and went with him to the floor.

Daniel hit the downed man again and again and Tarbell did not defend himself even with his good arm. The blonde reached to his hip and then he was sitting up with the buckknife and he dragged the blade deep through the outside of Daniel's left armpit. Daniel let go and stood up, reeled back stung into the hallway. He stepped on the stock of the shotgun and saw it and picked it up. Looked down at his left arm and tried to work his fingers and elbowjoint.

Tarbell rose full in the doorway with the wet buck-knife in his right hand, a chunk of his scalp pushed up like half-laid sod. His orbital bone was fractured and one eyeball sat lower in his face than the other. He came with the knife. Daniel got hold of the shotgun grip in his right hand and he cocked both hammers with his thumb as he raised the weapon up and then he pulled the trigger. Tarbell was not there anymore. Daniel started into the bathroom but he staggered at the threshold. The man was down by the toilet. He'd lost part of his arm and shoulder on the side he was shot.

Daniel leaned heavy against the doorway framing. Drew himself up and went inside. He knelt and reached into the man's jacket for more shells. Tarbell lay there dying and he spat thick red phlegm at Daniel. He seethed to the end, lonely and hollow soul unready to be sent on. Daniel got up again and broke the shotgun, shook the shellcasings loose and reloaded. He stood over the man and aimed the muzzle at his face. The gun bucked and breathed fire and the head of Tarbell blew apart and painted the room.

Daniel stood over the body until fire climbed to the second floor and licked the windowglass at the other end of the hallway. He let the shotgun drop to the hardwood. By the time he got downstairs the entire front wall of the house curled in flame. Something erupted in a storage closet off the main room and set the floor afire. Daniel covered his mouth and went though a series of corridors that led to the side entryway. He left the house and climbed a rise toward the gravel lot. From across the clearing he could see Wallace slumped over in the front seat of the car, his head turned awkward by the window frame. Daniel turned and walked the other way. Rounded the eastern side of the building and stumbled down the grade toward the shore.

Down and down he went, feet slipping in the grasses. His clothes were soaked through on his left side. Blood pooled warm in his shoe. He'd already gone shades paler and he reached the dock at a stagger. When he got to the end of the dock he lay down, his feet toward the burning house. Fire had taken the back porch. The lake-facing rooms burned behind their burst windows. Smoke poured from the siding and the seams below the roof.

The support beams gave from below the porch and Daniel watched the structure collapse and spill fire out along the hillslope. He had trouble breathing and his heart beat too quick. The lumber below had been soaked through by his blood and now it dropped thick to the cool baywater, dissolved somewhere in the dark. The fire's reflection played in the lake, spun peculiar colours some feet below the surface. Daniel's skin hurt from the heat and he reached for water with his good hand, cupped it out and wet his face. Nonetheless, he was shivering as the house sloughed its roof and began to list.

Lying there bloodied, his body wrecked and gone strange with shock, Daniel started to cry. He'd no way to stop it. Daniel sobbed hard enough that he couldn't see and it took a very long time for him to get his hand up to his face to cover his mouth and stifle the sounds that came out of him. To wipe his eyes clear. He thought that he would die. That he would never see his daughter again. He thought that he would die, but he was not dead yet. Nor was she.

He studied the skies, shifted on the dock and started making feral noises. He rolled back and forth and ground his head against the planking. Bit his teeth together hard. He got up.

FORTY-FIVE

The house burned on while firemen ran hoses to the
lake and started pumping water. Constable Smith stood
near to the body of Wallace King and watched them
douse the flames. Wallace's shirt was gone. Someone
nearly trod in the cordoned off area and the constable
took that cop by the collar and shoved him clear. Smith
came back and looked at the dead man. He'd known
him by sight, known where the man was born, where
he lived. Another officer came over to him.

"We got the car," he said.

"Where?"

"Country Road Six, just outside town."

"Stay here with Wallace."

"Sure."

They found the car in a farmer's field with mangled
fencewire trailing from the undercarriage. Wild brush
wound over tortuous in the lines. The tires were torn
and flat to the rims. The engine idled yet and thin
smoke carried from the tailpipe. A bull roamed beyond,
thick-horned and boulder-headed. The animal came
up to the car and snorted, watched the constable with
black eyes. The constable stopped and stared back at
the bull, its flicking tail. He drew his pistol and let it
hang at his side. The bull sidled on and the constable

walked toward the car with his sidearm's safety off. Three cops followed him.

He passed by the rear, driver-side corner of the car and he couldn't see anything through the deep-tinted glass. The other cops had their pistols aimed at the vehicle and they were hissing at him to hold up. Constable Smith went calm to the driver door and rapped the muzzle of his sidearm against the window. He reached for the handle and tried it. The door unlatched. The constable hesitated a second and then he pulled the door open.

Daniel sat upright with his chin to his chest, still as could be. One enormous hand hung inside the steering wheel. Scars in the skin. The constable put his fingers to the side of the man's thick neck. Cold as cellar wood. He held the back of his hand in front of Daniel's mouth and nose. After awhile he let the hand drop. He knelt to better see the man. The leather upholstery of the seat swamped with blood and Daniel's left shoulder tied with a tourniquet made from Wallace King's shirt. Daniel's own belt fastened around it all. His shoes were thick with beachmud. The constable felt the man's jeans and the collar of his shirt. All he wore sopping wet except for the tourniquet. The other cops were behind the constable now, holstering their pistols one by one as they took measure of it all.

"He's long gone," one cop said.

Constable Smith nodded and got up slow.

"Shot?" asked another.

"No. I don't think so," Smith said.

The constable told one of the other cops to call it in and then Smith sent them all down to the road to meet the owner of the farm. The farmer got out of his pickup in his jeans and undershirt and the cops stopped him fifteen feet from the truck before he got close enough to see the damage to his land. They talked him away from the scene. Constable Smith watched the officers go. He had traces of red on his fingers and he wiped them on his pants. The constable leaned his elbows heavy to the roof of the wreck. He stared into the fields, farther yet to the distant town. There were streetlamps gone dark that had been lit when they'd drove out earlier. Somewhere in a valley to the east the sound of heavy engines fired, low growl of truck motors. In the near homes lights had come on here and there. Others still dark throughout. Houses of that town that held sleeping souls and those that slept little or not at all. He could see thin columns of chimney-smoke against the lightening sky.

After a few minutes the constable took his arms off the car. Sunk to one knee again. He looked up at Daniel's face and exhaled hard. The eyes were closed and he was glad for it. There the constable saw the glint of clean metal and reached up to the dead man's neck. His fingertips to the cold length of a broken silver chain. In touching it the chain loosed and slid clear off the dead man's neck but Smith caught it. He took it all up, the links pooling in the ridges of his palm. He stared awhile. Then he pocketed the chain and stood.

ACKNOWLEDGEMENTS

This novel wouldn't ever have been written without the support of my family, in Canada and England, and especially my mother, father, and brother. They are responsible for all of the things that matter in these pages. All well as every other page and line I lay down.

The keen editorial eye of John Metcalf has been on this novel for years now, and he reshaped the book into a much more dynamic and effective work. The single most important thing that happened to me so far in my writing career is Metcalf finding a story of mine in a journal, and calling me up on the phone, and writing to me about it. Without that, and without Metcalf, I might be somewhere, but it sure wouldn't be somewhere nearly as good. I've said it before, but it's still the truth, that John Metcalf and Biblioasis changed my life. The staff at Biblioasis, including Dan, Chris, Natalie, Meghan, and Casey, and more, have championed my work for awhile now, and they are the real deal when it comes to publishing. Much respect to you all.

Sincere thanks to fellow writers who offered their support to this novel, and for my writing in general. Foremost to John Irving, who has thrown his considerable literary weight behind both of my books, whether in the form of a quote, or an interview, or a kind mention to somebody about the writing. He has also shared some wise words on what I should do with myself as I keep on trying to do this for a living. I am proud to call him a friend. I've also been fortunate to have the recent support of Donald Ray Pollock, one of my favourite writers to ever pen a word, as well as Waubgeshig Rice, who kept an eye on the validity of the terrain, and the Jiu-Jitsu. Also, thanks to all of the folks in the literary community at large, in Toronto and elsewhere, who have read and supported my work over the years.

I received funding for this book from the Canada Council for the Arts, the Toronto Arts Council, and the Ontario Arts Council. Without that funding I would be living under a bridge near to the river. Thank you for giving a guy a chance to write some books without having to stop and just lie face-down on the floor while listening to Enya.

Finally, I would like to thank some key readers who helped me get this novel right, including Jenna Illies, Naben Ruthnum, and, to a very significant extent, Kris Bertin. Without the notes I got from them, you'd have a substantially different book, and in writing and revising the work over so many years, I needed their perspective to make sure I'd stayed honest about how good this book was and how good it could eventually be.

Special thanks to Jenna, for putting up with me over so many months. I did not expect you to come into my life, but I am very, very lucky that you did.